THE LIZARD

THE LIZARD

Dugald Bruce-Lockhart

MUSWELL
PRESS

First published by Muswell Press in 2020

Typeset in Bembo by M Rules
Copyright © Dugald Bruce-Lockhart 2020

Dugald Bruce-Lockhart has asserted his right
to be identified as the author of this work in accordance
with under the Copyright, Designs and Patents Act, 1988

Printed and bound by CPI Group (UK) Ltd, Croydon CR0 4YY

This book is a work of fiction and,
except in the case of historical fact, any resemblance
to actual persons, living or dead, is purely coincidental.

A CIP catalogue record for this book
is available from the British Library

Hardback ISBN:9781916129269
Paperback ISBN: 9781916360211

Muswell Press
London N6 5HQ
www.muswell-press.co.uk

No responsibility for loss occasioned to any person or
corporate body acting or refraining to act as a result of reading
material in the book can be accepted by the Publisher, by the
Author, or by the employer of the Author.

For Mouse and Frog

You've got a devil inside you, as well, but you don't know his name yet, and since you don't know that, you can't breathe. Baptise him, boss, and you'll feel better!

NIKOS KAZANTZAKIS,
Zorba the Greek

Prologue

According to Ellie I was too eager to please. Unable to make a decision; not my own man.

Which is why she dumped me.

Why I left for the Greek islands in the summer of '88.

And ended up in jail for murder.

How far back the seed was sown is impossible to tell. Nothing comes from nothing. Be it fate or free will, life boils down to continuous binary code: a never-ending series of choices; yes or no; in or out; fight or flight. Until death ends the equation. Humans overcomplicate it; we invent shades of grey, hover in a limbo of moderation and deem it intelligence. Only the mad and the brave change the world. The rest look on in wonder.

I went to Greece to embrace the binary code, to get off the sidelines and become a player. To live in the moment. Or, as Ellie put it, to become my own man.

Was I accountable for the horror, that fateful summer?

Looking back, it's easy enough to pinpoint the sliding-door

moments where I went wrong. But then, what use is hindsight? As Kierkegaard wrote: 'Life can only be understood backwards; but it must be lived forwards.'

Cold comfort when you've taken another man's life.

I

1

I stepped off the Athens airport-transfer bus at the port of Piraeus on the morning of 27 May as the sky turned pink. The combination of heat, diesel fumes and the swelling army of backpackers was compounded by coiled street lamps that bathed the environs in a weird orange murk, through which squat ferries along the harbour concourse loomed like giant slugs. In the shadows lay a scattering of ghostly kiosks selling pretzels, water bottles and bread rolls, where island-hoppers assembled in droves to stock up on supplies; a hungry, apocalyptic exodus.

A far cry from the Greece I'd seen in magazines.

Trawling the ring of travel offices with their overenthusiastic ticket touts, I found what appeared to be the best deal for a one-way journey to Paros, took a seat at a café along the harbour wall and, ordering an iced coffee to ease the headache that had grown steadily since my 4 a.m. arrival, settled in for the wait as the port lumbered to life.

As we drew nearer to departure, the café filled up, and it wasn't long before a fellow traveller sporting a tie-dye neck scarf came over to share my table. He gave me a nod and pulled out a sun-bleached copy of Paulo Coelho's *The Alchemist*. Then, with an artful flick of his Zippo lighter, he lit one of his Camel cigarettes and ordered a Heineken. I checked my watch – not even 8 a.m.

Exactly the sort of man Ellie would go for. Independent to the hilt. A cool contender, suave and assured, with a natural breeziness I could only dream of.

Sucking the sugar granules from the bottom of my glass, I focused on the seagulls dive-bombing the pretzel kiosks, assuring myself that I needn't feel intimidated. Yes, I was a little on the conventional side, and certainly not someone who looked natural holding a cigarette, but who cared? I'd just arrived. In a matter of days I'd fit in with the best of them.

At which point, an official voice cut through the hubbub of the café, barking departure instructions.

The *Apollonia* was ready to board.

We left Piraeus bang on nine o'clock, contrary to all the warnings I'd been given on Greek efficiency. Standing on the top deck with my fellow bleary-eyed passengers, I watched Athens retreat into the heat haze; the sea was so calm it was hard to distinguish which was actually moving, the ship or the land. We simply seemed to separate.

As the steel deck throbbed with increasing urgency beneath my feet, mainland Greece disappeared from the horizon and we passed the first cluster of islands, apparently uninhabited. Pressing on past these scrubby, rocky outposts into deeper water, the ship soon picked up the open swell and started its gentle roll. As the sun climbed higher, I eased off my shirt, exposed my pallid flesh to the salt air and embraced my new-found anonymity.

St Andrews University and its trickle of tea shops, golf courses and cobbled streets seemed a universe away. Good riddance, too. Alistair Haston, student of moral philosophy and German – no more. I was starting over, shaking things up. A blank canvas upon which to draw new lines. Cleaner, stronger lines. I'd have to return to uni after the summer break to complete my fourth and final year, of course – I was hardly going to chuck in three years of study – but for now, it was goodbye to books and intellectual enlightenment. Logic had been my undoing. Ellie wanted a 'doer', not a thinker. I was after the innate wisdom of my primaeval forefathers, where the only qualification needed was an ability to hunt and fight: a stripped-back, honest existence. The hunter-gatherer society. Hunt down the supper and fight the neighbour off your turf – or your woman. Sod the degree. Air. Food. Water. Sleep.

I could hear Ellie's snort of derision. I couldn't be further removed from my ancestral alpha males than I already was. *People-pleaser extraordinaire.*

Stepping back from the railing – I could feel the beginnings of sunburn on the tops of my shoulders – I slipped the shirt back on and, cursing my lack of foresight for not having packed any painkillers, made my way through the throng of semi-naked bodies down to the covered deck below in search of something to ease the now pounding headache. The iced coffee seemed only to have had the reverse effect; I needed something stronger, chemical.

The lower deck was populated by Greeks primarily, in their forties plus. Some were grouped around tables, smoking and playing backgammon and cards, others slept curled up in the banks of shiny plastic armchairs. I spotted a couple of octogenarian women dressed in the traditional all black.

Faces lined like cracked mud, silver crucifixes around their necks. One of them eyed me with vague disinterest, the way a tortoise might eye a dock leaf. I smiled but it wasn't returned.

I averted my eyes, turned towards the bar to see what was on offer and scoured the shelves in search of pharmaceuticals. Unable to spot anything promising among the fake coral necklaces, batteries and 'Sea Captain' hats, I cast an eye over the selection of beers as a possible alternative and noticed a faded poster on the wall: *Michael Jenner. Eighteen years old. Missing since July 1986, last seen on Mykonos. Anyone with information should contact the police or the British Embassy.*

Two years ago. They were still holding out hope – unless it was an oversight and the poster had been left to rot on the walls. Striking fellow. Unruly red hair and emerald eyes. There was something familiar about his expression: his eyes were alive and lit up – a pull at the side of the lips that suggested something was happening just off-camera, a shared secret.

I remembered that feeling sitting on a train with Ellie and a group of second-year students returning from the summer holidays. They'd been celebrating and lamenting, in turn, the follies of holiday romances. Ellie had reached under the table and squeezed my hand – a silent complicity that we were one, invincible, above such frippery. I wore the tiniest of smiles. Certain. Complete. A feeling that all I needed was right next to me.

Yeah, right.

Six weeks before, meeting up in the rain after her twelve o'clock anthropology tutorial, Ellie and I hadstood, hand in hand, under the cloisters of St Salvator's Quad, waiting for a lull in the deluge before making a run for it. She'd been asking me all term if I'd come out to Greece and visit her relations in Athens – her paternal uncle was an influential shipping magnate who controlled half the tankers in the Med, and she assured me her cousins would show us a good time. A self-professed yachtswoman, she boasted she'd commandeer her uncle's luxury catamaran, knock the landlubber out of me and give me sea legs. Not wanting to lose out on other options, however, I'd dithered for two months, unable to commit. Finally, realising all too late that friends and family had all made arrangements elsewhere, I decided to take the plunge, or risk facing the summer months alone. So I wrapped my fingers around Ellie's, took a deep breath and told her that I'd love to join her and her Greek cousins for the summer break, thank you.

She turned to me, eyes moistening, tucked a lock of wet hair behind her ear and told me that something just wasn't right; she couldn't quite put her finger on it. Although, when I told her to stop the tears, the finger found it easily enough: 'We're wasting each other's time – you don't know who you are, or what you want. You rely on me and it's weighing me down. I can't carry both of us.'

With that, she stepped out across the sodden grass in a melee of auburn hair, lever arch files and denim, and left me there, confused and admonished.

I tried desperately to reopen negotiations, but her gatekeepers were well prepped and my advances rebuffed at every turn. As for my friends, they were useless. They simply nodded along, bought me another pint of cider and black, and returned to the slot machines: *Taking it a little seriously, poor bugger.* So I sought guidance from my moral philosophy tutor, collapsing onto his tobacco-stained chaise longue in floods of tears, claiming that life, studies, and the whole notion of a career was meaningless if one was 'out of love'. How could

I begin to think clearly, see straight, eat, sleep or breathe even, in such a state — let alone finish my degree? Ellie was my life, my reason to get up in the morning. 'Without Ellie,' I concluded, 'I might as well be dead.' But all he did was pour me a brandy, suggest I was critically co-dependent, and recommended I see a shrink.

After five days pining away in my bedsit, disgusted by my innate fickleness, I set off through the quad, past the New Picture House with its poster of Tom Cruise and Kelly McGillis straddling a large motorbike, and made my way to the travel office in the students' union, where, approaching a stringy sales assistant in a 'The Cure' T-shirt, I announced I wanted to do the Greek islands. *Without Ellie. Alone. Teach myself to sail — that'll show her.* Fine, I'd use up a term's living allowance in one swift stroke of the pen, but if I put my nose to the grindstone, I'd claw back some of the deficit. And anyway, weren't all students in debt?

Morag, the travel agent, couldn't agree more, and issued me with a one-way ticket to Athens.

Back at my halls of residence, having picked up £20-worth of drachmas and £50 in travellers' cheques from the bank on North Street, I immediately set to packing a rucksack — just the essentials: no camera, nothing to read, not even a notebook. And as a grace note, buoyed up by my proactive decision-making, and in the vain hope I might provoke a reaction, I wrote a disingenuously cheerful letter to Ellie, telling her not only of my plans to head, solo, to the Greek islands, but also claiming that I was ready to be just friends, despite my profound belief we were made for each other. She never replied.

Six eternal weeks . . .

*

A shout from across the cabin cut through my melancholia. Leaving Michael Jenner to his secret smile, I swung around to witness the flustered arrival of the barman, chequered apron flapping from his waist, barking at no one in particular. Leaning across the bar towards him, I was ordering an Amstel beer, when a voice piped up behind me. 'Mythos every time, mate.'

I turned and came face to face with a grinning Australian. He was in his late twenties, complete with a wide-brimmed leather hat and mahogany tan. 'The Amstel's piss and they water it down anyway.' He wiped his hand on his T-shirt, took off the hat and ran a hand through his matted blond hair. 'Stay local.'

Continuing to grin, he lit a cigarette.

'On your own?'

He lifted his chin and blew the smoke straight up in the air without taking his gaze off me. For a moment, I couldn't answer; I was struck by his extraordinarily translucent eyes. The colour was wrong – it didn't quite fit with the rest of his face.

'Pretty much,' I replied finally, unnerved by the directness of his stare. 'Heading to Paros. Second stop, I think it is.'

'Looking for work?'

'Actually, I am.'

'Paros? There are way more bars and clubs on Ios.'

'Didn't fancy the "Ios Cough",' I replied, remembering Morag the travel agent's advice to stay away from Ios – every year, countless tourists died from alcohol poisoning, to the point where the authorities would turn away the inbound ferries for days at a time in a bid to restore order. A hellhole party island to be avoided at all costs.

'Fair play,' he said, holding my gaze. 'Still, depends where you go.'

There was, in fact, a more telling reason: Ellie's cousin owned a restaurant on Paros, near the port of Naoussa on the north of the island – the Tamarisk. Ellie had earmarked it for our itinerary. Somewhat pathetically, I was entertaining the hope she might stick with her summer plans, head to Paros with her cousin and visit the family restaurant ... where, fancy that, I'd run into her.

But the Australian didn't need to hear that.

He blew out another long stream of smoke. 'I've got a few contacts over here. You wanna job, I can hook you up, no sweat.'

'Thanks,' I replied, still thinking of Ellie.

It was, of course, stupidly unlikely. And in any case, what was I going to do – stake out the restaurant and wait for her to show up? I had a tiny budget; I had to work. Besides, if Ellie knew I'd been lying in wait, she'd run a mile. The idea was to play the aloof game, the independent game – not become a stalker.

'No worries,' said the Australian. 'What's your thing – what do you do?'

'Probably going to do some labouring first,' I replied, looking around for the barman, who had once again disappeared. 'Build up a resistance to the heat and stuff. Might get down to Ios later in the summer.'

Unless I did hook up with Ellie – convinced her she'd made a terrible mistake ...

Wake up, Haston.

'Right,' he said, flicking his ash on the floor. 'Like working on a building site isn't gonna fry your skin to shit.'

'True.'

Still, faced with ten or so islands to choose from, the possibility of bumping into Ellie had at least helped make my

12

decision: Paros was as good as any. And according to Morag, there was plenty of work, it had more to offer than the other party islands, and boasted some of the best beaches in the Cyclades.

'I'll take whatever comes my way,' I concluded, noticing the tattoo on his neck, just behind his right ear – a lizard. Dark green.

'Right on.' He clapped me on the shoulder. 'What's ya name, mate?'

'Haston,' I replied, flinching at the physical contact.

'Like the car?'

'With an aitch.'

'I'm Ricky. Wanna play a game of quarters?'

Before I could admit I didn't know what that meant, he put an arm around me and said: 'Come with me, I'm going to introduce you to some friends.'

On the sun deck, Ricky brought me before his 'crew': there was Matt, a six-foot-four Aussie Rules football player who looked like John Lennon; Diane, a Kiwi who taught maths at a secondary school in Wellington, and who, whenever she spoke, sounded like she had a chunk of phlegm stuck in her throat; and finally Parrish, a slow-drawling Texan who was studying medicine at Chapel Hill in North Carolina.

They were all stoned.

Nonetheless, they welcomed me like I was a long-lost friend, and didn't seem to notice or care that I was a straight-laced, conservative ex-public schoolboy whose only experience of drug taking was limited to soluble aspirin.

Along with the first few cans of beer came a barrage of personal questions, which I at first deflected but found increasingly palatable with the aid of alcohol. Soon enough I felt like

13

a celebrity. I'd never imagined that studying philosophy and German would ever sound cool. And when I mentioned my break-up with Ellie, the group edged in tighter – drunken solidarity for the plight of the English bloke with a broken heart. Diane pushed Matt out of the way, squeezed in next to me and laid her soft legs across mine. She kissed my neck, put a slender arm around me and said she'd cure my woes – 'Bushman style', whatever that meant.

'We're gonna get you shit-faced,' declared Parrish, cutting to the chase. 'Fucking blotto.'

A cheer rolled across the deck.

'Welcome to the club, ya Pommie bastard!' yelled Ricky, spraying his can of beer over my face. 'The club's about spreading the word, and the word is love.' With that he planted his face on Diane's lips and the two of them rolled onto my lap, as, out of nowhere, a chant struck up for 'quarters'.

I joined in, the infection of goodwill spreading like sun cream. Matt whipped off his shirt and ordered us to follow suit – house rules. We obeyed, including Diane, who revealed she was wearing a silver-spangled bra. The bra lasted a matter of seconds before she unclipped herself and threw it at a pair of lanky Swedish girls who were spectating from the railings behind their sunglasses and straw hats. She then drew a circle around each puffy nipple with a tube of green sunblock and made me complete the left breast, 'to help me get over my girlfriend', while everyone vied at once to explain the rules of the game.

From the tumult of drunken shouts, I managed to glean the essentials: the idea was to bounce a 'quarter' – an American quarter-dollar coin, which Parrish duly provided – into a glass that contained a shot of Jack Daniels. If I made it, I'd get to choose who drank it and would be allowed another turn. If I missed, I'd have to down the glass and refill it for the next person to have their turn. The game ended when someone puked or passed out.

'Fuckin' simple, mate,' said Matt, clapping me on the back. 'Didn't ya girlfriend teach you this one?'

I laughed and admitted she had failed in that respect. Diane gave Matt a slap and told him to have 'some fuckin' respect' – and then kissed him. She then kissed me.

Ricky kissed Parrish.

Parrish tried to kiss me.

I gave him a nifty slap, which drew a cheer, followed by another wave of onlookers keen to witness the antics.

Preliminaries out of the way, the game got underway as George Michael's 'Faith' riffed from the ghetto blaster. And as the new member of the club, I had the honour of starting. I held the coin between finger and thumb, took aim and bounced the thing sharply off the table, plonk, straight into the shot glass.

I was astounded.

'The guy's a fuckin' natural!' screamed Matt, slapping me across the back.

'Rookie's luck,' came the riposte from Ricky as he scratched his tattoo. 'Won't cop that shit again.'

I slotted another. And then two more.

Competitive by nature and with an unhealthy taste for praise, I was hooked. I picked on Ricky and made him drink each round; I was in awe of him and wanted to make an impression, as well as punish him for his earlier jibe. After my third successful toss, I invented a victory dance: a four-limbed robotic crabbing motion that had them in stitches. The others took it on too. Every time someone scored, out came the dance. The dance drew cheers from the club, which in turn drew an increasingly larger crowd of spectators. Before long, over half of the top deck were doing it.

I was high as a kite on sheer camaraderie, something I'd not felt since my dismissal by Ellie. The conviviality grew, the noise increased, and time slid by in a wash of pickled sunlight.

Then it all went wrong.

A series of extra forfeits were put into force, at which point the club ganged up on me. In one fateful round, I slugged three shots from Matt and Diane, followed by a quintuple: for swearing twice; for pointing at Ricky with my finger rather than my elbow; followed by putting the empty glass back on the table without the Jack Daniels in it – which I forgot to call 'liquid'.

Things turned hazy.

I remember the ghetto-blaster on full whack – 'It's the End of the World as We Know It' by R.E.M.; Parrish and Matt were dancing naked with two Russian girls, braids in their hair, rings and hoops in every nook and cranny of their faces; a steward showed up, told them to put their clothes back on or face arrest; I remember the crowd jeering him back to his lair; I remember wanting to get out of the sun; I remember Ricky breaking out his video camera, filming Diane and me doing shots; I remember him encouraging her to kiss me; I remember her kissing me – the camera lens in my face.

After that . . .

Nothing.

When I came to my senses I was no longer on the boat.

I was lying on the ground at the foot of a dry-stone wall opposite a café; no shirt on my back, my chinos soaked in piss, and my hand resting in a puddle of golden puke.

I checked the contents of my rucksack and took stock.

On the plus side, I was on dry land, I had all my clothes – minus a T-shirt – and was still in possession of my wallet. But my passport and travellers' cheques were gone.

I had 1300 drachmas in change.

Seven quid.

Wiping the vomit from my fingers, I closed my ears to the increasing shouts of disdain emanating from the restaurant and staggered back and forth across the harbour square to see if my passport and cheques had fallen out nearby. I tried all the cafés in the immediate vicinity and asked at the tourist information centre by the windmill. I tried the ferry kiosk and the two travel agencies.

No joy.

Stumbling across the dusty tarmac, blinded by the brightness of everything around me, I headed towards the town end of a heavily populated sandy beach and took advantage of a shop bristling with floatation devices to pick up a bottle of water. Ducking out of the sun, I knocked over a postcard stand and inadvertently discovered where I was – Paros.

That was something, at least.

I paid eighty drachmas for the water, made a wavering beeline to the beach, and wading through the piping-hot sand to the only shade unclaimed by any beachgoers, I tossed the rucksack to the ground, flopped back against the trunk of the thickest tree and without pause emptied my litre bottle of water. Without ID there was no doing anything, let alone the fact I'd need a passport to claim back the lost travellers' cheques. But then, if I told the police, they'd ship me straight back to Athens and the British Embassy; from there, the authorities would put me on the next available flight to the UK. Game over.

No way could I go back now.
What would Ellie say?

For the next six hours, I sheltered from the scorching heat under the boughs of my olive tree, debating whether I should take a bus up to Naoussa in the north and try and track down Ellie's cousin – although, were I to find her, it wasn't clear how she could help, apart from lend me money. Give me a job? Why would she feel the need to do that? I didn't even know her name; I was to all intents and purposes a stranger. Would Ellie have mentioned me? Possibly. But then she might also have told her we were no longer together. Besides, the fact that Ellie's cousin owned the restaurant didn't mean she would necessarily be in residence. Furthermore, Ellie had planned to take me to her uncle's house in Athens before travelling the islands, and even then, the plan had been to go sometime mid-June. Two weeks away at the earliest.

I remained stewing in my hangover, kicking myself for not having done the groundwork on finding out exactly when – or indeed, if at all – Ellie was planning on her Greek excursion, until, at dusk, I pulled myself together, reminded myself I was there to reclaim my independence and not wallow in heartbreak, then ventured north along the bay to take advantage of the thinning crowd and have my first swim.

Standing waist-deep in the silky water, I started a conversation with a fellow bather, Roland, a traveller from Glasgow who had zero tan, a shock of ginger hair and was wiry as a whippet. He was working on a building site on the other side of the island and had arrived a month ago with the first wave of workers for the season. As he hoisted first one leg then the other out of the water to wash the flakes of paint from his pasty, freckled legs, I told him of my predicament.

'Aye, gotta watch yer back around here,' he said finally, ringing the water out of his ear with his little finger. 'Passports sell for a thousand quid on the black market.'

He then gave me the low-down on working on the islands.

Casual work was managed by locals, who paid around 2,500 drachmas for a day's graft – eleven quid. No food or water included, you had to get that yourself. Because I spoke another language, I'd get work *kamakying* – chatting up passing tourists in an attempt to lure them to lunch or dinner. There was no pay, but if you were good at it you could make decent tips, and you were always fed.

'And there's the usual stuff,' he continued, rubbing the paint from his scalp. 'Washing dishes, selling watermelons on the beach, bartending – that kind of thing.'

'Any chance of you putting in a word to your boss?'

I was staring an opportunity in the face.

He blinked at me with a crooked smile. 'Ever worked on a building site before?'

'Sure,' I lied. 'I mean, I can't do any of that plastering stuff, but I can paint, strip walls, that kind of thing.' I was fit and willing – that had to count.

'I'll ask my boss in the morning,' he chuckled, picking yet more paint out of his hair. 'He'll say "yes", but don't get your hopes up, it'll be dogsbody stuff at the hands of one his lackeys.'

My spirits rose immediately. Manual labour, working my passage for an honest crust of bread – exactly what I needed. It would impress Ellie no end.

'Yeah, if you're happy with any old shite, I'm sure there'll be something for you.'

He told me to find him at the Koula campsite café in the morning at six-thirty, and we'd take it from there. I thanked him, to which he gave a cheery 'nae fuckin' bother', then loped off across the beach into the twilight.

I flopped back into the brine, congratulated myself on seizing the moment and watched the silhouette of Paros Mountain sharpen against a bruised sky.

Welcome to Greece.

It was all looking good.

As I swam further out to avoid the jutting rocks below my feet, a guttural shout brought my attention back to the beach: Roland was standing at the campsite gates, his pale figure visible against the dark mantel of the cypresses: towel round his neck, rinsing his feet under the freshwater tap, hand raised mid-salute. 'Watch out for a fat, lazy cunt called Leo,' he yelled, his voice echoing off the cliffs across the bay. 'He'll eat yer lunch if you turn your back on the bastard.'

2

An apricot dawn brought a lightness of spirit, and a not-unsuccessful night's sleep under the mosquito-infested cedars along the beach wall renewed a belief in my hunter-gatherer potential.

Cajoled off my patch by an overfriendly stray dog, I walked north along the bay, stashed my kit in a clump of bamboo behind an old goat hut, then returned to the campsite to find Roland. He was already up and waiting for me, and proving true to his word, took me on the back of his moped to the building site depot where he introduced me to his boss, Kyros, a massive man in a string vest and tight shorts who, despite being so hairy he looked like an ape caught in a hammock, was charm itself: *Yes, of course there was work for me, when could I start? Now? Perfect.*

In seconds, it was all tied up. Roland set off for the resort of Piso Livadi on the east coast to continue work on a bijou new-wave hotel perched above the strand, and Kyros introduced me to his nephew, Leo, an equally massive man who had a mane of hair down to his shoulders and wide, hairy nostrils. All lion, for sure. He couldn't speak any English, but via a series of hand gestures we got off on the right foot.

What was Roland worried about?

Two weeks passed.

The spring flowers sloughed off their adornments under an increasingly sweltering sun as I acclimatised myself to the rhythm of the island, cutting my teeth on a near hand-to-mouth existence. By night, I slept on the roof of the goat hut, high enough off the ground to keep the mosquitoes at bay and remote enough for the police not to bother me; by day I was at work, refilling the coffers. It was hard graft, at times monotonous, but it felt honest. Each morning at the depot we stacked scaffolding and timber onto our flatbed truck and, with Leo at the wheel, delivered the materials to the smattering of building sites dotted about the island. Afternoons, we painted rooftops. We never really spoke, but it didn't matter; I felt privileged to be simply sharing space with a bona fide local. At the end of each day when Leo dropped me back in Parikia, I almost missed his company.

I didn't go out at night. Without secure funds, I figured I'd build up some savings before allowing myself such frivolities. I spent some of my downtime writing in my makeshift journal – a half-used school exercise book I'd found discarded in the dried thistles by the roadside near the campsite – but I mostly snorkelled off the cliffs at Krios, touched by the cold, swollen fingers of the open ocean, the misty sea floor carpeted in thousands of black urchins.

I thought of Ellie less and less. My philosophy tutor would have labelled it 'denial': pushing all memories of her into a dark recess of my mind, stored out of harm's way, yet accessible in a crisis. But my tutor was history. I felt stronger – did I dare say it? My own man.

In fact, so certain was I of my metamorphosis, I decided a celebration was in order, and on the Thursday of my third week on the island, after Leo and I clocked off early from work, I broke protocol, dipped into my meagre savings and hired a moped to check out Naoussa, in the north of the island.

Time to pay a visit to the Tamarisk.

Naoussa, with its wind-beaten, untarnished rocky coastline, was a completely different vibe from Parikia. An authentic, full-on fishing port, where the boats were hauled up onto the bank to dispense their catch while the seamen mended their nets, where the locals seemed for once to outnumber the tourists. Not a favourite with the lager-drinking hoards, it was graced instead by bohemian intellectuals in studied flowing attire, looking for enlightenment and sardines.

I trawled around the castle walls of the old town with its spiderweb of tiny alleys, avoiding the main attraction of my visit – sweat breaking out along my neck every time I spotted a woman over five-ten with auburn hair – until I could stand it no longer, and made for the harbour.

But of Ellie there was no sign. And as I had suspected, the Tamarisk restaurant was a dead end. Yes, they'd heard of an owner who lived in Athens, but the only name they could give was of a certain Ella – an Italian who lived on the island and spent time between Naoussa and Paros, where she also managed a cocktail bar. Did they know if the owner in Athens was Ellie's cousin? No idea. They had never heard of an Ellie.

Disappointed, yet determined to embrace the positive – I

was cutting a new path, after all – I stayed for dinner and ate alone, watching the sun set. My table perched only five feet from the water's edge, I let my mind empty and became mesmerised by phosphorescence in the shallows, which would flash up every time a wave surged onto the hissing sand; a hypnotic, almost erotic dance of light, urging me into the water to taste her deeper oblivion, if only I would dare. Then, as night thickened, came a boisterous live band, playing traditional Greek songs with bouzoukis and mandolins. Soul-searing music, sad and happy at the same time.

I assured myself that I didn't need Ellie. I missed her – of course, I had to admit it – but missing her was acceptable. It was important to grieve, vital, even – to make way for the new. But I didn't need her. I felt immediately lighter.

When the locals began to assemble and dance, I wondered if I was going to be invited to get up – which was when I caught sight of the only other non-Greek: a freckled, strawberry-blonde-haired girl trying to read a copy of *Cider with Rosie* at a table just behind me.

I asked if I could join her.

She obliged.

Her name was Charlotte Molenaar. She was Dutch, twenty-three years old, and worked at an investment bank in Rotterdam. We ordered a bottle of red and chatted about everything and nothing – from sea urchins, Greek food and sun cream to Swiss chocolate, Yeats's poetry, and how to make a friendship bracelet, which she demonstrated by undoing hers and starting over from scratch. She gave it to me as a memento.

There was more wine and more music.

With every toss of her waist-length locks, she enraptured me further, inviting me into her playful worldview that was far, far removed from Ellie's cool political savvy. Childlike in her wonder, she hung on my every word, from my teaching of the position of the Pole Star, the reliable, due-north centre point amid the relentless rotation of celestial bodies, to my recently acquired knowledge that one should only eat the purple sea urchins, not the black. And to top it all, she couldn't get enough of my matchbox trick – creating an 'erection' using three matches that fused once lit, causing the middle match to rise in a woody tumescence.

Eventually we were dragged to our feet by the locals and joined in the dancing until the kitchen closed. Over the course of those brief, music-swept, wine-soaked hours, I fell in love. I wanted to drink her in, absorb her into my skin and leave a single set of footprints on the earth.

At 1 a.m. when the waiters kicked us out, we walked hand in hand to her hostel, where she asked me to wait while she fetched something from her room. I was itching to kiss her in the lobby, but thought she'd appreciate the privacy, so I suggested I accompany her to her lodgings. 'It's a sweet gesture,' she replied, unhooking her arm from mine. 'But James will be asleep and he hates being woken unnecessarily.'

I felt the ground tilt.

She returned with a book of Yeats's poetry and told me I should read the one called the 'Song of the Wandering Aengus'. With that, she smoothed down her dress, kissed me on the cheek and told me not to lose the friendship bracelet.

Then off she went to bed.

I sat in the shabby foyer of her hostel, wondering if 'James' was a safety net, and considered knocking on her door to find out, but couldn't summon the courage. Finally, after fifteen minutes' popping and cracking from ill-fated insects electrocuting themselves on the fluorescent flytraps, I left the hostel and set off back across the plateau under the canopy of a thousand frozen lights to my goat hut, the copy of poems wedged into my shorts.

When I reached the highest point on the mountain, I stepped off my moped, kicked it over into the dust and stamped against the unforgiving earth, screaming obscenities into the night until I was at risk of breaking an ankle. Then, in a final act of indignation, I hurled the anthology of poems as far as I could into the thyme.

Ellie was right: I was a loser.

The next day I was fired.

I left early for the depot, keen to rid myself of the sour taste from the previous night, and on arrival, found Leo with his arm in a sling and a fuming Kyros in tow. I asked the former if he was okay, but he wouldn't even look at me. Kyros stepped forward, and clenching his massive fists, told me that according to Leo I had broken his arm by pushing him off his moped.

I was dumbfounded. Aside from the fact I'd never witnessed him ride a motorbike, let alone own one, the story was preposterous. But when I opened my mouth to demand exactly when and where this act took place, Kyros gave a dismissive wave of a hairy hand and turned his back on me in disgust. With that, they drove off and left me among the timber and scaffolding, utterly perplexed.

I couldn't go to Roland for advice, as he'd upped and left the previous week for Santorini to get in some sightseeing before returning to Scotland, so I remained contrite and kept my mouth shut. Leo was a stout lad, and as I'd never had a proper fight in my life, I didn't fancy my chances. Besides, being local, I figured he'd have connections.

When I finally returned, shattered and humiliated, back at the goat hut, I discovered someone had been through my rucksack and stolen the 10,000 drachmas I'd hidden away in a rolled-up pair of socks. They'd also taken my gym shoes and a T-shirt.

I was fucked.

For the next four days, I trawled the main strip of Parikia in search of work – anything to try and get back in the game – but without success. At night, I moved from rooftop to beach to building site to find a secure berth where I could expect a peaceful night's sleep, now my goat-hut hideaway had been compromised; and in a bid to eke out the remaining 3,000 drachmas, my diet was reduced to white bread and – when I could get away with it – the leftovers from other people's plates.

Inevitably, I ran out of money.

In desperation, I slogged back and forth across the quay-side into every restaurant and café, offering my services for the job that all the island workers loved to hate, *kamakying*, until finally, a Parisian chef agreed to give me a try-out the following night – unpaid, naturally; tips only.

That evening, I sat out by the lone church on the cliffs at Krios with my rucksack and watched the shooting stars, wondering what I'd do if I failed to make any tips. Put in a phone call to the parents – ask them to wire over some emergency funds? Out of the question. Aside from the fact I'd need identification to access the money, it was a question of pride. Hunter-gatherers didn't phone home. Besides, I'd only worry them unduly.

What then?

Steal, most likely. It was either that, or go to the police, admit my stolen passport and loss of funds, put myself in the hands of the British Embassy and call the whole thing off.

As midnight came around, unwilling to face the kilometre walk back around the bay, I pushed through the tiny chapel door into the cool interior and made use of the altar. Not the most comfortable of beds, but it was at least mosquito-free.

And yet sleep eluded me. If I couldn't provide for myself, if I couldn't guarantee food on the table, what use was I to anyone else? What right did I have to call myself a man?

As it turned out, I never made it to the restaurant, because the next day I ran into Ricky, the tattooed Australian, or, rather, he ran into me.

3

I had just finished using the Koula campsite shower to freshen up for my first night on the new job; the humidity had jumped over the course of the day and a sultry haze settled in above the island. Crossing the concrete apron between the shower block and the campsite entrance, I heard the screech of car brakes and turned in time to come face to face with an open-top jeep heading straight for me in a cloud of dust. I froze and awaited the impact, but it never came. The vehicle slammed sideways to a stop just inches from my feet as the engine cut out. 'Haston, you Pommie bastard! I've been searching this island for days. Where the fuck have you been?'

Twenty minutes later we were pulled up on the edge of a shingle beach in the sleepy village of Pounta, four miles south of Parikia, smoking cigarettes as we listened to the ticking of the cooling engine. Ricky had insisted on taking me for a spin, promising to drop me off at the restaurant in time to start work at eight.

He was quick to dismiss my outrage at being abandoned on the ferry, and he also swore he didn't have my passport or travellers' cheques. According to him, I'd disappeared below deck for a 'tactical vom' and never returned. Seeing as Santorini was the last stop and I hadn't reappeared, the gang had assumed I was either on Paros or Ios. Cracking on without me, they continued the party for several days straight in Fira, the stylish capital perched high above the cliffs. After that they parted ways.

'Diane was gutted, mate,' he grinned. 'Fancied the arse off you.'

From the twinkle in his eye I couldn't tell if he was bullshitting me – I figured the glint to be a permanent fixture – but I found his energy invigorating, and so, giving him the benefit of the doubt, I filled him in on my own little adventures – in particular, the strange incident with Leo 'the Cunt' – and enjoyed the sensation of catching up with an old friend, despite the fact we'd known each other for a matter of hours, much of which I couldn't recall.

'We should probably head to the restaurant,' I said, noticing the time on the dashboard clock. 'Chef's Parisian – surly bastard. Don't want to piss him off before I've started.'

'No sweat,' replied Ricky, flicking his cigarette across the bonnet of the jeep. 'But mate, I got to show you something first.'

He spun the vehicle around and we rejoined the main road back to Parikia. About half a mile into the journey, we turned off up a dusty byway that took us up and over a wide network of undulating olive groves and sun-bleached farm terrain with its scrawny goat-herd inhabitants before turning south again and effectively doubling back on ourselves as we approached the northern edges of Alyki, the ancient fishing village once famous for its salt production – so Ricky told me.

Bouncing along a track full of potholes, we approached a villa nestling among some cypress trees in the middle of a neatly laid out olive grove. It had a pristine ten-metre pool that looked over Alyki harbour below, and every meandering cuboid wall and turret was laced with climbing bougainvillea and jasmine, like a cover shot from a travel mag.

'Don't tell me you live here, you jammy bastard,' I shouted to Ricky above the whine of the engine.

He didn't reply, just grinned and continued fighting with the spinning steering wheel as we rolled up to the west side of the villa and parked alongside the patio steps.

I followed him around to the front of the building and he tossed me a set of keys. 'After you,' he said, gesturing to the ceiling-to-floor windows.

Expecting any minute to be surprised by an irate owner, I unlocked the doors, stepped over the threshold and wandered hesitantly in. Chequered marble flooring, antique furniture and Turkish tapestries spread out before me, leading up to a wide, open-plan kitchen resplendent with copper and steel cooking utensils hanging from elegant hooks on the wall behind low-slung industrial lamps.

'What's all this then?' I asked, thoroughly impressed.

'A proposition,' replied Ricky.

I turned around to find him pointing the lens of his video camera at me.

'Still got that thing?' I said, getting a flashback from the ferry of him thrusting it in my face as Diane tried to put her tongue in my mouth.

'Go on,' he grinned. 'Say something witty.'

'I'm all right,' I replied. 'So, what are we doing here?'

But he ignored the question: 'Sony camcorder,' he said, pressing 'record'. 'State of the art.' He filmed me for a

moment, then without a word handed me the camera, sauntered back outside, stripped down to his pants and backflipped
into the pool.

Keys in one hand, camcorder in the other, I walked out
and stood by the edge as Ricky raced himself for a length of
front crawl. Eventually he pulled himself up onto the side
and shook his head, dog-like. 'The villa belongs to a client of
mine,' he panted. 'An artist. Travels the islands every summer
so he can paint. I help him with his itinerary and organising
his affairs; do a bit of this and that. He hires a yacht every
year, which I help him source and occasionally crew for him.
It's a lot of work and I could use another set of hands about
the place.'

'Doing what, exactly?'

There was that glint again.

'Stick around, he'll tell you himself,' he replied, blowing
water from his nose, then he gestured at the machine in my
hands. 'Just point and press. Automatic focus.'

'Tell me,' I replied, putting the camera down and wondering if this was a wind-up, whether we were trespassing. *But
then how did he get the keys?*

'He's on Santorini with the yacht,' said Ricky, finally. 'I
have to go and bring him over. You hang out here, practise
your front crawl, work on your tan and maintain a presence
about the place. See you for ouzo and calamari when we get
back.'

'I'm supposed to be at the restaurant in an hour,' I said,
putting Ricky's air of mystery down to a penchant for the
dramatic, and already thinking how much better I'd sleep
there than on yet another mosquito-infested building site.

He didn't reply, but hauled himself up to his feet and went
off to the jeep, returning moments later with a leather satchel,

out of which he took an envelope of cash and proceeded to count out a fistful of dollar bills. 'A hundred up front,' he grinned, with another of his trademark winks. 'Call it house-sitting money.'

I stared at the notes in astonishment; it was practically my entire budget for the trip in one swoop. Misreading my hesitation, however, Ricky sighed, peeled off $50 more, and tossed the lot onto a sunlounger.

'No need to thank me,' he said, picking up his video camera and pointing it at me. 'But say something witty before I change my fuckin' mind.'

Two beers later, he left for Santorini to collect the client.

As the sun dipped below the horizon, the storm that had been threatening all day finally broke. Confined indoors, I explored the villa briefly – apart from the kitchen and larder, the place was effectively empty, including the basement – and after choosing the middle-sized room upstairs, flopped down on the bed to watch the lightning display through the windows, upon which I fell instantly asleep.

The following morning, after the best night's kip I'd had since Ellie broke up with me, I shook off the lingering dis-belief at my change of fortune, and for the next forty-eight hours did as instructed: stayed on-site, keeping a watchful eye over the villa and its surrounds, dined on the assortment of artisan groceries the kitchen was stocked up with, and divided the daylight hours between laps of the pool and forays through the neighbouring olive grove. At night I sat out on the patio, working my way through the crate of Mythos Ricky had left me, watching the fireflies dance beneath a rotating Milky Way.

With no one to talk to, nothing to read, and no desire

33

whatsoever to tune into the incomprehensible TV channels, my mind naturally turned back to Ellie. But it was different now: I understood that it wasn't our time, and that there was always next term – although, if she could see me in my present state, I wondered, she might perhaps change her mind. The truth was, I'd moved on and was starting to feel whole again; not one of the mad or brave who would change the world, but rather a necessary cog and cohabitant of planet Earth, tumbling unfettered and unjudged through time. No further need for self-definition than simply to be there. Like a lizard on a rock.

Beyond the binary code.

On the morning of the third day, however, my vigil came to an abrupt end when I came downstairs to find the dining table laid for breakfast and an array of packing boxes strewn about the sitting room. The client had arrived.

As I inspected the incongruous chinaware, baffled that I hadn't been woken by their arrival, the patio door opened and in walked a heavyset silver-haired man in a kimono and sunglasses, smoking a Café Crème.

'*Guten Tag*,' he smiled, '*Sie sind der Haston, glaube ich.*'

I couldn't reply. The left side of his face was disfigured by scar tissue and there was no movement in the facial muscles. 'Don't worry, you can say what you like,' he added, taking a seat at the table. 'Honesty is always the best policy. I'm Heinrich – pleased to meet you.' Then he took off his sunglasses to reveal he had no left eye, only a concave dent where the skin had been grafted over the socket.

I tried to think of something intelligent to say, but nothing came, so, I simply shook his hand, joined him at the table and poured him a coffee.

'*Danke sehr,*' he said, extinguishing his cigar in the ashtray, 'Ricky tells me you study German at the University?'

'*Ja, das stimmt,*' I replied, filling my own cup. '*Aber ich habe keine Ahnung was ich damit machen soll.*'

'A degree is a degree,' he continued in English, just the slightest hint of an accent. 'And you never know when these ugly languages can come in useful.'

I told him I agreed and helped myself to a croissant.

'Ricky tells me you are looking for work on the island?'

'I'm up for anything really, just paying my way.'

Cue the job offer . . .

He nodded and stirred his coffee.

But it didn't come.

'Ricky has gone into Alyki to fetch supplies and have the engine on the yacht looked at by a mechanic. So, for now, it is you and me.'

After breakfast, he said I should take it easy for a while and hang by the pool while he sorted himself out and moved in, so I duly obeyed orders. Then around midday he reappeared at the patio doors in a pair of shorts, a stripy, collared shirt and a Panama hat. He also wore a patch over his left eye that gave him the air of a retired pirate.

'Hey, lazy Englishman,' he yelled, 'Come inside, I have something to show you.'

I pulled on a T-shirt and followed him down to the basement, where the air was cooler and smelled of paint. Walking to the end of the corridor, Heinrich unlocked a door and flicked a switch. 'Please,' he said, with a bow of the head, stepping back to allow me through. 'A little hobby of mine.'

The room had been turned into a portrait gallery. At first guess, around six or eight different subjects: reclined, standing, lying on a sofa – men and women of different ages and sizes. All nude.

I walked round the room and studied them more closely. They were predominantly watercolours, but also a few charcoal sketches. 'They're wonderful,' I said, for want of any better adjective. 'It's as if they are trapped in the paper.'

'Thank you,' he replied, taking a slow walk around the room, gently straightening some of the frames. 'I presume for someone like you it is easy to meet people. No?' he asked, adjusting his eyepatch. 'You're handsome, intelligent. People warm to you easily, I expect.'

To hide the flush, I turned away and pretended to examine one of the nudes, who was lying on a chaise longue, breasts arching to the ceiling.

An offer was imminent – I could sense it.

'For me it is not so easy,' he continued quietly, indicating his broken face 'Each of these people you see was brought to me by Ricky. He tells them he has a friend who is an artist, looking for willing participants to model for him – to paint. For a fee, of course. And I pay Ricky to recruit them for me.'

He slid a finger behind the eyepatch, attending to an itch. 'But there is something else.' He took a few steps away from me then turned, hands flopping loosely at his sides. 'I have slept with all of them.'

Outside the cicadas stepped up their chant.

I turned back to the gallery of complicits: there were at least three male subjects; one of them looked in his teens. 'His name is Esteban,' said Heinrich, following my eyeline. 'From Barcelona, studying at the London School of Economics. Nearly twenty-one. The money will help him with his studies.'

Was there was a picture of Ricky somewhere?

36

'I paint them, and pay them for their time,' he continued, resting a hand on my shoulder. 'Afterwards, I invite them to stay for dinner. We talk. We relax. Eventually, if the feeling is right, I suggest a way of earning double the money over again. They are in no way forced to do anything they don't want to do. Nearly always, they are willing – thanks to Ricky's skill in selecting the right people. There are no tricks, no drugs. Sometimes they don't even want payment, but I insist.'

Unaccountably, I felt a stirring in my groin.

'A beautiful occasion deserves a beautiful memory,' he continued, getting to his feet. 'I would like you to help Ricky find me more subjects.'

'You think I have what it takes to be a pimp?'

I might have needed the work, but I still had a moral code.

'That is an ugly way of putting it,' he replied with a shrug. 'There is nothing sleazy or "incorrect" about what happens. I am looking for people open to adventure, to living fully and experiencing life's riches.' He let his hand slide down my back as he stepped away. 'For every model you bring, I will pay you five hundred dollars.'

I spun around to face him, but he was still staring at Esteban.

Five times my starting budget.

Was he serious? All I'd hoped for was to cover my costs on the islands, to live hand to mouth and pay my way. I hadn't expected to earn any real money.

But – selling sex?

'I suggest we go upstairs and have a drink,' he said, breaking the sense of intoxication that had crept over me. 'Ricky will be back any moment now. We shall have some lunch and relax. Then, if the boat is ready, maybe you would like to go for a sail?' He patted me on the shoulder, locked the gallery door and ascended the steps to the ground floor, whistling as he went. 'Oh, and tonight we will have a housewarming,' he added, calling down from the top of the stairs.

I hadn't actually said yes.

That night I was officially welcomed to the villa.

Every available bath and sink was filled with ice and booze. A pool table was set up in the rear lounge, a table-tennis table in the atrium by the rubber plant, the sitting room waswired for sound with top-of-the-range quadraphonic speakers;, and, naturally, Ricky's camcorder was recharged to capture the festivities.

According to Ricky, the housewarming was the traditional way to mark their arrival on a new island and it kick-started the recruiting process. Heinrich announced that he wouldn't attend; he didn't like large gatherings and wanted us to get to work without cramping our style. I wasn't convinced that anyone would come with zero notice but Ricky was cock-sure. As we went about Parikia that afternoon, organising the party essentials, we dropped into the various clubs and bars, and Ricky spread the word. Apparently, that's all it took. Within hours the whole island would know.

'No pressure to join in, though, mate,' he said, whipping the top off a beer and handing me the bottle as we unloaded the jeep. 'Make your mind up in the morning.'

I told him I'd keep him posted. Moral concerns aside, there was also the issue of confidence. Could I hack it? Did I have the right skill set?

Then Ricky raised his beer and silenced my head-talk.

'Happy hunting.'

*

Before nightfall we said our goodbyes to our host, who was heading off into Parikia to have dinner with a friend. I offered to give him a lift in the jeep, but he protested he could use the walk – it wasn't far. I watched him traipse through the wasteland down to the dirt track at the bottom of the valley, where, all of a sudden, a motorbike appeared out of nowhere in a cloud of dust and stopped to pick him up. There appeared to be a brief issue with the bike's engine, whereupon, removing the helmet, the rider revealed herself to be female, which surprised me – way taller than Heinrich.

'Run out of shit to do?' came an accusatory voice behind me.

'Just checking out Heinrich's date,' I replied, clapping a hand on Ricky's shoulder, as I turned to face him. 'I thought he had trouble meeting women.'

'Probably his sister. He said they might hook up.'

His sister?

'Why not introduce us, then?'

'Maybe he doesn't want her finding out what he's up to,' said Ricky, lighting up a cigarette. 'Come on, let's have a tequila.'

'There's no one here yet.'

'Exactly. Someone's got to get this fuckin' party started.'

At eleven o'clock the first guests started to arrive.

First to cross the threshold were Svenja and Jens, a Belgian couple in their early twenties who were travelling southern Europe for the summer before going back to college in Bruges. They were an unlikely pair: Svenja was a diminutive peroxide blonde, garrulous, fiery – a pixie-cut hairdo framing her elfin features; Jens was a six-foot-two sleepy giant, his docile demeanour accentuated by drooping eyelids, freckled arms and legs covered with a matting of thick, sun-bleached hair. They arrived in a white camper van on which the words *Hoch die Tassen* were painted – 'Bottoms up'. They were staying at Golden Beach in Drios for the next month, and not just for the windsurfing. Drios was host to a select nudist colony where 'swinging' was a particular favourite on the list of after-hours activities. They'd windsurf, play backgammon and drink beer at the Bamboo Shack bar by day, then shag each other's partners on the beach by night. From time to time the police would turn up, but all that happened was a few drachmas changed hands and the police would move on and leave them to it – or else join in.

Around midnight everyone rolled up at once. A cavalcade of mopeds, quad bikes and jeeps bouncing their way up the farm track to the villa delivered a whole host of revellers of all nationalities and ages – at least one octogenarian – in varying degrees of dress and from every walk of life. A local farmer and his teenage son turned up on a lugubrious mule and told Ricky they were offering rides to any takers who might feel up to it later on.

By 1 a.m. the party was going off, at which point Ricky deemed me official cameraman, with instructions to capture 'anything funky, sexy, or weird.'

Amazed at just how many people he had managed to drum up, I roamed the villa with the camcorder and with the aid of alcohol soon shook off any reticence about getting involved. I was particularly taken with a pair of Canadian punk sisters, Sky and Lela, who had identical tattoos up their arms and studded leather collars round their necks. I chatted them up, discussing Jack Kerouac's *On the Road*, before they popped some speed and took to the dance floor. They'd come with Stu 'Sun-in', the manager of the Dubliner, along with three of his off-duty waiting staff – Debbie, Ian and Jess, all badly sun-burned, all from Nottingham, dressed in Kiwi rugby shirts they'd bought at the Rugby World Cup the previous year.

I earmarked them both as potentials for Heinrich.

I also met Ricky's girlfriend Amara, a stunning vision in a simple white dress, sleek-limbed and sultry – a cascade of chocolate hair down to her hips, and seductive doe eyes, such a dark shade of brown they were almost ebony. She introduced herself into camera singing along to INXS's 'Need You Tonight,' before breaking off and telling me she was on holiday before starting drama school in Athens. She was over visiting Ricky on a break from helping out at her father's res-taurant on Naxos – 'best fish on the island.' When I finally looked up from the viewfinder to reciprocate the introduc-tion, Ricky put a proprietorial arm around her and instructed me to get some fresh film cassettes from the basement.

At only just eighteen she really was something: unwittingly oozing sex appeal, yet oblivious of her effect on men.

Dangerous.

At 2 a.m. Ricky announced it was time to get in the pool. Under his instruction, I grabbed the camcorder and stood on the poolside filming the melee, which turned from being a playful water fight into something a whole lot steamier, thanks to Svenja and Jens, who kicked things off with a little fellatio on the pool steps.

The sexual exhibitionism was infectious. At one point, there were four couples at it in the water: two up against the sides of the pool, one on the diving board and a couple in the shallow end – a brash New Yorker with platinum blonde hair, who ran a voice-over agency in the Big Apple, and the spotty-faced teenage son of the Greek farmer with the mule. She was hoisted up on his hips, screaming as if being

41

knifed, while pulling at his hair and repeatedly shoving his face underwater.

The romp moved from the pool to indoors as new members joined the action. Then out came the cocaine.

I was behind the sofa on my knees taking my film-making duties to heart, framing Jess's bouncing breasts in close-up as she was taken from behind by Ian the skinhead – a good-looking boy if he'd had a full head of hair – when Ricky pulled me to my feet and handed me a CD case with four lines of white powder chopped out. He disengaged from Amara, produced a rolled-up $20 bill and dispatched the first two lines. At first, I hesitated, my conservative reflex cutting through the alcohol-induced euphoria, reminding me I didn't do drugs. But I wasn't going to be outdone by Ricky – not in front of his beautiful girlfriend. So I followed suit.

I was struck by how painless and instant the procedure was. No strange palpitations or angst; it was as easy as licking ice cream off a spoon. And it made me taller. Sexier. More animal.

So I did some more.

By the time the sun rose above the olive groves, the villa lay quiet. Lela and Sky were curled up together under a blanket on one of the sofas amid several other overnighters who had slept where they fell. Heinrich was asleep in his quarters – he'd slunk back in around half one. Amara was with Ricky in his room.

As for me: wired with cocaine, I was using up the last cassette on Svenja and Jens, who had worked their way through several guests, including the octogenarian, and then had reunited at close of play for a keep-it-in-the-family, lights-out missionary – as Ricky put it.

Engrossed in my directorial debut, I kept a steady hand and

wiped the sweat from my forehead, moving along the bed to get a close-up between Jens's writhing legs, when all of a sudden he jerked violently, rolled off Svenja with a groan and passed out. Unsure as to whether this was ejaculation or heart attack, I stopped filming and went to help him, but Svenja had other ideas. She pulled me onto her, forcing her tongue into my mouth while a free hand fumbled for my erection. I pushed the unconscious Jens to the side of the bed, shuffled out of my clothes and thrust myself inside her, uncaring that not only had another man been there moments earlier, but that the same man was still present, lying unconscious, his scratchy leg resting against my thigh.

I lost all sense of time, but I seemed to be taking for ever, the effect of the drugs hampering my performance. When I rolled onto my side to allow my pounding heart brief respite, I noticed with a start that Ricky had crept into the room and was filming me with his video camera. How long he'd been there, I had no idea. Had Svenja seen him? Had she suggested he join us? She and Jens had started the orgy, after all.

Staring wildly at the red light on the camera housing, I was about tell him to fuck off, but he held up a finger to his lips and motioned me to carry on.

So, I did. I was making films – why not star in them too?

The next time I turned towards the door, he'd gone.

When the inconsequential ending finally came, it was getting light. I withdrew, dislodged Jens' hairy arm from across my back, and, plumping the pillow under my head, turned to Svenja to engage in some post-coital pillow talk, but she was already asleep.

Not in any condition to drift off, I slipped out of her arms and pulled on my shorts, made my way downstairs through the sitting room, with its debris of crashed-out bodies, and stepped out through the patio doors into the fresh air, a smile forming at the corners of my mouth.

Nietzsche would approve.

Walking over to the perimeter wall, I picked up a stone and hurled it as far as I could down the dusty track. The noise disturbed a large woodpecker-sized bird from his resting place in the scrub, and it set off, swooping low to one side of the villa, its undulating flight a blur of gold against the dark green of the cypresses.

'That was the golden oriole,' piped up a voice from behind me.

I turned to find Heinrich holding two cups of coffee.

'Quite rare here; they usually stay on the mainland.' He handed me one of the coffees and I nodded my thanks, unable to tear my gaze from the hollow that was his left eye.

'How was your night?' I asked, forcing myself to look at his good eye.

'Very pleasant, thank you.'

'And your sister?'

'My sister?' he replied, his brow creasing. 'What do you mean?'

So, Ricky was bullshitting me again. Still – none of my business.

'I've been thinking about your offer,' I said, taking a sip of coffee. 'I accept.'

Okay, it wouldn't earn me Brownie points with the uni's careers advisory service, and it wasn't something I'd necessarily share with family and friends, but I'd have been insane to pass it up. I'd be able to make some serious savings. Pay off my overdraft. Put it towards a car . . . rent my own flat, even.

'All you have to do is bring them to me,' he chuckled, putting a hand on my shoulder. 'I will do the rest.'

'For five hundred dollars a time?'

He nodded, swiping a mosquito from his ear.

'If they sleep with you,' I added.

'Oh, they always do,' he concluded with a smile.

With that, the German ambled off to the pool, kicked off his sandals and let the kimono fall away, revealing his naked body in all its corpulent pink glory.

And with a heavy splash he was in.

I took a step towards the patio and narrowly missed planting my foot on a dead lizard, lying stiff and twisted on its side, half-eaten by ants. I stared at it . . . I couldn't think if it reminded me more of Heinrich or Ricky; there was a little of both. The missing eye, in Heinrich's case. And Ricky? Well, there was the smiling curl of the dead creature's jaw, for a start. But then Ricky was all reptile, wasn't he?

If you can't beat them, join them.

I felt a further rush of confidence; if it was that easy to get people to sleep together, recruiting potential models for Heinrich would be child's play.

Any fool could do it.

4

It was the easiest money I ever made.

Under the guiding arm of Ricky, July evaporated in a whirl of amphetamines and 'blow' as we successfully brought in model after model for our German artist. It was impossible to tell where work stopped and play started. The only lines drawn were the rows of white powder purveyed by the Australian and his cohorts of hangers-on; a nutrition-free but enjoyable diet that I found increasingly agreeable with the passing of each week. It gave me strength. Gave me wings. Put me on a level with Ricky and spurred on my competitive zeal; I was determined to prove that whatever Ricky could do, I could do better.

I didn't see it as pimping. After all, who was I to judge how consensual adults wished to spend their time and money? It was a work opportunity to die for, and a way to have fun and meet people – women in particular. This was the new me, the inner alpha male I'd been so clearly lacking. The whole point of the trip was to shed my wings of indecisiveness and 'grow a pair'. Well, thanks to Ricky I had. Now I was sharing them – and getting paid for it.

As for Ellie . . .
Ellie – who?

The recruiting itself was inventive and, on the whole, executed with professional acumen. Ricky was on point. My role? Sidekick, occasional decoy, and of course, cameraman.

Aside from Lucy, the screaming voice-over agent, and Sky, who were both recruited at the housewarming, the nine remaining models from July's catch came from an assortment of sorties in different parts of the island. Elizabeth was a fifty-year-old, divorcee primary-school teacher whom Ricky had come across in Naoussa; the first casualty of his favourite method of recruiting, which was to set up an easel and chair and do caricature sketches for willing tourists. A simple enough ruse: whenever he sketched someone he fancied was good fodder for Heinrich, he gave them the portrait for free and explained that his teacher, a retired but famous artist in residence on the island, was looking for models to sit for him for a fee, and that they would be perfect.

Working as a double act – it was uncanny how people could be lured into dropping their guard in the presence of a rolling video camera – Ricky and I used the same tactic to snag Gary, a Welsh professional footballer; Shane, a South African airline pilot; and finally, two savvy French women in their thirties, Isabel and Martha, who worked for Crédit Lyonnais in Paris. They had recently given up on men and started dating each other, but felt there was no harm revisiting old ground – they were on holiday, after all.

Then there was Charlene, the biochemist postgrad from Texas State University. Not a total success story, but a result nonetheless.

I invited her and her three excitable tie-dyed college

48

friends, Tina, Arlene and Dana, on the yacht for a day trip to Antiparos to visit the stalactite caves. The plan was to land the entire group – a 'full house,' as Ricky put it – but thanks to the help of incessant tequila shots, followed by the popping of numerous Ponderol pills, a diet tablet that you could buy over the counter, which, taken in excess, could induce a speed-like euphoria, the return leg of the journey turned into a floating orgy. So, while Ricky and I had our share of the fun, the only recruit still standing by the time we reached the villa was Charlene. Luckily, as well as being a dedicated tourist – courtesy of her student travel guide, *Let's Go Greece*, she had regaled us with all the must-dos and must-knows about Antiparos – she was also a serious art enthusiast, and willingly offered herself to Heinrich 'for the betterment of his craft.'

However, she was also one of the few that got pissed off with a camera in her face – something she revealed eloquently enough once we were back on board the yacht, after our two-kilometre hike from the caves at the summit of Antiparos mountain.

'You guys ever turn that thing off?' she said, pushing her hand into the lens and jamming the eyepiece into my temple.

'Gotta capture the moment,' I replied breezily. 'Life's too short.'

'Bullshit. If you're filming it, you ain't livin' it.'

With that, she stripped naked and somersaulted off the prow of the yacht into the water. My confidence thrown for the first time in weeks, I had no comeback. So I sheepishly turned off the camera and pretended to busy myself below deck.

It was later, during this same episode, that Ricky and I had a 'moment.'

I was at the tiller, proving my helming capabilities while

Ricky dangled his legs through the starboard rail, sipping on a tequila. Charlene and the girls were crashed out on the foredeck, catching the last of the rays as the day drew to a close. Ricky suggested I reef the sails and go under engine power. 'More comfortable for the ladies – less tilt.'

'Go for it,' I replied, nodding to the mast. Yes, he was team leader, but his insistent need to give the orders was starting to wear thin, and for the first time since my arrival at the villa – thanks in part to my interlude with Charlene and the video camera – I felt a pang of shame that I'd agreed to take part in such a tasteless enterprise for financial gain.

'You're the fuckin' captain,' he replied. 'Show me how it's done.'

Unable to risk losing face in front of our guests, I tied the tiller off, rolled in the genoa and reefed the mainsail, then flicked the engine on and took up position at the wheel.

'Done like a pro,' he beamed.

'Taught by the best,' I replied, unable to hide a smile.

Ambushed by his flattery, along with several shots of tequila, my negativity soon slipped away, as I reminded myself that the work was a temporary means to an end – a tactical necessity 'with benefits.' Everyone was having fun; ultimately it was harmless and, therefore, there was no need to quit before time.

And so, as the dying light cast a soft-focus veil over our bronzed bodies, Ricky and I fell to swapping compliments in the unselfconscious way that only inebriation will usually permit among men. Two hunter-gatherers admiring each other's prowess. Post-kill. Masters of the moment.

I told him that had he been a girl, I'd have kissed him.

He told me I should do so anyway.

I considered it for a millisecond, then laughed it off and

told him about Ellie. Everything. How she'd invited me to spend the summer with her in Greece, expenses paid – by her wealthy ship-owning uncle – but that I'd blown it with my inability to commit. I told him she'd been my soul mate; that I'd never find another.

He suggested I look the family up; a shipping business wouldn't be hard to locate. He even offered to tap into his connections and have her tracked down on my behalf.

I laughed and called him a pussy, then we broke out the Ponderols and the party got underway.

The last three recruits to complete July's blistering tally were: Reinhardt, a svelte writer from Austria, who had driven his Harley-Davidson over from Vienna, looking for enlightenment; Sarah, an edgy graphic designer from London, who had fallen out with her gay male travelling companion after too many amphetamines at the fish festival in Piso Livadi; and finally Masha, a wide-eyed university student originally from Russia who was training to be an actor in Berlin and desperate to practise her English.

The fee for my endeavours? Two and a half thousand dollars in cash, safely stashed away under my mattress at the villa. A tidy sum for four weeks' work.

In terms of specifics – as to what happened once a client agreed to go back to the villa to be painted – well, that was between subject and artist. No longer a necessary part of the equation, Ricky and I had to remove ourselves and let Heinrich practise his magic alone. Ricky usually went off to Parikia town to check in on one of the two bars he had a financial stake in – the Dubliner, and the Saloon d'Or – whereas I took the opportunity to snorkel off the rocks at Pounta in search of edible sea urchins, or practise my windsurfing at the surf school. With the exception of Charlene, all business with the models was conducted during daylight hours. On that one occasion Heinrich entertained into the night, Ricky slunk off somewhere in town, while I joined the Belgians in Drios and spent a snug night crashed out in their camper van.

As for the video footage, it was catalogued by Heinrich for posterity. Sometimes it contained graphic sexual acts – such as whenever we filmed a drug-fuelled party at the villa – but more often than not it was just banter and larking about, captured during the recruiting process. Either way, Heinrich wanted to keep the tapes as a memento – his 'collection of friends,' as he termed it. Ricky transferred the cassettes to VHS using the television and his VCR player, then we'd watch them all together over a drink or two before handing them to Heinrich, who stored them in the basement along with his portraits. The only copy I got to keep myself was the one that included footage Ricky had taken of me in bed with Svenja at the party, which I kept hidden in my rucksack for a couple of weeks – for personal use when alone at the villa – before concluding that masturbating over a filmed recording of myself in a sexual act was not necessarily a healthy thing, and duly recorded over the tape with a TV chat show.

The point being I was having enough fun with the women I met, and unlike Ricky, I didn't need celluloid proof to confirm it. But I was always careful to make sure that whenever I got lucky, Ricky and his camcorder were nowhere in sight.

An exhausting, exhilarating month. Worth every second.

It should have been the moment to take a well-earned break, to hang up my spurs, cut free from my hosts and explore the other islands, but I was hooked. The thrill of the chase was one thing, but the lure of easy money was irresistible. And there was more to be made – much more. Besides,

I had unfinished business to attend to: a recruiting sting that would land me another three Gs and put a monstrous cherry on an already sizeable cake.

Operation Svenja.

The idea had taken seed a week after the housewarming in June, when Heinrich and I were reviewing the tapes from the camcorder. He had been captivated by the effervescent girl – whom Ricky had now dubbed 'our blonde pocket rocket' – and offered me $2,000 if I could bring her to him. So, I tracked both Svenja and Jens down one night in Parikia, and over several piña coladas told them straight up how they could make some serious cash. As far as I was concerned, it was a dead cert: they were swingers; they'd both be up for it – two for one.

But I'd misjudged them. 'Just because we're swingers doesn't mean we are prostitutes,' Svenja had announced, her button nose wrinkling in distaste. When I passed this on to Heinrich, explaining that the whole idea was a no-go area, he simply offered me $1,000 more, and disappeared off to bed.

Three thousand dollars in one pop.

There had to be a way.

As Ricky and I set about our work, I kept the Belgians in play by accepting their offer of windsurfing lessons. They took me twice a week to Pounta surf school, where the beach was sheltered and slow-shelving, offering beginners' boards which I got for free, due to Ricky's connections with the manager, Sadie, a professional windsurfer from the Australian Gold Coast.

As the weeks passed by, however, I couldn't find an angle. No matter how free and easy the Belgians were, they were not going to receive money for sex. It simply went against their creed. Distracted by my successes elsewhere, I was ready to accept defeat and give up on the idea, worried that my obsession was in danger of turning me into another Ricky; but then the solution suddenly popped up out of the blue – from the Belgians themselves.

We had just finished a day's windsurfing on their home turf, Golden Beach, the nudist colony that lay to the south-east of the island along the windblown Drios peninsular. Sitting around a smoking souvlaki tin amid the swathes of myrtle and bamboo, they told me of their imminent plan to up sticks to Santorini, and asked me if I fancied joining them on their travels. Uncomfortable with my duplicity, I none-theless lied and told them I'd be delighted to do so, and in return asked if they'd care to attend a leaving do at the villa to mark the occasion.

The offer was accepted without hesitation and a date set for the following night.

Operation Svenja was go.

Leaving the Belgians to their barbecued sausages, I returned to the villa, prised Ricky and Heinrich away from their mar-athon video binge on the World War II German series, *Das Boot*, and told them of my success. Heinrich was ecstatic – Ricky less so. He was concerned that Amara was coming over for the weekend and we'd be forced to include her. I pointed out that it would only help the situation: the more people round the dinner table, the more opportunity for Heinrich to have Svenja to himself to ensnare her with his magic.

It was action stations all round.

Heinrich offered to cook, but Ricky told him to relax – he'd need to preserve his creative energies for more pressing concerns. Ricky would hire in a chef for the occasion; a mate of his worked as a sous-chef at the Dubliner – cooked the best lamb kleftiko on the island. It would be Ricky's treat. His way of saying thank you to both of us – to celebrate 'a seriously awesome summer.'

The next morning Ricky ordered me off the premises while he put preparations in place, so I spent a few hours alone, practising gybing on the windsurfer at Pounta, musing how – if I decided I was ready to splash out and buy my own board – I'd get the bloody thing back to the UK. When I returned to the villa later that afternoon, I found the table had been moved to the patio, complete with white table-cloth, silver candlesticks and what looked like expensive china. Off to one side was a souvlaki grill and a clay oven on wheels, next to an impromptu bar with a stupendous array of spirits.

I stood, gobsmacked, as Ricky emerged from the villa in a sarong and sunglasses. 'Don't thank me, thank Yannis,' he said, flopping into a chair.

'Who's Yannis?' I replied.

'Hey, Yannis!' he hollered through the patio doors.

'*Ella Ricky, ti theleis malakas?*' came a voice from within. *Malakas* was a word I'd picked up within hours of arriving out here – it meant 'wanker,' a standard form of address between friends.

'Come and mop the floor under our table, it stinks of piss.'

'*Filisei ton kolo mou,*' came the response. Kiss my ass.

'Fine. Two beers when you've taken your hand off your dick.'

On cue, Yannis loped over with the beers and an ashtray, set them down and waited to be introduced. He was around twenty-five or so, with slicked-back, long dark hair and a chiselled jawbone covered in heavy, fashionable stubble. He stood behind Ricky, rested a hairy hand on his shoulder and asked me in a voice as thick as gravel if I spoke Greek.

'*Mono ligo*,' I'd replied, feeling a need to impress. '*Emai apo tin Anglia.*'

'*Gamimeno, afto einai kalo*! English boy who speak Greek. You need to learn from this boy. Australian – he only drink beer. Enjoy, motherfuckers.'

I watched Yannis slink back into the kitchen and decided that he was someone you'd want to keep on the right side of. 'Don't worry,' said Ricky, as if reading my mind, 'we'll keep him out back and throw him some scraps.'

He laughed and lit two cigarettes.

'Where's Amara?' I asked, wondering if she'd be looking as devastating as she had the night of the party.

'Powdering her nose,' winked Ricky, taking a drag and passing me the other cigarette.

I misunderstood him and protested we shouldn't involve any kind of drugs that evening – this was a work event and a lot rode on it. Ricky told me to chill and assured me there'd be no Class As – just fun stuff, by which he meant spliffs, or maybe some ecstasy or Ponderols if we went out on the town after.

'Depends on Yannis's mate.'

Yannis had an assistant who was helping with the cooking prep. There was an extensive meat and fish mezze before the main course, and the extra set of hands was crucial – for clearing up after the event too. But Ricky assured me that no one other than the invitees would be present at the table.

At that moment, our German host arrived in a freshly pressed linen suit and navy eyepatch, sucking on a Cuban cigar.

'My boys, my heroes – here's to a marvellous summer.'

*

56

Svenja and Jens arrived fashionably late in their clapped-out van, and after an appropriate fuss was made over Svenja's and Amara's attire (the former wearing a figure-hugging orange pencil dress, accentuating her modest curves; the latter draped in a flowing, jet-black off-the-shoulder affair), dinner got underway under starlight, additional illumination provided by roaming fireflies and a low-slung crescent moon. Grilled halloumi, loukanika and octopus à la grecque, accompanied by fresh sardines, moules marinière and whitebait kicked off the first course, served alongside home-made taramasalata, melinzanasalata and tahini – washed down with a dry rosé.

Couldn't have got off to a better start.

With the ending of the main course, we all changed places – house rules as set down by Ricky. I'd been sitting opposite Amara and next to Heinrich, who was at the head of the table holding court, but now we let Svenja and Ricky take our seats, Jens staying roughly where he was, Amara and I moving to the far end of the table.

Up until now the conversation had been all-inclusive, everyone throwing in their contributions – from politics to sailboat design, to Mickey Rourke versus Al Pacino, to who might win the next football World Cup. But with the change of seating came new dynamics. Intoxicated by the wine and good humour, pockets of more intimate discussion started to blossom and we began to segregate.

Which of course was the plan.

And Svenja and Heinrich were getting on famously.

I first noticed the dizziness when standing by the pool talking to Amara over a Metaxa. She'd just confessed that she knew all about the recruiting scheme and that I should watch out for Svenja. The recruiting operations weren't to her taste and she'd be leaving after dinner to join up with friends in Piso Livadi along the coast. Surprised by her candour, but unsure as to what she meant by 'watch out for,' I turned in time to see Heinrich and the Belgian disappear through the patio doors, and in the next instant was hit by a wave of what felt like vertigo.

Embarrassed, I excused myself, sat down on the garden wall and put my head between my legs until the feeling subsided. When I looked up, it was as if time had suddenly jumped – fast-forwarded somehow. A moment ago, Amara was by my side, now she was fully ensconced talking to Jens on a sunlounger. Ricky was sharing a joint with Yannis, who had his feet up on the dining table and was sitting where Heinrich had just been seconds earlier.

It didn't make sense.

I got up slowly and found myself staggering towards the table, cursing Heinrich for continually topping me up. Another wave of dizziness hit me, but I managed to make it to the end of the table before my knees gave way. Ignored by the others, I hauled myself back up, filled myself a glass of water from the jug, and was about to join the table when Yannis's assistant came through the patio doors holding a tequila bottle, a lemon and a knife.

Tequila? The last thing I needed.

He looked up and caught my eye, pointed the knife at me and laughed. But only when he stepped out of the shadow of the patio doors did I recognise him.

Leo the Cunt.

What the fuck was he doing there?

Stunned, I stumbled towards him, wrenched the bottle out of his hands and shoved him to the floor. Around me, chairs were thrown back and a ruckus erupted – a mixture of Greek and English. And yet everything sounded muffled, distant, as if underwater.

'Leo the Cunt!' I shouted at Ricky, who was trying to pull me away from the fallen man. 'Get him out of here!' I tried to kick him but I slipped and fell, hitting my head on the stone paving. Leo staggered to his feet, aided by Yannis, who was shouting at me in Greek, but I couldn't hear, let alone understand him.

Ricky jumped out from my peripheral vision to calm Yannis down, just as Jens appeared from behind the table to help me to my feet, while in the background, I could see Amara standing completely still, cigarette in the air, with one arm folded across her, watching with a fixed smile.

Suddenly Yannis turned on Leo – whatever Ricky had said to him had worked – and within seconds was slapping him about the head as he pushed him across the garden. Leo stopped momentarily to pick up his bag, which had been hurled across the patio to his feet, then bounded off towards the perimeter wall, followed closely by the bellowing Yannis.

I collapsed once more to my knees. Ricky was mouthing words, but I had gone totally deaf. I turned again to where Yannis stood, hands on hips, shouting into the valley, and saw the shadowy figure of Leo scurrying across the wasteland into the night . . .

Then I blacked out.

When I awoke, I found myself alone in my room, sprawled across the bed, fully clothed, and with a dull pain in all my joints – not a clue as to how I got there. From the angle of sunlight through the window, it appeared to be well into the afternoon.

Cursing my inability to handle my liquor, I made my way out into the corridor and down the stairs, grateful that I'd been left alone to sleep it off, and stumbled into the sitting room, expecting to see a sated Heinrich entertaining his guest.

But the place was deserted.

Walking out onto the patio, I found everything as it was the night before: the table outside a mess of plates, glasses and drying food; chairs strewn about the patio; cigarette butts and half-smoked joints lying around; and inside, the kitchen in an equal state of disarray.

My immediate thought was that Heinrich had taken Svenja out to eat, not wanting to be bothered with having to clear up or cook. But as I wandered through the villa I realised that something about the room wasn't quite right. The mess from the evening's entertainment was untouched, but the array of paraphernalia that Heinrich had dotted about everywhere – art materials, videos and books – had disappeared.

I went back upstairs, and finding Heinrich's door ajar, I pushed it open: other than the bed linen, the room was empty.

Same with Ricky's quarters.

Equally, the bathrooms and cupboards along the corridor.

I went downstairs to inspect the basement: empty. The gallery was no more: the walls were bare, no paintings, no equipment to be seen. Not a sign that anyone had been there at all.

They'd cleared out and gone.

Shuffling back out into the air, I wondered if it had anything to do with Leo, or rather, with me throwing Leo off the premises. But that didn't add up; everyone had been on my side – even Yannis had helped to kick him out.

Fighting a wave of nausea, I leaned against the doorframe and surveyed the table and poolside area, trying to make sense of the situation. Apart from the mess, however, there was nothing untoward – nothing that told a story.

What the hell had happened?

5

I spent twenty-four hours holed up in the villa, occupying myself with physical tasks to ease the alcohol-induced paranoia. I cleaned the entire premises from top to bottom, inside and out; I swam endless laps of the pool and tried to read the one object Heinrich had left behind – a tattered copy of Ken Follett's *Lie Down with Lions*. But by the time night fell on the second day, I had to accept that, paranoia or no, I'd been abandoned and it was time to move on.

The following morning, assessing the situation with fresh perspective, I packed up the few items I still possessed into my rucksack and finished off the last remnants of food in the fridge. Standing, pot of yoghurt in hand, I leaned against the patio doors, and came to the conclusion that, in the end, my friendship with Ricky had been akin to a holiday romance. I should have known better than to think we'd stay friends – truth was, we barely knew each other; I was as ignorant of the real Ricky as I had been when I met him on the ferry. He was an act, a pastiche of himself: gregarious, brash and wholly self-centred, but I'd grown fond of the man. We'd had fun sharing time, and thanks entirely to him I'd made a shedload of cash ... And he'd made me forget about Ellie.

He owed me nothing.

Heinrich on the other hand – well, technically, if Operation Svenja had gone down successfully, he owed me three Gs. It was my sole and rather distasteful reason for even entertaining the idea of the project in the first place. Although judging by the speedy and unannounced departure, I had the feeling the plan had been aborted. My soul would remain intact. As for Svenja and Jens, if they hadn't already left for Santorini, I could pass by Golden Beach and see if they could shed light on what had happened. Chances were though, if they'd got wind of the deceit, I'd probably never see them again either.

Licking the last streak of yoghurt off the spoon, I pulled away from the glass door and felt my shirt stick momentarily. I turned to find a smudge on the edge of the window where the glass met the metal siding; rusty in colour and quite clearly the outline of half a hand – from the little finger to the middle finger, with the heel of the palm also visible. Peering closer at it, I assumed the stain was food, but then I noticed on the patio flooring, directly underneath, several drops of the same substance – leading inside about two feet. Wondering how I'd managed to miss it on my earlier cleaning stint, I fetched a cloth and bent down to wipe it away. I thought it might have been gravy, the onion sauce that had accompanied the lamb, but on closer inspection, it was more translucent. In fact, against the patio floor tiling it seemed a clearer, brighter red.

It looked like blood.

I wiped both the glass and the floor, and on returning the cloth to the kitchen, saw a flash of light out of the corner of my eye; a flaring – like sunlight on glass.

I stood up and peered through the oval window.

It was a car, high up on the ridge of Sotires plateau, sun reflecting off the windscreen as it approached the fork in the road where the track split east and south. Shielding my eyes from the glare, I watched it crawl down a dip in the road, where, entering the shade, it revealed its identity.

It was a police car.

Cresting the next rise, it pulled up to a stop in the middle of the road at the junction. A door opened and out stepped an officer, his peaked hat cutting a clear silhouette against the skyline. He made his way around the back of the vehicle, surveying the panorama, and was joined by a second officer who came around the front of the car, flipped open a map, and spread it over the bonnet. Having studied it a moment, he looked up and turned to face south, in the direction of Alyki. After a brief consultation, they got back in the car.

For a moment, nothing happened. The vehicle simply hovered at the junction, a shimmering metal beetle in the midday heat, uncertain which foot to put first. Finally, it took wing, swung slowly round and rolled down onto the farm track.

Towards the villa.

It was a feeling, an instinct in my gut.

I shot upstairs to my room, took my stash of dollars from under the mattress and headed back downstairs, stopping at the patio doors. Peering round the edge of the window frame, I saw the car bouncing steadily along, no rush, as it came ever closer. I waited until it was obscured by the row of cypresses, then slipped out into the air. Keeping low, I ran around the edge of the villa to the east side, where I knew there to be loose drain cover beside the bins. I took the cash, stuffed it into a plastic bag and shoved it deep into the cavity of the drain, replacing the concrete lid to conceal the hole.

Without pausing, I continued round the back of the villa to find the car had completed the 'S' bend at the bottom of the valley, and was now headed directly up towards the villa on the 150 yards of potholed track that led to the garden perimeter.

I ambled round the side of the property and re-entered the patio doors knowing full well I would have been seen by the occupants of the vehicle, hoping my nonchalance wouldn't arouse suspicion – *Just getting rid of some rubbish.*

If Ricky and Heinrich had been busted, if Operation Svenja had somehow backfired, resulting in them having to lay low, I wasn't about to let my hard-won cash fall into the hands of the authorities.

Outside, I heard the car crunch its way to the garden wall and stop. A beat later the engine died. Trying to look natural and unfazed, I took some lamb from the fridge, stuck the meat on a dried piece of pitta and wandered out through the patio doors onto the paving.

The two officers stepped out in unison.

I smiled and waved.

The taller officer, the one with the map in his hand, waved back and had a quick look at the pool before continuing towards me.

I cut them off before they got any closer. 'Good day,' I said cheerfully, taking a bite of my food.

Stay cool.

'English?' asked the leading officer, checking a notepad.

'Absolutely,' I replied with my mouth full. 'How can I help?'

At this point the rear guard turned away and walked round the side of the villa, out of sight.

'Is there anyone else here with you?' The officer took off his hat and wiped his forehead.

'Just me,' I replied.

'Your name is Mister Haston?'

'That's right. Alistair Haston.'

How did they know my name?

'There is no one else inside?' He smiled and took a step closer, tried to peer in the windows.

'On my own. What can I do for you?' I asked mid-chew, keen to show that I was relaxed, non-confrontational.

He said he had some questions.

I told him to fire away.

'Can I get you a drink?' I added, waving an arm in the direction of the patio doors, but not budging an inch. It was good to appear helpful, but not overly keen.

'Thank you, no.' He cast an eye over to the swimming pool, then to the cypresses. 'Big place,' he continued, pursing his lips.

'Yes, I'm lucky.' I smiled again and took another bite. 'Beautiful morning,' I continued, mouth full, fielding the silence. The second officer appeared from the east side of the villa and rejoined his boss.

'This is your jeep?' continued the latter.

'Rental,' I replied, deflecting.

No need to bring Heinrich or Ricky into it just yet.

He waited for me to continue, but I changed tack and asked him again if there was a problem. He assured me everything was fine. But he'd be grateful if I would come with them to the police station in Parikia.

'Can you tell me what this is about?' I asked, picking some lamb out from behind my teeth in an attempt to disguise the tremor in my voice.

He couldn't say. I would be told everything at the station.

I told him politely it wasn't a great time, but that they were

more than welcome to come in to the villa and ask me anything they needed to know, right then and there.

'It's okay. You come with us,' piped up the second officer.

I couldn't tell if it was a question or a command.

'Right now?'

'Now is a good time,' added his superior.

I might have imagined it, but the smile faded and his hand
dropped from his chest down to his hip. Which was when I
noticed the firearm clipped to his belt.

For a moment, there was just the *sree, sree* of the swifts.

I had no idea how to play this. Not mentioning my erst-
while hosts could backfire. I had done nothing wrong; I'd
been abruptly and rather inconsiderately sidelined. It was
important to play the innocent – I *was* innocent. If Ricky
and Heinrich had got themselves in some kind of trouble,
now would be the time to tell the police I'd been abandoned
overnight. On the other hand, Ricky and Heinrich might
equally have been compromised, having good cause to keep
me out of their deliberations – for my protection, even. It was
wiser not to jump the gun.

'Of course,' I answered finally.

I just needed to put on some shoes.

They laughed, agreed it was probably a good idea.

The police station was low-ceilinged, windowless and stank
of cigarettes. The main office, as such, consisted of a group
of desks that had been clumped together within a wall of
dented cabinets, strewn with coffee cups, stacks of files and
newspapers, along with assorted boxes of stationery. Off to
one side lay the superintendent's office, and beyond that, a
corridor lit by a row of glaring fluorescent lights that led away
to a heavy set of doors with bars across them – presumably

the holding cell or whatever it was called. Apart from my chaperone, the place was deserted.

The man who entered the room a good hour later was a trim, immaculately dressed officer sporting a perfectly combed side parting and a chiselled jawline. He greeted me cordially, introduced himself as Andreas and apologised for taking up my time – it was a question of formalities.

'About what?' I asked, watching his junior aide waddle out of the room; he looked barely out of school.

Andreas smiled, opened up an envelope and produced a British passport. He fingered through to the photo page, flicked a look at me, then back again. Satisfied, he tossed it onto the desk.

'You lost it?' he asked, a smile on his lips.

I picked it up, amazed. 'Stolen. On the ferry.'

'You didn't report it?'

I told him I was worried that if I reported it, I'd be shipped back to the UK, so I'd thought I'd save it for when I left.

He nodded, leaned back in his chair.

'It was handed in,' he said, scratching his chin. 'Lucky, no?'

'Somewhere I have a guardian angel,' I laughed.

Odd that it should turn up now, of all moments.

He pushed his chair back and crossed his legs. 'How are you enjoying Greece?'

'Been a fun summer,' I replied, thrown by the change of subject. 'Apart from losing my passport.'

'Of course,' he said, picking at a tooth.

'Wonderful island,' I continued. 'Looking forward to checking out some of the others.'

'Santorini is the most beautiful.'

'So I've heard.'

'And they have the best wine.'

69

I stood up to shake his hand, but he drew his chair forward and opened up a file. 'Do you know this woman?'

I picked up the photo and for the first time noticed the purr of the overhead fan. 'Yes,' I said, rubbing my thumb over the surface, baffled by the coincidence. 'I do know her.' It was Diane the Kiwi, from the ferry. A passport photo.

I told him I'd met her briefly on the ferry from Piraeus; that I'd been introduced to her by Ricky the Australian, who up until today had been living at the villa with me and Heinrich.

I tried to appear casual, but an alarm bell had gone off.

'I understood you are living alone at the villa,' he said, checking his notes; a cooler edge had replaced the former friendly tone.

'No, the villa belongs to a German artist, Heinrich, for whom I've been working – along with a friend of mine Ricky, an Australian.'

He looked up at me and frowned.

'Diane – is she okay?' I continued.

What the hell had Ricky done?

He ignored the question and asked me instead to tell him about my travels so far, my exact movements since arriving in Greece. So I sat down and told him everything – almost everything: when I got to my time at the villa, I didn't go into the explicit details of our work, explaining only that I had been paid to find models for Heinrich to paint. I left aside his sexual exploits. Of those, I was officially ignorant.

He nodded and flicked through his file.

'Heinrich?' he asked, without looking up.

'Yes, and Ricky. I was working with them at the villa.'

I picked up the passport and flicked through the pages.

'Did you have a sexual relationship with Diane?'

'Sorry?'

'This woman – you have sex with her?'

I laughed; told him I'd only known her a matter of minutes. Although we had kissed – or, rather, she had kissed me.

I started to feel sick.

When I pushed again as to why he was asking, he wouldn't say – suggested I talk more about the ferry trip. I explained that if he wanted to know anything about Diane, he needed to talk to Ricky; they'd spent time together on Santorini. If not Ricky, then the other two guys – Matt and Parrish. They'd hung out together.

Matt and Parrish? Did I know where they were?

No clue. I knew them no more than I had Diane.

What about Ricky – could I find him?

'I've no idea where he is,' I said, wiping my face. 'One minute we were having dinner together, the next minute they've cleared out.' I took a drink of water and told him how I'd woken up late in the afternoon to find they had packed up and gone.

'This is strange, no?'

'Very. I'm as in the dark as you.'

The nausea grew.

Should I call the British Embassy?

He then pulled out another photograph and pushed it in front of me: a woman with her arms around a man's neck in a bar. He was in a plain sweatshirt, wearing a Yankees baseball cap. She was in a black dress with a choker; dark hair, almost black – looked like it was dyed.

'You know this woman?' he asked, without taking his eyes off the photograph.

'No, never seen her before.' Although there was something familiar about the woman's face. But I couldn't place it. Could have been a pop star or actress – Angelica Huston in *Prizzi's*

Honor maybe, except with jet-black hair. 'Nope, neither of them,' I added, after giving a second look-over. Telling him she might have reminded me of someone was hardly going to help. Not if I wanted to get out of there any time soon.

He studied me a moment, replaced the photo in the folder, then jotted something down in his pad.

'Should I know her?' I added, trying to be helpful.

He ignored my question. 'So – the night your friends left you at the villa,' he said, loosening his tie. 'Was there a situation, an argument? Anything unusual?'

Before I could speak, a female officer knocked and entered the room. She was so tall, she instinctively ducked under the doorframe, though she wouldn't have actually struck it. Without waiting for a reply, she folded herself down to Andreas and whispered at length in his ear. All the while as she spoke, Andreas stared at me, a frown stitched across his brow, pen poised above the notebook. When at last she stepped back from the table and tucked her hair behind her ears, Andreas collected his papers and stood up.

'Okay, Mister Haston, thank you.'

'I can go now?'

'No, there will be more questions.' He gave me a brisk nod and followed his colleague out of the office.

Fuck the embassy, I needed a lawyer.

I paced the room and tried in vain to work out the connection between Diane and Ricky, and the evacuation from the villa. There was a piece missing, but I had no idea who or what I was looking for. When the door finally opened, a heavily built older man entered the room: cheerful and open-faced, a shock of unruly black hair on his head mirrored by a thick handlebar moustache. He told me to follow him into his private office. This one at least had a window, which he promptly shut. 'Mosquitoes,' he sighed, hitching up his sagging trousers. 'They will eat you alive.'

He poured two cups of water from the cooler, set them down on his desk and gestured to a chair. Unfastening his jacket fully, he sat down with a grunt and took out a file from his drawer. No introduction. No explanation.

'I don't mean to be rude; I need—' I started, but he cut me off.

'You recognise these?'

From the file he produced a selection of photographs and spread them across the desk. His hand hovered above them a moment, then he picked one out and nudged it across the table. It was a long-distance shot of a villa . . . I didn't recognise it; the landscape didn't look like Paros.

I shook my head.

'This?' Interiors, looked like bedrooms.

'Never seen it before.'

He produced the same photograph Andreas had shown me of the couple in the bar. 'And this woman?'

I was about to tell him she looked a bit like Angelica Huston, then thought better of it. He clocked my hesitation, but when I said 'no', he nodded and slid another picture in front of me. 'What about this?'

Heinrich's yacht. I knew it well, of course, and told him I'd been on it often – Ricky had taught me to sail on it, in fact.

He nodded and jotted something in his notebook. 'This?'

It was Ricky's jeep. I told him that too.

'And also this?'

It was a photo of Heinrich's villa on Paros. I explained it was where I'd been living for the last five weeks. I'd already

73

mentioned the fact to his colleague. 'Can you tell me what all this is about?'

He considered my question a moment, then tossed a pack of cigarettes onto the table. 'Please. Take one.'

I declined and waited for him to explain himself.

But he was in no hurry. He smoked in silence for a while then pulled his chair forward and placed his elbows on the table. 'Here is my problem,' he began, opening a file and spreading the contents on the table in front of me. 'The villa on Santorini, this yacht, the jeep, and the villa here in Paros – they are all rented in your name.'

Uncomprehending, I leaned forward to examine the papers, but he pushed my hand to one side and returned to the photo of the woman in the bar with the man in the cap.

'You don't know her?' he asked, pointing at the woman.

I told him I had no idea who she was.

'You are certain?'

'Yes,' I said, without hesitation. 'Why do you ask?'

'She was reported missing two weeks ago by her ex-husband. But – well, this happens sometimes. People come for a holiday and they stay a little longer.'

'Maybe she wanted to stay away from her ex?' I said, trying some humour.

Who the hell does she remind me of?

'Maybe,' he replied, the tiniest of smiles at the corner of his lips. He then placed the passport photo of Diane on top of the previous photograph. 'But her – you know?'

'Absolutely,' I replied. 'Diane. We met on the ferry – I told your colleague so.'

'Yes,' he said, thumbing the edge of the photo. 'Well, I'm sorry to tell you, but your friend is dead.' He tilted his head to one side and clicked his tongue. 'Her body was found by the cliffs near Fira, Santorini. She was raped, strangled, then had her throat cut. But she did not die there.' He paused and scratched at his greying temple. 'Her blood was found at the villa, a kilometre from the cliffs.'

A telephone rang. He waited until it had stopped.

'This villa,' he added, jabbing his thick finger at the photograph. 'With your signature on the rental agreement.'

6

'I have never been to Santorini,' I protested, horrified at the thought that the fun-loving, carefree girl I'd met on the ferry had lost her life, let alone in such a violent manner. 'These signatures are forgeries.'

He sat back and loosened his tie. 'There is no need to panic, Mister Haston.'

'Give me a list of the pertinent dates,' I replied, 'and I will prove where I was at the time.' Again, my stomach lurched.

Raped. Strangled.

'How do you explain the two villas, the yacht and the jeep all rented in your name?'

I told him – Ricky.

'He had your passport?'

'Obviously. He must have stolen it from me.'

He raised an eyebrow and examined a sheet of handwritten notes.

'But you were working for him?'

'We were working together. For Heinrich.'

I told him I'd also mentioned that to his colleague.

'If you were working together, why would he steal your passport?'

'To frame me. It was a set-up.'

He stubbed out his cigarette, wiped the sweat from the creases of skin around his heavy neckline, then wandered over to the door and checked the passageway. 'So you say.' He tapped a fresh cigarette out of the packet and lit it. 'Tell me about your work for Mister Heinrich.'

Exasperated, I told him I was responsible for recruiting models whom Heinrich would later entertain at his discretion.

'Entertain? How exactly?'

'I don't know. We were never present at the villa at the time.'

'Did he have sex with these models?'

Denying it now could only backfire later. 'I never witnessed it first-hand, but I believe he did, yes.'

'Did you have sex with them?'

I told him I hadn't, but I'd had a fun time partying with the people we met while working for him.

'He had sex with only women?'

'No. He was happy with men too.'

'With you?'

'No.'

'Your friend Ricky?'

Concerned he was going off-piste, I brought him back on point: 'You have to believe me,' I said, my voice tightening. 'I have never been to Santorini, I had nothing to with Diane's death. I'm being set up.'

He held up a hand. 'Until you can prove your passport was stolen and that you were not on Santorini, and did not rent the villas, the yacht and the jeep, you will stay here while we ask more questions.'

'I'm under arrest?'

'Not yet.'

I stood up, dumbstruck.

'But you believe me?'

'Of course,' he smiled, putting on his jacket. 'But this is not my case. Andreas is in charge.'

'You're his superior.'

'I will do what I can. If you have any concerns, please, my name is Mihalis, you can ask for me.'

'You need to focus on Ricky and Heinrich,' I said, walking over to him. 'They can't be far. They've probably taken the yacht.'

'Thank you, Mister Haston, for your advice.'

He gave me paper and pen and suggested I write down a list of people who could corroborate my story, then he tightened the belt around his considerable girth, wished me a good evening and left. At which point the junior officer slipped back in, checked the safety catch on the gun on his hip and took a seat by the door.

Keep calm. Above all, keep calm.

I wrote down all the names of the people I'd had dealings with: Svenja and Jens; Roland; Leo the Cunt and his boss, Kyros; Yannis, the sous-chef at the Dubliner; Sadie, the Australian windsurfing instructor at Pounta; and the farmer and his spotty son who had offered mule rides at the housewarming party. And then there was Amara: she was probably with Ricky, but a telephone call to the restaurants in Naxos would narrow down which of the owners had a daughter called Amara. She'd be a great witness; sweet-natured, straight up, she wouldn't lie. Even for Ricky.

It was gone 10 p.m. before Andreas reappeared with

fresh water and food: still perfectly dressed – not a hair out of place in his slicked-down parting. When he presented me with a matted bundle of dried flesh stuffed into pitta bread, which I recognised as chicken souvlaki, along with rubbery chips, I thanked him, gave him my list of contacts and asked when the questioning would take place and how much longer I could expect to remain at the station – *given that I'm not under arrest.* He said he'd pass on the list when his boss returned.

'I thought this was your case,' I replied, trying to remain placid.

'We are working together,' he countered, clicking his jaw.

'So, when will I hear?'

He couldn't say – they were mid-investigations.

I asked him if they had made any headway on finding Ricky and Heinrich, whereupon his expression turned to one of contempt. Stepping in close, he suggested I forget about the two of them and concern myself with my own situation.

'I'm just trying to help,' I exclaimed. 'You have to find them.'

His nostrils flaring, he opened his mouth to reply, but after a quick glance at the officer by the door, thought better of it and walked out into the corridor.

Grateful for the presence of a guard, I tucked into my cold supper, wondering if I had narrowly avoided a beating. There was something erratic in Andreas's demeanour that unnerved me; one minute he was all charm and politesse, the next, aggressive and brittle. When it came to asking questions, it was probably best to stick to his considerably more relaxed boss, Mihalis. Mihalis I could work on. Convincing Andreas would be harder.

*

At midnight, my sentinel was relieved by the tall female officer from earlier. No exchange of conversation took place, just a complicit nod and then a straight swap for the seat, where she sat perfectly still, like a heron. At around 1.30 a.m. I asked her if there were any blankets or pillows lying about. She pulled faces of incomprehension, so I acted it out for her, upon which she finally cracked a smile and produced a fire blanket from a cupboard. Only then did I notice how un-Greek she appeared: blonde hair tied up in a ponytail and pale blue eyes. Perhaps she was from northern Greece – they were said to be much fairer in complexion.

I thanked her and made up my bed underneath the table. Finally, I asked if I could turn off the lights. She understood that one, no problem.

'No.'

As I lay there watching a pair of geckos on the wall squabbling over lodging rights behind a framed photo of Naoussa, I had the growing suspicion that there would be no questioning that night, that everything would wait until the morning. It was perhaps their way of keeping me under wraps without actually charging me with an arrest. My knowledge of law was negligible, but from the many hours squandered in front of television detective shows, I understood that once an arrest was made, the authorities had twenty-four hours to follow it up and either find further evidence or release the suspect. But in Greece – who knew?

I tried to close my eyes – it was vital to be fresh for my interview with Mihalis in the morning; the most innocuous of details might be the one that led to Ricky and Heinrich – but sleep proved impossible. In order to help the police, I had to try and understand better for myself what had happened, and therefore, I remained wide awake, trying to second-guess the sequence of events:

Ricky steals my passport on the ferry, either to sell, or to use as leverage against future scams. Having met Diane on the flight with Matt and Parrish, he courts her on the ferry, and later on Santorini, eventually persuading her to be one of Heinrich's models . . .

Then what?

Possibly she opted to pose for Heinrich, but it had backfired. An accident perhaps – a sex game that went wrong . . . *asphyxiation*?

So, they have no choice but to get rid of the body. They come to Paros, believing that they've got away with it, carry on with their indulgent pastimes, renting yet another property in my name, except this time Ricky tracks me down as extra insurance, brings me into his web of deceit and reunites me with my passport when the shit hits the fan, implicating me in the killing while they run for cover.

But what about Heinrich, Svenja and Jens – Yannis, and his assistant? Where did they figure in this? If Heinrich was innocent, would he agree to take off with Ricky in the middle of the night, leaving me behind? Where did he think they'd be going at such short notice?

I tried to boil it down: I crash out in my room, apparently from too much booze – although I now suspected I'd been slipped something in my drink – and at some point, Operation Svenja is aborted. They either dismiss the guests sometime after dinner and get on with the clear-out, or they all go out together into town 'to party'. Heinrich and Ricky return to the villa, and along with hired hand Yannis – who had stayed behind to 'tidy up' – the three of them execute the evacuation. Svenja and Jens go home none the wiser,

Yannis gets paid for his assistance, and Ricky and Heinrich do a runner.

Amara?

She must have gone with Ricky – which meant she was potentially also in the know.

But it didn't add up. How and when did they hear of the discovery of Diane's body? If they'd known for some time, a few days, perhaps, then why go through the motions of a dinner party, only to leave halfway through? If they were in jeopardy – as the sudden departure had suggested – why didn't they leave as soon as they found out? Why risk being caught? If, on the other hand, they'd only found out the night of the dinner, which seemed more likely, someone must have told them in person.

Who?

And none of this explained the blood I'd found at the villa.

The following morning at six-thirty sharp, however, my detective work suffered a rude awakening when Andreas and his chubby junior assistant dragged me from under the table, took my mug shot and fingerprints, then read me my rights. The bodies of two tourists had been found in Alyki harbour; I was now officially under arrest.

'What the hell's this got to do with me?' I yelled, head reeling, as they frogmarched me down the corridor towards the cell. 'Where's Mihalis?'

'The bodies were found on your yacht,' replied Andreas, ignoring my question while tightening his grip on my wrist.

'I have no idea what you're talking about,' I retorted.

My yacht?

I jammed my heels into the floor and turned to face Andreas.

'Svenja and Jens?' I blurted, before I could stop myself.

Andreas threw his colleague a look, before yanking me by the arm and shoving me forwards down the corridor. 'If you say so.'

'But – wait. I told you, I didn't rent the yacht,' I exclaimed, trying to force the panic from my throat. 'I didn't rent the fucking villa. My passport was stolen. Ricky rented them. Everything.'

They killed Svenja and Jens?

Between them, Andreas and his assistant dragged me the remaining twenty yards to the door of the jail cell; all the while I insisted that the Belgians had been my friends, that I had been worried that something had happened to them the night of the dinner party at the villa – that I was innocent.

'You did not mention these people earlier,' barked Andreas, pushing the cell door open and shoving me forwards.

It was true – I hadn't.

Because of Operation Svenja.

'But this doesn't make any sense,' I protested, spinning around to face him. 'I'm telling you – we were friends. I had no idea they were in danger.'

'You are not fooling anybody,' Andreas said, closing the door.

'Where's Mihalis?' I asked once again, as the door slammed in my face. 'I need to speak to Mihalis!' But as I pressed my ear to the metal door jamb, all I could hear was the *clip clop* of receding footsteps. 'What about my lawyer?' I yelled, hammering my fists on the door. 'I demand to speak to a lawyer!'

But they'd gone.

Blinking back the stinging behind my eyes, I turned to face my cell: a dusty, concrete box containing a tin wash bowl, a stained toilet and a narrow seat built into the wall covered with frayed matting. A hole, high up with steel bars across it, served as a window. Aside from that, nothing but a straggle of flies and a lone hornet circling a bare bulb hanging from the cracked ceiling.

I slid to the floor.

Diane, Svenja, and Jens were dead . . .

Murdered.

And I was being framed for it.

Grinding my knuckles into the concrete, I reminded myself that I was innocent, that I should hang on to that at all costs. Mihalis or no – they would have to give me a lawyer, and any lawyer worth their salt would soon prove that I had been set up. I hadn't ever been to Santorini – how could they begin to try and pin Diane's death on me?

But Svenja and Jens . . .

As my attention turned from the wheeling insects to the blood seeping from my fingers, it dawned on me that if I hadn't lied, if I hadn't tricked the Belgians into coming to a leaving dinner at the villa, they would still be alive. A lawyer would need the background to the events – they'd need to know the whole story. Which meant they'd know that Operation Svenja was hatched, facilitated and orchestrated by me.

For the promise of $3,000.

7

Three interminable days turned into five, and then a week.

Other than the delivery of meals and water, no one came to see me, to ask me any questions or take a further statement. No one came to see if I needed anything; there was no talk of any legal representation, or even of a call home, despite my repeated demands. The few visits I did receive were far from restorative. The junior staff who dropped off my daytime meals wouldn't even look me in the eye. The night watchman who brought my dinner each day – a colossal brute with a scar above his left eyebrow – was downright sadistic: every time he visited my cell, he muttered something in Greek, smiled as he slid my plastic plate across the floor, and as he left, drew an imaginary knife across his throat.

To pass the time, and to fight off the growing claustrophobia, I practised a daily routine of sit-ups and push-ups, and tried to meditate; it was important to stay fit, calm and level-headed. I had to hang on to the belief that, at the right moment, Mihalis – wherever the hell he had got to – would make good his promise to help and step in. I had to keep faith in procedure, in the law. At some point a lawyer would have to get involved – the investigation couldn't possibly develop without one – and then the dice would roll in my favour. Mistakes happened. It was only a matter of time before I was proved innocent. No matter how responsible I felt for the deaths of Svenja and Jens, I hadn't committed murder; I'd been an unwitting patsy. Self-absorbed, certainly. Gullible, yes, and oblivious. But innocent.

And yet, as each day wore on, my optimism began to dwindle, along with my health. My clothes turned foetid; I couldn't wash properly, couldn't take any proper exercise or stretch out the knots in my back from the sleepless nights on the rock-hard bench; I didn't dare infect the sores on my skin with the discoloured water from the tap; I couldn't shave, couldn't shit, and my piss had turned brown from dehydration. I'd been bitten without respite by mosquitoes and the ants that patrolled the concrete floor – several of the bites infected from my incessant scratching. And I'd developed a wheezing cough from the pervading stench of faeces wafting through the open window above the drain that housed the run-off from the police toilets.

Where was my fucking lawyer?

On the eighth day of my incarceration, however, Andreas opened the door with a plate of fried eggs and ham in his hand, and wished me a 'good morning.' He seemed unusually relaxed – in good humour, even. Apparently, a change in fortune was on the cusp.

'Please – have some breakfast,' he added, with a smile.

'Is the lawyer here?' I growled, pushing the plate to one side and stepping over the threshold of the cell door.

'There have been some developments,' he replied, moving to one side to allow me through. 'You know your way.'

I started to shuffle down the corridor, then stopped.

'You can continue,' came Andreas's voice from behind.

Why the change in humour?

'Please. I have something that may interest you,' he added, then gestured for me to carry on down the corridor, as the tall female police officer appeared at the far end, her hands behind her back.

'I'm not doing anything without a lawyer,' I said, hugging the wall.

'Everything is ready,' he said, ignoring me. 'Something to drink?'

Remaining on my feet, I accepted a cup of water and hovered at the edge of the table in the middle of the cramped office, my eyes on the television balanced on top of a dusty VCR player. On the other side of the room stood Andreas with a VHS copy of *Das Boot* in his hand. 'It is a good programme, no?' he purred, taking a cassette out of the case. 'You have seen it? About a German submarine in the war.'

Then he stuck the cassette in the television and pressed 'play'.

'But I don't remember this,' he added.

After a flicker of static, the screen jumped to life. It was footage Ricky had taken from the ferry: the game of quarters ... Matt and Parrish, gyrating naked at the railings ... me doing my victory crab-dance, accompanied by one of the Scandinavians in her straw hat and shades ... a close-up of me trying to kiss the camera ... Diane folding herself into my lap ... Diane forcing my head down to lick the sunblock off her nipples ... kissing me ... kissing me in close-up ... me pushing the lens away from my face ...

Then the film stopped.

'That was on the ferry,' I said, without looking at Andreas. 'Ricky shot it – on his camcorder. We were all drunk – having fun.'

'You seem to know her pretty well.'

'I didn't know her at all. It was . . . we were drunk.'

I twisted around to see why Andreas hadn't responded, but a groan from the television brought my attention back to the screen . . . Another image had appeared: dark, grainy – the rhythmic creaking of bedsprings coming from off-camera. It was a shot of Diane in bed, a close-up, filmed from above and slightly to one side – a couple of feet away, perhaps. She was staring straight into the lens, mouth open, moving gently back and forth on the bed in time to the grunts from off-camera.

'And this?' asked Andreas, clicking a pen in his fingers.

Then the image disappeared and the tape went blank.

'I have no idea.' Ricky must have filmed it.

I told him that.

'Okay,' he replied. 'But you are having sex with her, yes?'

'No. As I keep telling you, I met her on the ferry for a matter of hours. They went on to Santorini – where I have never been.'

If Ricky was filming her, though – who was she in bed with? Heinrich?

'Yes, yes, of course,' he said, inclining his head as he fast-forwarded the tape. 'But this – was on Paros, no?' All of a sudden, the screen was filled with a close-up of Svenja, lying on her back in bed. As with Diane, she was rocking rhyth-mically back and forth, apparently in the act of sex. After a moment, she reached up with an arm and pulled the camera closer to her face. The image juddered a moment, then the

90

picture resumed: an extreme close-up of her mouth, lips parted, her breathing now audible above the noises in the background. A few seconds later, the camera pulled back and moved away to one side, revealing Jens on top of his girlfriend.

The footage I shot at the housewarming.

'Ricky – he filmed this?' said Andreas, the tape clicking to a stop.

For a split second I considered lying, but there was no point – it could only cause trouble later. 'I filmed it,' I replied. 'The tape is from a party we had at the villa, weeks ago. We took turns with the camera. It was all consensual, just fun.'

Andreas grunted something I couldn't catch, then cast his eyes back to the television and pointed the remote. The tape went fuzzy then flickered on again. This time it was me and Svenja in bed together; the same occasion, but later – Jens's body comatose off to one side, his arm draped over my back.

The sequence Ricky had filmed from the doorway . . .

'But now you are with her, yes?' asked Andreas.

I nodded.

'So, who is filming?'

'Ricky. It was all innocent fun at a party.'

But I destroyed the tape – wiped over it.

'Where did you get this?' I demanded.

The villa was empty – they'd taken everything.

'You were jealous of the boyfriend?' Andreas asked, changing tack and lighting a cigarette.

For a moment, there was just the whirring of the fan overhead.

'Absolutely not,' I retorted, understanding finally where he was going with this. 'They were swingers. It was their "thing." You seriously think that because I had sex with

Svenja, I murdered her and her boyfriend? They had sex with half a dozen people that night. Look at the tape.'

I stood up, fuming, but Andreas merely exhaled a long plume of smoke then gave a nod to his colleague. 'Good idea,' he said, as she handed him a second VHS cassette. 'Let's have a look.'

Another tape?

'You have no right,' I declared. 'They're private.'

'Sit down,' replied Andreas, ejecting the first tape and replacing it with the next.

'Where is Mihalis?' I snapped. 'I need to speak to him.'

This was ridiculous, the tapes proved nothing.

But where the hell did they find them?

'He is aware of the situation.'

'I told you – I have to speak to him. I demand to speak to him.'

Ignoring me, he pressed 'play,' and the television screen lit up once more. This time it was footage of the house-warming party at the villa, the punk sisters with the rings and studs in their noses . . . a close-up of Amara talking to the camera about her plans to go to drama school in Athens . . . a medium-wide shot of Jess on all fours, naked, before the camera pulled back and revealed Ian the skinhead taking her from behind.

He paused the tape. 'You filmed this?'

It was a trick question; my reflection could clearly be seen in the window behind Jess and Ian. 'Yes, but . . .'

As words failed me, Andreas fast-forwarded the tape through a blank section – had Ricky erased it to keep him out of the equation? – then the film cut in at the orgy at the pool: Svenja and Jens in the act of fellatio on the steps; Lucy, the brash voice-over agent from New York, bouncing up and down on top of the spotty teenager who had offered everyone at the party a chance to ride his mule. As the camera pulled in tighter, they slid sideways to continue their lovemaking up against the edge of the pool.

'You filmed this too?'

Again, I nodded. 'But this is out of sequence,' I said. 'It's been doctored – spliced.'

'Your point?'

I wasn't sure – but I knew it had to be relevant.

'You like watching people have sex?' he asked, moving on.

But I was focusing on Lucy's face – her platinum-blonde hair . . .

'The parties were private,' I said, my heart racing.

Who did she remind me of?

I looked up at Andreas, who was studying me intently. Before I could open my mouth, he tossed a photo onto the table in front of me; the one I'd been shown earlier with the woman in the bar with jet-black hair, her arms around the man in the Yankees baseball cap . . . *Angelica Huston with dyed hair . . .*

Lucy, the voice-over agent.

'In this picture, you notice, she has changed her appearance,' Andreas said, flicking the photo face up and taking a step back from the table. 'The American Embassy reported her missing a few weeks ago. But we know she was at your villa, because we have a witness. A local farm boy told us he was there too. The boy in the water, no?'

He waited for me to comment but I had no idea what I should say.

'I honestly didn't recognise her,' was all I could manage.

'But here she is at your party.'

I nodded. 'It seems that way. Certainly. Yes.'

93

I could feel sweat beading on the back of my neck.

He watched me a moment longer, then took a deep breath and pressed the remote. There was the same flicker of static on the television, then a picture. Lucy again, in bed. A shot of her from directly above – a close-up. She was moving rhythmically up and down the bed and appeared to have what looked like underwear in her mouth, pulling it from side to side between her teeth as she blinked seductively into the lens.

'This is the same woman, no?'

'It is,' I replied, pushing back from the table. 'But that's not me. I'm not behind the camera.'

Must have been Ricky. Or Heinrich.

'Maybe it is the farm boy,' he sneered, brushing a hand through his slick hair. 'You don't have to watch,' he added, coolly. 'You know what happens.'

A muffled shriek brought me back to the television: the screen was filled with Lucy's face, terror in her eyes, as she clawed and scratched at the edges of the underwear that was now tight around her neck.

What the fuck?

'Turn it off!' I yelled.

Thumping the table, I jumped up and tried to back out towards the door. But a firm grip on my shoulder stopped me in my tracks, and I turned to find the policewoman towering over me. Without speaking, she pushed me back to the table, then retreated out of sight again.

'Strangled,' came Andreas's steady voice from across the room.

I stood frozen, my gaze desperately fixed on his grim features, as an unidentifiable sound reverberated from the television speaker.

'And her throat cut.'

94

A pair of hands grabbed me from behind and spun my head towards the television. I tried to twist away, but I was too late: on the screen, there was a flash of silver as the blade of a knife swept up from nowhere, slid across Lucy's neck and opened her throat, blurring the screen in a deluge of red.

8

The interrogation endured for over six hours.

Professing my innocence, I repeated to Andreas everything I had already told him and Mihalis about my movements on Paros since my arrival in May, elaborating in greater detail, however, about the work Ricky and I did for Heinrich – everything I could remember about every minute of every day, including Operation Svenja. I held nothing back, knowing it was now vital to be as upfront and truthful as possible; to hide anything from the police at this stage would only backfire when it came to dealing with the lawyers. I admitted I'd been deceitful – that I was motivated by the promise of $3,000 – but I had no idea of the fate that would befall Svenja or her boyfriend. I explained that of the eleven models we'd brought in for Heinrich – those who'd agreed to be painted – all of them had agreed to sleep with him for money. And I'd honestly believed that once Svenja was alone with Heinrich she might be swayed by his charm.

When he asked me what I knew of the models once they had slept with Heinrich, I had to tell him I was ignorant.

They were always gone from the villa by the time Ricky and I returned – with the exception of Charlene from Texas.

'So there could be more,' said Andreas, scratching his head. 'More murders.'

I told him I had no idea; I was as horrified and dumb-founded as he.

'It doesn't make any sense,' I offered. 'But I will do everything I can to help.'

Throughout the interview Andreas broke off from time to time to either take or make a telephone call, and every time he returned, he'd softened fractionally. I felt that I was making good headway: that he not only accepted the possibility of my ignorance in the events, and that I had indeed been used, but also that, whether in his mind I was complicit in the crimes or not, there were other individuals – Ricky and Heinrich primarily – who had to be tracked down and caught.

He asked me to write down again all the names of the people who could testify to timelines and my whereabouts on given dates, explaining with a tone akin to an apology even that the first list had been mislaid after Mihalis had left Paros on annual leave – which at least explained the latter's no-show. Then, at around two in the afternoon, the police-woman entered the office to tell Andreas he had another call. On his return, he announced stiffly that I was to be trans-ferred to the police department on the island of Syros, the capital of the Cyclades, and that they would be handling the investigation from there on in.

I was so overcome with relief that I nearly burst into tears. And once escorted back to the threshold of my con-crete dwelling, I felt sufficiently moved to shake Andreas by the hand. But he recoiled and stared at me with a look of incredulity stamped across his brow. Chewing vigorously on his lower lip, it appeared he wanted to say something, but he evidently thought better of it, shook his head and slammed the cell door in my face.

That night, I dreamed of Ellie.

I was running over the top of theParos plateau under starlight – running for my life. From what, I didn't know. Suddenly a bus appeared on the road behind me. I ran into the dark to escape its beams, but it slowed down to a stop and the driver's door opened. The driver beckoned me on board. The driver was Ellie. Without any exchange of conversation, I made my way to the back of the empty bus and we continued the journey down the mountain. Then I noticed the hornets, hundreds of them, hanging half-dead from the bus roof. I panicked and tried to get off the bus, but Ellie wouldn't open the doors. She started to laugh – harder and harder until her throat opened up in a gush of scarlet. As the bus started to fill with blood, the hornets came back to life and flew towards me, like bullets ...

I awoke dripping with sweat and instinctively twisted over towards my cell door.

It was open.

The overhead light was off, but I could just make out the silhouette of a man I recognised as the officer responsible for bringing my dinner every night. He stood with his hands by his sides, breathing quietly.

I sat up and asked him if everything was okay.

He didn't say anything. Instead he took two steps into the room and with a quick swing of his leg kicked me hard in the face. The boot caught me on the side of the jaw and snapped my head back. There was a flash of white behind my eyes and a searing pain in my neck. I rolled backwards, my head slamming into the concrete seating buttress. I staggered to my feet but he stepped in, picked me up and threw me against the wall, and as I slid to the floor, threw a barrage of punches at my head and stomach.

I curled up, trying to get my breath as he stood over me, panting.

'English motherfucker like to suck cock, yes?' He undid his trousers, pulling them down and grabbing at my face.

Survival instinct kicked in. I bit his hand to the bone and slammed my fist into his groin, releasing a bellow from his guts as he toppled backwards, his head hitting the concrete floor with a sharp crack. I froze, fearing I might have killed him, but he simply rolled over and began to laugh. 'English pussy,' he said. 'I kill you now, *malakas*.' With that he tried to pull himself to his feet, but fell back again, laughing even harder, then collapsed and fell silent.

Whatever was wrong with him, I had no intention of staying for round two. I shot out of the cell, down the corridor and through to the office in search of sanctuary. In the reception area I found the television on, the door to a side office ajar, but not a soul present. I stuck my head round the edge of the doorframe but could confirm only the presence of a slow-spinning ceiling fan and a gecko on the windowsill.

Creeping back out to the reception area I looked for something to defend myself with, and, in passing, gave the heavy glass door to the front of the building a cursory push. To my utter disbelief, it swung open. Hesitating briefly, I was about to make a dash for it, then thought it prudent to scavenge for anything that might help me on my way. The place was deserted — I could spare another twenty seconds.

Behind the reception desk hung a jacket on a chair, belonging – I assumed – to the man who had attacked me. I rifled through the pockets until I found a pack of cigarettes, but no money. Still, I grabbed the cigarettes – currency of a kind – and, taking advantage of a water cooler, downed as much liquid as my shrunken stomach could take, then returned to the main office and rummaged through the drawers and cupboards to see if I could find my passport – until a cry from down the corridor brought an abrupt end to the search.

I hurried back into the reception, checked for signs of life outside the station, and wavered by the door: other than a stray dog sniffing at a rolled-up hedgehog in the ditch, the coast was clear.

When I heard the approach of stumbling footsteps echoing from within the building behind me, I debated my options for a fleeting second, then concluded that on no account was I prepared to stay and risk a severe beating; he could quite feasibly kill me. So I stepped over the threshold into the night . . .

And ran.

II

9

I hovered under a flickering street light, coughing and spitting, spinning left and right, wondering what the fuck to do
next. My instinct was to head for the beach, where I could
hang back at the water's edge and remain in the shadows, but
I also knew I had to get to the villa and retrieve my stash of
money. Without it, I didn't stand a chance.

Except the villa was several kilometres away – I'd have to
hitch a lift.

At two in the morning?

Veering off-road up an earthy bank, I rolled down into
a dry flood drain, and keeping as low to the ground as
possible, continued along it as far as it could take me, until
I surfaced at the main square behind the Bank of Greece,
where I continued uphill towards a pine-tree nursery.
Once in the park, I cut diagonally across and headed for
the Parikia ring road, with which I was familiar, and
which I also knew would take me to the southern edge of
town without passing too many people en route; although
at this time of night I was counting on it being only the

hardcore partygoers in search of something to soak up the booze.

Halfway across the enclosure, I noticed a bandstand with a pair of park benches on either side; on one of them a figure lay motionless, apparently asleep. Stifling my wheezes, I advanced through the shadows, and on discovering him to be a crashed-out tourist, I plunged my hands into his shorts pockets, found his wallet and yanked out the notes: less than 400 drachmas.

A cab ride, if nothing else.

I tossed the wallet on top of him, apologised under my breath, then slipped away. Minutes later, having shaken off the attentions of a pack of stray dogs, I found the place where the ring road met the north end of the main promenade, where, heading out into the open, I joined the ranks of roving clubbers.

Swept along by the crowd, I noticed my bloodstained shirt was attracting the occasional stare, so I tossed the offending article over the harbour wall. Now I was just another mosquito-bitten, topless Brit who didn't know any better – my limp no more noticeable than the stumblings of the boozed-up revellers on their quest for grease.

As I passed a group of hammered Scandinavians outside the Saloon d'Or, playing keepy-uppy with a beer can, I spotted a lone taxi parked up opposite the famous Parikia windmill. Hobbling over as fast as I could, I leaned in at the driver's window, promised him my state of attire didn't reflect a likelihood of throwing up in his ride, and asked him if he'd kindly take me to Sotires.

He wasn't aware of any tourist accommodation up there.

I assured him there was – I'd direct him.

He gave me a high-five and a 'no problem', then asked

me if I'd had a fight with a woman. It took me a moment to realise I'd forgotten to rub the blood off my chin and neck.

English football fans, I told him, offering him a cigarette.

He laughed, accepted the smoke, and we set off.

Before long, we were out of the main drag of Parikia and its web of neon into the shadows of the outer town, with its twisting, darker purlieus. I lay back in the seat nursing my throbbing jaw, tuned out to the jangle of Greek music on the stereo and watched the jiggling crucifix that hung from the rear-view mirror.

Running from the law was undeniably foolish, but what was I supposed to do – sit and take a kicking? Besides, it wasn't my fault they'd left the doors open.

The villa was further than I'd reckoned. When we got to the turn-off at Pounta, I noticed the meter was about to exceed my funds, so I told my singing driver to pull up, explaining that I'd changed my mind: a friend of mine was camping on the beach and having a party – I'd go to Sotires later. He couldn't care less. Pocketing the change, he asked for another cigarette, and noticing the angry sores on my skin, suggested I try using insect repellent. I thanked him for the advice.

'English tourists are crazy,' he scoffed. Then he turned the car around and skidded off to Parikia.

I crossed the tarmac road and, keeping parallel to the dirt track, climbed through the parched wasteland towards an Orthodox church that lay half a kilometre from Heinrich's villa. Despite my deteriorated physical condition, I made good headway, buoyed up with the anticipation of being reunited with my money. For now, visibility was good, but it looked like it mightn't last long; on the western horizon an intermittent pulse of sheet lightning lit up a growing bank of cloud. A summer storm was on its way.

I pressed on and put together a plan: get my money from the villa, hide until first light and then check into a hotel in Alyki, from whence I could plan my evacuation off the island. Next step, head for the sanctuary of the British Embassy in Athens, tell them the whole story and wait for the dust to settle. There was no point trying to call them from Paros – not at this time of night. Even if they believed my story and were to act immediately, Athens was a five-hour ferry ride away. I still had to evade capture in the interim. And I certainly didn't fancy my chances with the Paros police, now that I'd assaulted an officer and done a runner. The embassy was the only safe option. Once I had the ear of the British authorities, I'd be listened to and my innocence ascertained in no time. The police could then turn their attention to where it belonged, tracking down the Australian and Heinrich. Wherever they were.

Drenched in sweat, I reached the church on the plateau, propped myself momentarily against the south transept wall and let the rattling in my chest die down. My foot had stopped hurting, or else had gone numb, and my muscles were benefiting from the sustained exercise. I felt a little looser, brighter in spirit, and with the prospect of clearer water ahead, I'd almost forgotten about the itching on my arms and legs.

I could do this.

A distant roll of thunder prompted me to resume my march, and, traversing fifty metres of the chalky high street, I wandered off-piste again, moving cross country on the donkey path that meandered through a scattering of olive trees and rejoined the main causeway a couple of hundred yards down the hill. Cutting through a scrubby field dotted with sleeping sheep, I made it to the rocky outcrop on the hillock from which the villa and surrounding valley were finally viewable.

Still no sign of the police.

I continued four hundred yards further along the track, chose a narrow gulley as my approach route, and skidded down the scree to the valley floor. I then wound my way back around to the olive grove from the south and crept along the outer edge of the trees until I came upon the perimeter wall of the villa.

The bank of cloud blotted out the stars to the west now, and the lightning drew closer, the air increasingly thick and sulphurous. Climbing over the loose stones, I headed across the garden, past the pool and, following the paving round the villa, aimed for the drain cover on the east side where my money was hidden. Keeping the oleander on my right shoulder, I hugged the shadows, and at the last minute slipped across the path to the bins.

Almost there.

Wiping the sweat from my eyes, I knelt down by the drain and hoisted the concrete cover into my lap, stuck my hand down the hole, and groped around for the plastic bag. But before my fingers could locate it, a cry from across the garden stopped me in my tracks.

I wrenched my neck towards the pool and saw a figure run diagonally towards the patio doors. He hit halfway, halted, crouched down into a squat and pointed at me. Instinctively I ducked. A split second later a gunshot ripped through the air.

Diving face down onto the concrete, I rolled onto my side as another shot rang out, accompanied this time by the whine of a ricochet as the bullet spent itself somewhere over the olive grove.

Stunned by the violence, I bolted for the cover of the oleander but was cut off by a second figure looming out of the borders of the hedge. I froze, not knowing which way to turn, and in that moment he launched himself into the air and brought us both down onto the paving, knocking the breath from my lungs.

Locked together, we rolled across the concrete until I managed to force a knee into his crotch, then threw a punch in what I hoped was the direction of his face. He grunted, hauled himself upright and picked me off the ground in the process. Level with his head, I found he was wearing a balaclava and tried to rip the thing from his face, but he was far stronger and had me pinned.

As he wrestled me towards the hedge, I managed a kick to his kneecap, and for a second his grip loosened. I whipped out a hand and my fingers found their way to his throat, but before I could apply any pressure, two gunshots erupted in quick succession from the west wall of the villa.

With a cry, he released me and slumped to the ground.

There was a moment's silence.

And then chaos.

A motorbike spluttered into life as a clamour of incomprehensible expletives flew to and fro across the garden. My hooded assailant came back to life and tried to crawl towards the patio as a surge of blood swilled out from underneath his stomach.

Astounded he was still alive, I veered off in the other direction and made for the outline of the hedge, but stopped midway across the tiles when I caught sight of a gun-brandishing figure flying out from the bougainvillea, the motorbike hot on his heels, engine revving at full pitch.

As the pair gesticulated above the din, I ducked into the undergrowth, fought my way through the maze of flesh-stripping branches, and crawled through the dust to the foot of the perimeter wall. Checking for the whereabouts of my attackers, I dragged myself over the top, fell down onto the wasteland on the other side, and continued across the scrub, half-running, half-limping, until I was deep within the shadows of the olive grove, where I collapsed, spent, against a tree trunk.

Shaking with the rush of adrenaline, I kept an eye on the garden wall and attempted a series of deep breaths to calm myself down as I frantically tried to work out what the fuck was going on.

They'd outnumbered me three to one. There was no need for weaponry, let alone bullets. There'd been no warning, no attempt at negotiation, or indeed communication – they hadn't given me a chance.

It was an ambush.

My skin pricking in anticipation of more gunfire, I lowered myself into a crouch and shuffled my way to the valley floor, turning every few yards to check I wasn't being followed. When I reached a rutted farm track, I stopped again and took refuge behind a corrugated-iron hut to tighten my laces.

A pair of torch beams roamed the wasteland in the immediate vicinity of the villa. Then the motorbike drew up to the perimeter wall and swept the upper reaches of the olive grove in fits and starts with its powerful headlamp. I was poised, ready to make another run for it should the lights advance down the hill, but to my relief they turned and retreated into the shadow of the villa.

Close by an owl screeched and flew for cover as a prolonged

flash of lightning lit up the valley, followed by a violent thunderclap. The storm was almost overhead.

I stayed put, kept my eyes fixed on the villa.

How had the police got here before me?

Even if the officer at the station had radioed immediately for help, they would have had to pass me on the way. And they hadn't – of that I was certain; I'd travelled the only route that accessed this part of the island, and there was no way they could have overtaken me without my noticing . . . which meant they had already been in place.

But that didn't add up either. Of all the places I could have run to, how did they know I would head for the villa? No one saw me leave the police station, no one followed me; I had the whole island at my disposal, I could have gone anywhere. If anything, the villa – the scene of my arrest – was the least likely destination. And yet there the police were, set up and waiting.

How did they know?

Cutting through the grumble of thunder, I heard the wail of a siren. Seconds later, up on Sotires ridge, a police car punctured the night with its flickering blue lights and hurtled along the upper reaches of the plateau in the direction of the villa. My chances of escape were next to zero; the entire constabulary of Paros would have been alerted by now, and it was only a matter of time before every police vehicle on the island descended on the area.

Keeping my eyes peeled for a promising hideaway, I stumbled onwards in the direction of Alyki as the first volley of fat raindrops struck the dust about me. I was clueless now, no idea where to go or what to do. I was only delaying the inevitable. They were going to catch me; it was just a question of when. Robbed of my hard-won earnings, the odds had turned fully against me. With no food or water, not even a shirt on my back, I'd have to surface eventually.

My only hope lay in somehow leaving the island.

I struck out towards Alyki, crossed through a builders' yard, then reached an inner ring road, from which a network of cobbled alleys fingered their way to the seafront. On no account could I risk the harbour: Heinrich's yacht would be a crime scene – there would be forensics and round-the-clock security in attendance. I had to get out of Alyki and head further east, to the string of small villages and hamlets that lined the coast. There the fishermen left their boats beached on the shoreline; if I found one with a set of oars, I could risk rowing to the island immediately off Drios. From Drios, I could make my way across the six-kilometre stretch of water to Antiparos. But at night? Without sleep and in the middle of a storm?

I turned east along the pavement, hugging the walls of the assorted tourist shops and cafés along the ring road, preparing to cross the main road where it bottlenecked at the eastern perimeter, opposite a scuba outlet. From the shadows, I scanned the forest of masts on the furthest quay, where Heinrich's yacht lay at anchor. I couldn't make out any telltale signs of the authorities, but I knew they were there. It was vital to keep a wide berth.

It was only ten yards of tarmac I had to cross; I'd be on the other side in seconds, but still I couldn't quite leave the safety of the buildings. Only when a gust of wind barrelled down the street, heralding the imminent arrival of a downpour, did I take the leap.

In that same instant, a motorbike pulled out from nowhere a hundred yards west, opened the throttle and spun round towards me.

Too late.

I stood in the gutter and watched, mesmerised, as it careered straight for me, and at the last second slammed on the brakes, skidding to a halt on the wet road.

The rider flipped his helmet. 'Get the fuck on and hold tight.'

I stared in amazement.

'Now!'

Another downdraft of wind, and then the heavens opened.

I jumped onto the back of the bike, wrapped my arms around the driver's waist, and off we shot through the bouncing hailstones, down the cobbled streets and onto the tarmac road that led to the windswept beaches of the east, while all around the storm turned the dust to mud.

As the rain chased us into the night we didn't pass a soul. Just me and my former mentor from the Koula campsite.

Roland the Scot.

10

The stone-walled dwelling comprised a windowless living-room-cum-kitchen, a single bedroom off to one side, along with a shower unit, basin and toilet. There had been no conversation, no explanation on arrival at the hideout. No 'Fancy meeting you here,' or 'How the hell have you been?' Roland simply gave me a towel and a fresh T-shirt, then set to preparing me some food, while outside the storm battered the island.

Clutching a bottle of water, I stood bewildered and exhausted on the clay flooring, confronted by a display of maps, newspaper cuttings and flow charts that covered every wall.

Like the operations room of the CID.

As I searched the trails of paper, my eyes fell on a series of photographs, and on closer inspection was astonished to find two familiar faces: Ricky – in prison attire; a police mugshot from Thailand, dated 1984. Skeletal, covered in acne and sporting a ponytail. And then Heinrich, less recognisable. Same outfit, but earlier: 1981. Wispy blond hair – both eyes intact.

Roland sidled up with two plates of stew. 'It's where they met.'

I couldn't take my eyes off the photograph of Heinrich; with both eyes, he was a good-looking man, muscular, svelte. He had gained nearly forty pounds since the picture was taken.

'A pretty couple, eh?' said Roland, mouth full of food.

I took a plate off him and scanned the walls.

'I'm no chef, and it'll make you fart like a bastard,' he said, 'but it'll do the trick.' Then he stuck on a thick pair of spectacles and grinned.

'I appreciate it, thanks.'

His eyes were magnified so much that he looked like a goldfish.

Below the photos of Ricky and Heinrich were headshots of two men in uniform. 'That's the chief on Paros – Mihalis,' I said, taking the first photo off the wall. 'He promised to help me but then took annual leave. A good guy.'

'The other guy's the deputy,' said Roland, adjusting his glasses.

'Andreas – he's a snake,' I added, replacing the photo as I turned to face the Scot. 'What is this? You undercover, or something?'

He put down his plate, belched, and took up position by the kitchen counter. 'I'll start from the beginning.'

'Start at the end. You were in Alyki in the middle of the night, waiting for me. You knew I was at the villa – you knew I'd been arrested and broken out. How?'

'I'll get there,' he said, holding up a hand.

'What the fuck is going on?'

'You're safe. Relax.'

Relax? They'd tried to kill me.

A squall shook the front door as the drumming of the rain

116

on the roof swelled to a crescendo, and for a moment he stared at the paper trail, lost in thought. When he finally spoke, his guttural voice had tightened. 'Two years ago my brother went backpacking around Europe before startin' uni. Wanted me to go with him, but I was in the middle of a builder's contract and couldn't just up and go. So he went on his own, reckoned he'd make pals along the way. Four weeks into his trip he rang me, told me he was in Greece, hanging out on Mykonos with an Australian guy and a German painter. Gettin' paid a load of cash to recruit models.'

'Sounds familiar,' I said, forking stew into my mouth. 'Filming them too? Making videos?'

I was about to add 'murder' to the list, but Roland interrupted me: 'I'll get there — hold your horses.' He stuck a finger in his ear and dug around to clean it. 'He wanted me to come out and join him — you know, all expenses paid and stuff,' he continued, wiping his waxy finger on his trousers. 'So, when my contract finished in Glasgow, I took time off and made a plan to meet him at a hotel on Santorini. But when I got there, he never showed.'

I nudged the food about my plate. 'Something tells me this doesn't end well.'

He gave nothing away, stuck a finger in the other ear and continued with his story. 'I took the ferry to Mykonos to see if he'd gone back to his mates, but had no idea where to start — he never gave me an address. I tried a couple of rentals, asked if they'd hired out any properties to a German and an Australian. Of course, there were loads of them. Greece is a favourite playground of the krauts especially — all that wife-swapping, keys-in-the-bowl stuff. But I was stuck, 'cos they refused to give out confidential information. So, I went to the police to see if they could help.'

117

'No joy, I guess?'

'Wouldn't even give me a fuckin' cup of tea,' he said, executing a karate chop in the air. 'But that's off the record.'

Was his compulsion to entertain meant to calm my nerves or his?

'They wouldn't take me seriously,' he continued, dropping the fighter stance. 'I wouldn't let it go, though, told 'em my brother's life was on the line. They made a few calls, found out that he hadn't left the country – well, not via the airport, anyway. But still they refused to report him officially missing. Every year tourists go AWOL apparently, but they are usually pissed up in a bar somewhere, having too much of a good time to leave. To declare him officially missing would be a waste of their resources.'

'It's all about money,' I said, wondering how much longer he'd take to get to the point, and when I'd be able give him my story. Although, if his didn't end in murder, we were in entirely different ballparks. 'If you can't cough up the cash – "not interested",' I added, choosing to humour him. After all, Roland may well have saved my life.

The lights flickered and there was a crash of thunder directly overhead. A second wave of rumbling followed, and from the bedroom I could hear the hail pelting against the lodging's sole window.

'I went back to Athens,' continued Roland, raising his voice above the barrage. 'Told the British Embassy what I knew and that they had to help me find him. My bro was a quiet lad, not a gobby bastard like me. Lived by the rulebook. Definition of reliability and good sense. If he was missing, there was something wrong, no doubt about it. They said they'd do what they could, and I didn't leave until they showed me the poster, which they said they'd send to all the islands. After that, I was told it was a waiting game. So I went back to the UK.'

The hail backed off and a brief silence fell upon the room.

Roland leaned over and handed me the clipping: Michael Jenner. Eighteen years old. Missing since July 1986.

'I saw this poster,' I said, putting down my plate. 'On the ferry from Piraeus.' The family resemblance was clear: wild red hair and freckles. Feline, widely spaced eyes.

'Aye, the police never took them down. Because officially he's still missing.' He took the clipping off me and stuck it back on the wall, then went over to the fridge.

Officially?

'Beer?'

I nodded my thanks, then suffered a coughing fit. 'Didn't yer ma tell you not to smoke?' he continued, popping the cap with a flourish of his gangly arms.

'The cell in Parikia,' I wheezed, 'right over the drains – been breathing shit for week.'

He nodded sagely and brought over my beer, but before he could sit down there was a scratching at the door. Quick as a flash he took out a knife from the kitchen drawer, and with a finger to his lips gestured for me to hide in the bedroom. Then flicked off the lights.

For a moment, it was just the rattle of the storm.

And then, above the thunder, I heard a dog bark. The light snapped back on and Roland flung open the door. There was a rush of wind followed by his growling brogue: 'I've nothing for you, yer mangy beast, bugger off and get some kip.' He laughed, slammed the door against the elements and sauntered back inside. 'Belongs to Yorgos. Just because I fed him three weeks ago, he thinks I'm open all hours.'

'Yorgos?'

'The farmer who owns the gaff. He's cool. Nae threat.'
I heard the kitchen drawer rattle as he replaced the knife.
'Good guard dog, though. Must have smelled you.'

I crawled out from under the bed, heart hammering in
my chest, amazed at his transformation from geek to action
man. 'Maybe he wanted out of the storm,' I coughed, trying
to sound nonchalant. 'You should let him in.'

But Roland had moved on. 'When my brother and I
were wee, our parents were killed in a car crash, so we
were brought up by our grandparents. We'd been left some
inheritance money for when we turned eighteen. Mike
wouldn't touch his portion till after uni. I was gonna buy
a flat. But when he went missing, I used it to hire a private
detective.'

'Out here?'

He shook his head. 'Welsh guy. Jack. Ex-marines. Started
the autumn Mike went missing. Uncovered a report from
the authorities in Mykonos about the shooting of a Michael
Jenner who had resisted arrest and done a runner. According
to the records he was wounded but got away in a stolen car.
During the chase, it crashed and burst into flames. They never
recovered his body.'

Roland turned away and ran a hand through his hair.

'They killed him.' I whispered.

Outside the wind rose briefly, then fell quiet again.

'Jack came back the next day to make more enquiries, but
they told him the document had gone missing overnight and
the officer responsible had taken sick leave. A week later the
guy hadn't returned and still they wouldn't talk to Jack. So
he hired a solicitor, put in an official request for the docu-
ments. But the police denied there ever was a file. No record
of a shooting. Or of a car having crashed and caught fire.

They claimed the officer invented the story and wouldn't be coming back.'

'Jesus Christ,' I said, turning back to the photo of Mihalis, remembering how my list of witnesses had somehow gone missing, along with Mihalis's convenient departure for annual leave.

The police were complicit.

'One of them knows something, for sure,' said Roland.

And one of them had probably killed his brother.

Mike had been arrested and done a runner . . .

Just like me.

So, who was responsible – Andreas or Mihalis?

Roland figured there'd certainly be a handful of individuals responsible, and not necessarily just on Paros, either.

Thinking this was a good moment to begin my story – he appeared to have concluded his account – I drew breath to speak, but was prevented by a further scratching at the door. 'Might as well not go to waste,' Roland said, picking up the pot of stew. 'You had enough, right? Or do you fancy a week o' the shits?'

'I'm good, thanks.' I took a swig of my beer. I could have done with the extra nutrition, shits or no shits. But nerves had shredded my appetite. I was grateful for the alcohol.

Wondering exactly where I should begin, I waited while Roland tossed the stew outdoors, but when he returned and closed the door, it turned out he hadn't finished. 'Jack went back to Greece that winter, and this time he cross-checked Mike's name with the rental agencies on Mykonos. Immediately he came up with a hit. A four-bedroomed villa on the outskirts of the capital.'

'Same with me,' I interrupted, sweeping up a pair of binoculars off a side table and tapping them against my palm.

'The rental papers for the two villas, the yacht and the jeep were all under my name. Ricky stole my passport.'

Roland pressed on and became increasingly fidgety, from time to time shaking his hands in the air as if attempting to dislodge an insect. 'When Jack asked around the neighbourhood, the locals confirmed three men had been living there: an Australian, a German and an "English guy with a funny accent". They didn't know about the German, but they knew the Australian's name was Ricky. He was a bit of a hero on the island – you know, celebrity type. Fingers in many pies. According to the restaurant next door there were all-night raves at the villa, which the police never shut down. Then one day in July, the tenants simply buggered off.'

'Snap,' I said. 'One night we're having dinner; the next morning the villa was empty. Gone. Like ghosts.'

Roland clicked his beer bottle against his teeth as another volley of rain shook the hideaway. 'With the help of his "old-boy" network,' he continued, 'Jack called in a favour on an MI6 contact in Athens who gave him a photofit list of all the possible Australian "Rickys" and "Richards", and all the German, Austrian and Belgian "Heinrichs" that had entered the country in that three-month period. When he got back to Mykonos, he had the locals ID them from the photos.' He passed me the clipping of their mugshots and gave his hands another flick at the wrists.

'Richard Jones and Heinrich Weber,' I said, reading aloud from the caption I'd missed first time round.

The names seemed too normal.

'Now that Jack knew their full identities, they were traceable. Turned out Ricky and Heinrich spent time together in a Thai jail. Heinrich was in first, for raping a teenage girl in Koh Samui. Ricky followed three years later. Drug smuggling. But they were released within days of each other. Heinrich's rape sentence was overturned after an appeal. In Ricky's case, the Thai government admitted they'd made a mistake, and off he went.'

'More like a fix.'

'Serious money changed hands, no doubt.'

'But no paper trail?'

'Case closed.' He wandered over to the kitchen and opened a cupboard.

'Dessert?' he asked, holding up an overripe banana.

I shook my head.

'Fuckin' love a banana, me.' He peeled it and stuffed one half straight in, followed by the other, rendering his cheeks hamster-like. 'Full of potassium too,' he mumbled, as an afterthought.

'So, Heinrich funds the manoeuvre,' I said, replacing the binoculars. 'He earns Ricky's loyalty for effectively breaking him out of prison, and Ricky is expected to return the favour.'

'Exactly,' concluded Roland.

He crossed the kitchen and tossed away the banana skins.

'So – the videotapes, the recruiting . . .' he said, wiping his mouth. 'Let's have it.'

I filled him in on everything that had happened to me since my arrival in Athens and meeting Ricky on the ferry, right up to the moment Roland picked me up on his motorbike; going into particular detail about my time with Ricky at the villa, and of his incessant use of the camcorder. I told him how I'd been informed of the deaths of Diane and the Belgians while at the police station; and finally, I recounted how I'd been forced by Andreas and his assistant to watch the gruesome film of Lucy's murder.

For the first time since our arrival at the hut, he stood perfectly still, staring at me with unblinking focus. When I'd finished, I slumped down in the tatty armchair. 'Doing it is bad enough,' I concluded. 'But to film the thing. Why? I mean, Jesus fuck, why would you do that?'

'Aye, well, this is where it gets ugly,' said Roland, returning to the kitchen to run his head under the tap. He then picked up his story where he'd left off, recounting how the rental-office folk on Mykonos informed his detective, Jack, that a videotape had been found in the basement after the villa had been cleaned. The owner, a woman in her sixties, handed the tape to the police once she discovered it was pornographic.

'Three films,' said Roland. 'The first, was of two men together. The second — of a woman with a group of, I think, three men . . .' He broke off and looked over at me. 'The third was a "snuff" film.'

I stared at him, uncomprehending.

'Where they kill someone and film it. For money.'

Unable to compute what he'd said, I could only stare, dumbfounded, as he began to pace the room, bouncing from corner to corner without further eye contact.

'An older woman this time. Raped and then strangled. All on tape. Couldn't identify the attacker, but the camera caught a reflection in the mirror. There were a group of onlookers, visible only from the waist down, apart from one guy sat in a chair, who she recognised as Heinrich. When she went to the police they thanked her, said they'd look into it. But that was the last she heard.'

I knew Heinrich and Ricky were crooks, but . . .

'Once again, when Jack made his enquiries, the authorities denied any knowledge of the tape. So he fetched the land-lady of the villa and took her to the station, where she gave a description of the guy she'd handed the tape to. But the guy had gone back to the mainland for family reasons. They couldn't help any further. Jack went to the British Embassy, but they washed their hands of it. Told him to deal directly with the Greek CID. When he did so, they assured him they'd get on it, but he heard nothing more. Every time he asked about developments they just said it was being taken care of.'

The rain fell silent.

Roland unpinned the clipping of Mike and ran a twitchy finger over it. 'Jack reckoned there were more tapes on the black market, and he was keen to get going, but my cash had run out. Couldn't afford to employ him any more. He returned to the UK and that was that.'

At last it all fell into place: Ricky and Heinrich were not only running a far-reaching and abhorrent criminal operation, but they were paying the police protection money to boot. And just like me, Roland's brother had got in with the wrong crowd, been made the fall guy. Except I made it, and he didn't.

'But who buys that kind of thing?' I said, unable to let it go.

'You fucking tell me,' snapped Roland. 'Sick bastards.'

'We recruited eleven models,' I continued, 'Surely not all—'

'Nope,' interrupted Roland, getting there first. 'They'd have sold all the tapes of Heinrich's models having sex with him – or with Ricky, or both, or whatever – for sure. But for the nasty stuff, for the snuff films, they'd only target people travelling solo. Those on a loose itinerary, who weren't expected to be anywhere soon.'

Like Lucy – getting over a divorce. And then there was Diane, travelling Europe all the way from New Zealand, with no particular agenda or plans in mind, carefree and going where her fancy took her. 'The Belgians were an unlikely target then – being a pair,' I said, massaging my temples to ease the onset of another headache.

'Which is why they killed them both.'

Roland suggested we venture outside to escape the foetid humidity of the hideout and make the most of the newly washed air. Anxious to be breaking our cover, I asked him if it was a wise idea. 'No one knows you're here, pal,' he replied. 'It's all good.'

I followed him out, keeping my eyes peeled as he rounded the back of the tumbledown farmstead, picked up a shovel – 'just in case' – and made his way to a fallen eucalyptus.

A sudden snuffling noise heralded the arrival of a bedraggled red setter that sniffed its way over, tail wagging, and curled up at our feet. Roland produced a second banana, peeled it and chewed thoughtfully, staring at the stars as they lit the night canopy.

I took the moment to study my new environment. A spooky idyll; a verdant oasis surrounded by high cliffs. Nothing like the rest of the island; tall, gnarly firs and poplars laden with hanging creepers gave it a Jurassic feel, as if at any moment a prehistoric reptile might emerge from the vapours. Off in the distance, I heard the steady rush of water.

'In the next valley it's another story,' Roland mumbled, tossing the peel into the undergrowth. 'There's a waterfall near the entrance of the caves where the tiger moths breed. Tourists come from all over to watch them at it. A fuck-fest of furry beasties. But here, no one ever comes.'

'I'm a fugitive,' I said, bringing us back to my present predicament. 'You're hiding me. Why?' In all this, I still didn't know how Roland fitted in, and how he knew where to find me. But Roland ignored me and knelt down to stroke his companion. 'I haven't a name for him,' he said with a smile. 'Not sure Yorgos does either.'

The setter looked up at me, panting. 'How did you even know I was arrested?' I said, pressing further. 'I thought you left for Santorini. And what about Naoussa? The building work . . . did you ever do any? I mean, why were you even at the campsite if you were trying to track down your brother?'

'Ricky,' he said, correcting me with a wave of his hand.

A scuffling noise from the nearby copse caught the setter's attention and he shot off to investigate. Seconds later, a flapping of wings exploded from the thicket and a large, unidentifiable bird took flight. Roland cleared his throat and his body became more erect. The fresh air had calmed him. I sensed I was about to get the truth.

'In May this year,' he began, 'Jack phoned out of the blue. Told me a man named Heinrich Weber had passed through Athens airport, and he was sure Ricky would follow. I flew straight over from Glasgow, checked into a hostel at Piraeus harbour and waited to hear word.' He punched a fist against his chest, belched, then continued. 'After three days, Jack called and told me that Ricky had gone through immigration in Paris and was on a connecting Lufthansa flight to Greece.'

'How'd he find out?'

'His mate at MI6, I guess. Anyway, as a final favour, he set me up with a Greek soldier who'd been laid off because of diabetes. Same guy who had helped Jack with his investigations on the islands the year before. He'd been given a healthy golden handshake from the army and agreed to work pro bono until he found steady work in the private sector. Wasn't about the dosh. Early retirement didn't suit him – he wanted a piece of the action.'

I pulled the shovel out of the ground and tapped it against the exposed roots. An idea was forming, murky, distant – but growing.

'The soldier waited at the airport,' continued Roland, 'got a positive ID on Ricky when he stepped off the plane, and followed him to Piraeus. He met up with me at a prearranged location that Jack had set up by telephone. We teamed up and followed Ricky onto the ferry.'

'Jack did all this for nothing?'

He nodded. 'At first, he claimed he didn't mind about losing the fee; reckoned he could expect a decent reward at the end of it – you know, some kind of bounty. But later he admitted he was looking to rejoin the police force – Interpol, ideally. Wanted to pick up a posting in Europe. Spain. Greece – or Italy. Somewhere warm and sunny – that was the key thing for Jack. I guess he saw this project as an investment.' He assumed a karate stance, aimed a chop at a firefly and missed, then turned to me once more. 'Anyway, by this stage Ricky had met up with a group of backpackers—'

'Matt, Parrish and Diane,' I said, interrupting him. 'Matt was Australian. Parrish an American. And Diane . . .'

' . . .Was a Kiwi. I saw the whole thing. Watched how he groomed you and nicked your passport. How you left the ferry at Paros, hammered, chucking up everywhere.'

'But then . . .' I broke off.

'We tailed you.'

I stood motionless, as the rain dripped from the trees.

'As soon as Jack told me Heinrich was back in Greece,' continued Roland, 'I put two and two together, realised they were about to do the whole thing again.'

'So, you used me,' I said, as the penny dropped, 'to get to Ricky.'

But I could only focus on one thing, the 'we' in the story – the diabetic ex-soldier.

'When you were crashed out under the tree at Livadia beach,' continued Roland eventually, 'I checked into the Koula campsite, sent my man to find you work on a building site, and then waited for the right moment to "bump into" you. The rest – well, you know the rest, eh?'

I stood there, head spinning.

Leo the Cunt.

'You're working together?' I said, tossing the shovel at his feet.

Roland stared at me, grin fixed firmly in place. 'Leo turned up one night at the villa,' I said, before he could answer. 'I kicked him out.' Just the memory of his smug face made my blood boil. 'The guy lost me my job at the building site,' I continued, 'I wasn't gonna share any time with the fucker. Not on my turf.'

'Fair enough.'

'What was he doing at the villa?'

Roland slipped off the tree trunk. 'Check this out.'

I followed him back to the hideout, where he disappeared into his room and returned with what I quickly recognised as one of my old socks. 'Ten thousand drachmas,' he announced, tossing it into my lap. 'Count it.'

It took a moment to sink in.

'You stole it from the goat hut?'

'Leo did.'

'After I'd been fired for "breaking his arm"?'

'His idea, not mine. Had to make sure you were up shit creek enough to accept Ricky's offer of a job when it came, so – well, we did what we could.'

'You played me,' I said. 'Just like Ricky did.'

'Please don't compare me to that cunt,' he said, sitting down and stretching his neck to one side.

'Why was Leo at the dinner?' I pressed, as the setter began to whimper outside the front door.

Roland jumped up and performed a further series of stretches, in between increasingly vigorous bouts of hand-shaking. 'We needed proof. Leo tailed Ricky every time he left the villa, hoping to witness an exchange of the sex tapes with one of his 'mules', or ideally, with the police contact. Wanted to photograph them. But Ricky outsmarted him. Somewhere along the line, he engineered a hand-off that Leo never caught. We hit a dead end.'

I remembered Ricky talking loosely of his business; it was always a 'bit of this and that', never anything more.

'So we came up with another plan,' continued Roland, chewing at his lower lip. 'Leo would find a way in at the villa somehow, and get photos in situ. Risky but necessary. Leo wasn't exactly model material – he knew Ricky would never recruit him. Reckoned you'd flip if you even set eyes on him. But knowing of the relationship Ricky had with the manager of the Dubliner, he got a job as sous-chef at the club, and when he heard about the dinner, persuaded his boss to let him join in for the night.'

'Yannis.'

'Aye.'

'Yannis might have said "no",' I said, pacing the room.

'We got a lucky break,' replied Roland.

'And I fucked it up.'

For once there was no witty retort.

Roland went on to explain how, between them, Leo and he kept watch over my antics whenever possible throughout the entire period of my stay at the villa; from my recruiting missions with Ricky, to my windsurfing lessons with the Belgians. They took turns on a round-the-clock basis. Once I'd compromised the sting for Leo and was arrested, they staked out the police station. Ricky and Heinrich having fled, they had to rethink their operation. But whatever they did next, they knew it had to include me.

'You didn't think I'd been involved enough already?'

'If anyone knew anything about Ricky, it was gonna be you.'

'What made you so sure?'

'What other choice did we have? You knew his crew. His movements. His likes and dislikes.'

'I don't know where he is,' I replied, the anger building. 'He's gone to ground. Probably left the country, for fuck's sake! I may have been in his circle of trust, but not any more. I'm dead to the guy!' I shouted.

When I'd finished seething, Roland recounted how he'd suspected the police would engineer a fugitive situation in order to shoot me on the run – in the same way they had done to his brother. But Leo and he had no idea how they would achieve it. The night I broke out, Roland had been hiding close by the police station with his bike, but I had been too quick and disappeared off the street before he could catch me. He drove straight to the villa to warn Leo, but was unable to make contact, as there were already police in place.'

'Leo was at the villa?'

Roland held my gaze, unflinching, as the truth dawned on me. The man from the bushes, the one who jumped me as I was looking for the money in the drain cover – he wasn't an assailant, far from it. Hence the balaclava, the disguise.

Leo tried to save me.

And he'd taken a bullet.

*

131

Roland insisted it was time to get some sleep; I'd need every ounce of strength for what lay ahead. But I didn't give a shit. Leo had died for me, and the self-obsessed Scot hadn't even asked what had happened to him. So I told him. Gave him a blow-by-blow account. I owed Leo that, at the very least. But when I explained how the man crawled across the concrete with blood pouring from his stomach, Roland remained unmoved.

'I heard the shots. It was either you or him.'

It could have been both of us.

'Leo was doing what he wanted,' he continued, locking the front door. 'The army left him high and dry. He was grateful for a sense of purpose. I told him we were dealing with a lethal gang of bastards, but he was adamant. It was his choice.'

'It wasn't his choice to be shot,' I said.

Leo and I were no more than a means to an end.

Expendable.

For a moment, I watched him as he jerked his way about the room, hands flicking, twitching – scratching at his thick ginger mop. I realised that he wasn't flicking away an insect, or an evil spirit, even: all those months of pain and frustration over his missing brother – and now Leo – had left him consumed with guilt. And it was verging on madness. 'How did you know I'd go to the villa?' I asked, changing tack.

'The same way the police knew,' he grunted. 'Because of the money. Except Leo and I saw you plant the money in the drain. The police were told by Ricky.'

'He'd gone by then.'

'He knew you had a large amount of cash hidden in the villa. It didn't matter exactly where the money was. What mattered was that you needed it.'

I headed over to the photos on the wall. 'So the police

primed the guard at the cell to attack me and then let me escape, setting up an ambush at the one place to which I'd have to return.'

Shot escaping arrest. No further questions asked.

Roland concluded his account, telling me that after I'd kicked Leo out at the dinner party, he and his Greek accomplice became worried for the Belgians' safety, but their position was compromised, so there was nothing that they could do. 'Not that I'm blaming you,' Roland added, by way of conclusion.

As far as I was concerned we were both to blame. For Leo, too.

'Leo and I retired back to the hideout for the night,' he continued. 'Next day we saw the ambulance and police at the harbour quay. Heard that two tourists had been found dead in a yacht.'

Roland's brother, Diane, Lucy, Leo and the Belgians. *Six souls.*

'Who in the police is responsible?'

'More than one of the bastards, at least,' he replied. 'One on Paros, maybe, another on Mykonos.'

'And Santorini,' I added. 'But why bother going through the charade of interrogation? They could have let me escape earlier.'

'They had to make it look legit,' replied Roland. 'Had to play by the book. And also, they had to put pressure on you – to make you run.'

So, Andreas's apparent softening during my final interrogation had little to do with him believing me and everything to do with the fact his case was about to be passed on. He didn't want to find himself facing a complaints procedure – or worse. He was washing his hands of me.

'What do we do now?'

We were utterly fucked.

'We have to find Ricky,' replied Roland without hesitation.

'What about the British Embassy?'

'Not a hope,' he snorted. 'I'm in the same position as before.'

'Except now you have my testimony.'

'The word of an escaped prisoner? I need more proof.'

I walked away from him to the kitchen and doused my head under the tap, as I'd seen him do. 'Why should I do this for you? I'm on the run for murder. I need legal help.'

'What makes you think they'll listen to you?' He kicked at one of the chairs and made his way over to me. 'The only way you'll clear your name is to prove he's guilty. We've got to catch him.'

Outside, a blackbird heralded the break of day.

'And anyway,' he continued, scratching his chin, 'say there is an outside chance they'll listen to you in Athens – how d'you expect to get there? Alone? Without help?'

He was right: I didn't stand a chance. There was no way, having caught me – or me having turned myself in – that the police would risk official procedures; the staged breakout from jail was proof enough. I had to stick with Roland. We needed evidence. We needed Ricky.

'Okay,' I said, finally. 'I'm in.'

'Let's get some rest,' said Roland, kicking off his shoes. 'In the morning, while I find us a yacht, you figure out how to track the fucker down.'

And then what?

11

By the time I hauled my aching body out of bed, Roland had already been out into Piso Livadi and returned with water, food and a change of clothes: a lightweight tracksuit, several T-shirts and a pair of plimsolls, along with a packet of black hair dye, a baseball cap and some cheap sunglasses. The combination of clothes and accessories would serve as a disguise when it came to leaving the hideout.

His plan was simple enough: to persuade a boat and crew to take us straight to Naxos or, ideally, Santorini, in return for cash in hand, from where we could plan our next move in relative safety. 'So, get thinking, my wee pal,' he said, with a twinkle in his eye. 'Where has that bastard fucked off to, eh?' And as he kicked his moped into life, he instructed me to apply the dye as soon as possible, rehydrate and rest. On no account was I to leave the hideout – he'd be back in a heartbeat.

The first thing I did was shower.

Standing naked in front of the cracked mirror, I was struck

by the sea change that Alistair Haston, moral philosophy and German student at St Andrews University, had undergone: my face a deep chestnut brown; white creases at the corners of the mouth and eyes where the sun hadn't penetrated; dark freckles across my nose; platinum-white eyebrows under a sun-bleached, shoulder-length mop of salt-curled hair. In fact, this 'other me' looked deceptively healthy, despite the ten days' incarceration. Cheeks hollowed out. Trim. Not an ounce of spare flesh. And yet the truth was quite the opposite: I was undernourished, dehydrated and shrivelled. And not only physically; the inside of me had crashed and burned within a shiny shell that told a pack of lies.

I took a pair of kitchen scissors, cut my hair as short as I could, then applied the black dye to the wayward tufts – to my eyebrows as well as the hair. Having rinsed it out, I changed into my new outfit, added the sunglasses and returned to face the mirror.

Alistair Haston no more.

Welcome, the dodgy 'clubber' from the Eastern Bloc.

By four o'clock, I was desperate for air. Roland left shortly after midday and had yet to return. I'd read and reread every article on the walls and done everything the Scot had instructed me to do: I'd rested, rehydrated and dyed my hair. I'd also thought long and hard about where Ricky might be, but, as I'd suspected from the outset, I was onto a loser. I had no clue. More than anything, however, it was Roland's lodgings that unnerved me: hemming me in with its menacingly thick, warped stone walls, inducing a return of the debilitating claustrophobia I'd suffered in the Parikia jail cell.

I needed fresh perspective – on everything.

I threw open the door and found the red setter curled up

by the stone steps, tail thumping the ground as I approached. A short walk would do us both no harm. Roland had stressed that we were quite safe in the valley: nothing up here for the tourists. It only had one access road – the almost impassable, potholed track that led to Yorgos's farmstead – and was too far off the beaten track for the police to bother with. They'd be concentrating their efforts on the coastal areas – the ports, harbours, and yachting marinas – on the assumption I'd be trying to get off the island.

And they wouldn't be wrong.

Donning my cap, shades and Roland's binoculars, I found a key hanging on the back of the front door, locked up and, keeping a vigilant eye out for any sign of trouble, set off with my canine companion in the direction of the waterfall.

As we trekked further into the vale, accompanied by the chant of cicadas, I felt my spirits lift, experiencing a renewed optimism for Roland's plan – so much so that my current predicament receded momentarily into the heat haze, and I found myself admiring my altogether un-Greek surroundings.

A spring welled up from the ground half a kilometre from the farm and became a tiny stream, sparkling its way through an expansive meadow of eucalyptus and bamboo, around which clumps of long-stemmed, vibrant flowers spread out in every direction. As the waterway progressed, I found an abundance of lemon and pomegranate trees, fig and cactus. Emerging from the shadows of the cliff peak, the stream bent north and took me under an ancient carob, from which I plucked one of the flattened black pods from a low-hanging branch. Rumour had it that they were as sweet as chocolate. The first bites of the chewy, dark fruit confirmed it; but not chocolate – more like a creamy vanilla. I plucked a second, and then, inevitably, as we negotiated the shrubbery

137

towards the end of the ever-narrowing, steepening valley, my thoughts returned to Ricky and Heinrich . . .

Would they carry on with their work on another island? Or would word have reached them that the police hadn't neutralised me, causing them to go to ground and shelve their activities temporarily – or even pack it in altogether and leave the country?

Putting myself in Ricky's position, the reality was that he and Heinrich would have disappeared under the radar, despite any help they may have received along the way. Telling anyone of their whereabouts would be on a need-to-know basis – and there'd be few contenders, if any. The police perhaps. It would be expedient to keep them in the loop – open communication would be needed to ensure safe passage around the islands – but it would also be a risk; there was no saying the police wouldn't turn on Ricky and Heinrich to cover their own backs, should investigations compromise their position.

I turned my face to the sun.

Who, in the police?

It was either Andreas or Mihalis – had to be. The former had been as charming as his groomed, silver-screen good looks had promised, but as time drew on, he had turned; the pleasure he took in my discomfort had been plain enough. Whereas Mihalis – moustachioed, unkempt and unflappable – had been genuinely affable and sympathetic, and I believed he was sure of my innocence. But then there was the whole façade of Mihalis taking annual leave . . .

Were they in it together: good cop, bad cop?

My train of thought was interrupted by barking from my outrider: a man and woman were edging their way down the rocky scree at the end of the valley, towards the setter, now crouching at the foot of the fallen boulders, one paw raised as he threw his head back and alerted the intruders of their trespass on his turf.

I froze, stock-still, in the dust.

How the fuck did they get there?

Scanning the vicinity for somewhere to hide, I realised I was utterly caught out – the nearest cover was over a hundred yards away. And by the time I turned back to face the rocks, they'd already spotted me.

'Hi!' Shouted the woman.

American.

'Is this your dog?'

'*Ja* – he's cool,' I called out, affecting a German accent. 'He is not biting. *Keine Sorge!*' I set off towards the rockfall, and in a bid to change my physicality, lengthened my gait, rolled my shoulders and let my head jut back and forth, pigeon-like. On my arrival, the setter relaxed and came bounding back to heel, tongue lolling.

The dog clearly wasn't fooled.

'You speak English?' The man's turn this time; he was trying to keep up with his partner, swatting at this face as he kicked up the mosquitoes from their drowsy lair.

'*Ja*, no problem. Everything is okay?'

They arrived together, sweating and beaming. I put both of them down as being in their late forties. Just because they were hikers – American to boot – didn't mean they were tourists. With an island-wide search underway, there was no saying who the police might have roped in for the task.

'We were in the tiger moth caves,' the woman said, blowing her nose.

'They were mating,' the man added. 'Randy little critters.'

'Bill!' She dug him in the ribs and laughed. 'Figured we can cut through to Piso Livadi at the end of this valley, is that

139

right?' She held out an Hellenic Military map and jabbed a sinewy finger at it.

Was this a test?

I studied the map, feigning miscomprehension.

Paranoia kicked in and I felt sure that any slip on my behalf would trigger the flash of a badge and a call for ID.

What the hell was I to do?

Tell the truth, for a start.

Which meant they'd pass by the hideout.

Was there any harm in that? There was nothing to see; the only window into the dwelling gave out from the bedroom. The room with the paperwork was windowless.

'You all right?' She was staring at me, puzzled, as she stuffed the handkerchief into a pocket of her tight-fitting shorts and folded the map.

'Yeah. I'm just thinking ...' And like that, my accent slipped.

The man frowned. Had he clocked it?

'*Moment mal* – there is a farm road down here,' I continued, sucking the air through my teeth, German lilt back in place. 'And I think you can travel on this. *Ja, ich bin sicher.*'

For fuck's sake, Haston.

'Hey guy, there's nothing down there for you.' The dog was sniffing at the man's crotch. There came a repeat of his frown – it must have been a facial tic, or the sun in his eyes ...

Don't hide – keep eye contact.

'What's his name?' the woman asked, tickling the animal's back while trying to pull the inquisitive doggy nose from her partner's groin.

Good question.

Before I could make up an answer, the setter shot off in the direction of the farm. I managed to produce a disdainful chuckle, assuming the role of the long-suffering owner, while I thought of a viable name for the animal.

German or English?

I couldn't decide, so I changed tack. 'Please. You can go. Follow, he is showing you the path.' I hitched my tracksuit bottoms up and made as if to get on my way. 'He is lazy, you know? Leave him, he will come.' I laughed again and set off in the opposite direction towards the caves, heart thundering in my ribcage.

'Thanks for your help, buddy.'

'*Kein Problem.* Good afternoon,' I turned and waved.

'Yeah, thanks,' she added, tapping her walking stick on the hard earth and setting forth. 'Good luck.'

As the two of them strode down the valley to the farmstead, I turned off the donkey trail, sweating profusely, hot in the cheeks and with a heightened heart rate, berating myself not only for my poor spy skills and the crass stupidity of unnecessarily putting myself in a vulnerable position, but also for how close I'd come to falling apart in the presence of a pair of harmless hikers.

Reaching a flattened slab of clay, I slumped down to watch through the binoculars as the couple drew up to the farm, pushed their faces against the window of the lean-to and appeared to confer. After a minute or so, the dog suddenly became excited, turning his attention to the stone wall; and as he bounded across the yard, another couple appeared from behind the myrtle hedge. The latter wore a leather jacket and jeans, along with a baseball cap and shades; the former was in a lightweight suit, carrying a bike helmet.

Heart in my mouth, I watched as the newcomers stopped in front of the lean-to and held a brief conversation with the ramblers before taking a slow turn around the farmstead,

examining the brickwork and the roof. When they reappeared round the front of the main building, the woman
knocked on Yorgos's front door, but when no one answered
she rejoined the others.

They huddled together a while longer in conversation, and
then all four of them simultaneously turned in my direction –
the American man gesticulating wildly. Flattening myself
closer to the ground, I hid the binoculars from the sun to
avoid reflections.

Shit.

I counted to ten, then, elbowing my way into shadow, I
risked another peek through the binoculars.

They weren't dressed like police ... they had the air of
locals. Nothing unusual about them – other than the woman
was taller than both men. Didn't look like crooks ...

Estate agents?

Roland had explained that the valley next door was a
nature reserve, put in place to protect the moths as well as
the rare wild flowers; but it didn't extend to Yorgos's valley.
After all, his farm had been built on it. Perhaps they were out
scouting for development prospects?

Estate agents? Like fuck.

But then, if they were police, or plain-clothed CID, why
weren't they coming after me?

I waited, glued to my lump of earth as, overhead, a bird of
prey's plaintive cry echoed off the valley walls. Finally, as the
air began to cool, the Americans left the scene, ambling off
into the dusk. The Greeks took one more turn around the
property, gave a cursory look into the bedroom window of
the hideout, and then they too disappeared down the track.

I waited until nightfall, then made my way back.

*

By the time the moon had risen above the cliffs, cutting a silver path across the valley floor with its pulse of chirruping night crawlers, it had turned midnight.

Still no Roland.

I wanted to assume that no news was good news. He wouldn't have taken this long only to return empty-handed. He must have found a willing charter and was perhaps in a bar or restaurant in Naoussa marina, chatting up the potential crew, mid-negotiations, discussing the fee, timings, or even to which island they could take us.

I considered organising the place in prep for our departure but decided against it. This was Roland's turf; he'd have his own way of doing things. Besides, other than the paper on the walls, there was precious little to pack. Instead, I drank the last beer in the fridge and went to bed.

Later that night I woke up with a start in a puddle of sweat.

Outside the setter was going berserk.

I stumbled into the sitting room, and finding no Roland crashed out in his chair, made my way to the front door, wondering if the excitement heralded his arrival. I was about to turn the handle but instinct stopped me, and instead I waited for confirmation that it was indeed the Scot. As the seconds passed, however, the setter circling the building with his frenzied barking suggested this was no welcome-home serenade: he was raising the alarm.

Pulse racing, I crept back to the kitchen, took the knife from the drawer and stalked back to the door.

Now what?

The fact that Roland hadn't returned didn't mean ipso facto that there was an intruder on the premises. It could be anything out there: a hedgehog or a snake – I'd seen how rats in particular could send dogs crazy. And if I waited long enough, Yorgos would venture out to see what was up. It was his property, after all.

Or was I being chicken?

I reached for the handle and found the door ajar, which was odd. I was sure I'd shut it before going to bed. I hadn't locked it because Roland wouldn't have been able to get in. But I'd definitely closed it, on account of the mosquitoes.

Maybe the latch had slipped.

Clutching the knife handle tighter, I inched the door open and stepped out into the shadow of the roof guttering, where I was assaulted by a chorus of frogs. Over to my right, just beyond the reach of the stone wall, the setter was sniffing at the ground in front of the main building. He looked up and bolted in my direction, whining excitedly. But when I reached out to stroke him, he shot off again, nose pressed firmly to the ground. Seconds later he returned again, pawing at me and jumping up on his hind legs, then repeated his foray into the scrub.

I stepped out of the shadows and surveyed the area further afield. Under the glare of a full moon I could see as clearly as if it were day, and yet, with the exception the dancing fireflies and the tumult of amorous frogs, there was nothing of note.

What had he seen?

The dog wound his way back to me and I held out my hands to greet him, but at the last moment he veered off towards the threshold of the hideout and froze, a paw raised off the ground. 'Come on, matey,' I said, as I walked over and scratched his ear. 'If it's a rat we'll find him.' I entered the lean-to and turned to see if he was following, but he was motionless, paw still suspended in the air.

'What is it?' I urged, encouraging him in. 'Water?'

He lowered his foot and lay down on the ground, halfway through the entrance. Still his eyes were fixed on something in the room.

Baffled, I came out of the kitchenette and studied him.

Was he spooked by one of the clippings – a photograph perhaps?

Pushing past the armchair, I approached the display for a closer look, and in doing so knocked my knee against the side table. Or, so I thought.

I looked down and found the side table was indeed where I'd expected it to be, but tucked up behind it was something that I had missed on my way out, and it was the object I'd struck.

A cool box. Bright blue and the size of a small suitcase, with a thick plastic basket handle. Whether or not it belonged to the Scot or Yorgos, on no account was it there when I went to bed.

In the doorway the dog whined, head tilted to one side.

A cool box?

Wondering if in fact it had been there all along but that I'd never noticed it, I put down the knife and lifted off the lid.

It took me a moment to register what I was looking at; not because I didn't recognise it, but because never had I dreamed of seeing such a thing, let alone at close quarters. It was lying in a pool of blood, an inch deep at the bottom of the box.

Roland's severed head.

Smiling at me.

12

Stumbling along the rutted farm track in the greying light, I clasped the kitchen knife tighter in my hand as Roland's death-grin materialised in the gloom ahead of me, his smile stretching in a silent scream of terror.

I felt the vomit claw its way back up my throat . . .

Ricky killed him.

Cut him, stabbed him – *beheaded him.*

A startled hoopoe shot out of the myrtle in a blur of wings, inches from my face. Instinctively I ducked, lost my footing and stumbled into a weedy crevice, narrowly avoiding impaling myself on the knife.

Clawing at the dust, I scrabbled to my feet.

Get a fucking grip.

Stop. Check the surrounds . . .

Across the valley, the outline of Piso Livadi was now visible, the flat light rendering the town and its satellite dwellings an assembly of eerie cardboard cutouts glued to a backdrop of slate-grey sea.

In the distance, a cock crowed.

Breathe.

It had to have been Ricky – or one of his entourage. The police had no need for threats or psychological games. Having staged a breakout to shoot me on the run, they'd have killed me on the spot, given half the chance – or, at the very least, arrested me. It made no sense to silence Roland and let me live when they had the perfect opportunity to wrap the whole thing up.

Why had Ricky done this?

Was he harbouring feelings of compassion for his former playmate? Had the vestiges of friendship, camaraderie, brotherhood or suchlike prevented him from dispatching me, as he had done Roland? Perhaps he felt the macabre gesture was a sufficient deterrent to keep me at bay.

But how had he found the hideout?

Only one other person had known about it: Leo. I'd assumed he'd died at the villa, but if, in fact, he had made it, or at least, had held out long enough for the officers on-site to question him and extract the information of our where-abouts, the police could feasibly have passed the information on to Ricky – they were in cahoots, after all. But that was making assumptions about Leo's loyalty; there was no saying he would have divulged anything at all to the police. Nor was it a forgone conclusion that the police would feel any need to share such information with a wild card like Ricky.

Did it even matter?

The message was clear enough: *leave well alone*. And I intended to adhere. If I stayed any longer in the islands, I risked being caught and killed by the police, long before I'd got anywhere near seeing a lawyer, let alone a trial. Ricky's psychopathy wasn't my business, and, as grim and desperate as Roland's situation had been – also for Jens, Svenja, Lucy,

Diane; all of them – it wasn't my war to wage. Roland had been resourceful, almost military in his campaign, yet he ended up with his head ripped from his throat. I didn't have his aptitude or drive. Horrific as the murders were, my personal connections with the victims were too superficial to warrant risking my life, selfish though that might be. I was a twenty-year old university student with his whole life to live.

Right now, only one thing mattered. Get the fuck home.

The raggedy petrol station was built into the red-clay cliffs, flanked on either side by a row of poplars. The building itself, a tumble-down shack barely thirty square feet. Two rusting pumps occupied the cracked concrete concourse, behind which, an attendant in a sea captain's hat sat nursing a Turkish coffee, a copy of a newspaper hanging off his knee as he stared out across the valley towards the resort of Piso Livadi, shimmering in the early morning haze.

Plenty of cover. Good views of the road in both directions . . .

Ditching the kitchen knife, I pulled my cap down firmly on my head, stepped out onto the tarmac, and taking up position at a picnic table under the shade of the poplars, set in for the wait.

The quickest and safest option was to aim for Antiparos, Paros's neighbouring island, which, at the closest point – the village of Pounta – was just over two kilometres distant. How to get there, though? It was too far to swim. And even if I broke cover and tried to hitch a ride on a yacht, the nearest marina was several kilometres north, in Parikia, the capital – a definite no-go. I had faith in my change of appearance, but with the police on the alert, any single white male in his twenties might draw attention from the police. If I was asked for ID, it was all over.

There was, however, another possibility, something I'd contemplated while hanging out with Svenja and Jens in my downtime from recruiting. It was weather-dependent and it meant calling in a favour, but as far as I could see, it was my only option. And Pounta wasn't far – only ten or so kilometres to the west . . .

I just needed a lift.

As I sat waiting for my ride, the sun climbed higher, the temperature soared, and my thoughts returned to Roland, wondering how long it would be before some animal – Yorgos's red setter, in all probability – dug his head up.

I couldn't have just left it in the cool box; with my fingerprints all over the hideout, along with the paper trail on the walls, the police would only conclude that I'd tracked Roland down on behalf of Ricky and Heinrich, and subsequently killed him. I had no choice but to dispose of the evidence. But I'd also felt compelled to honour in some way the man who had, in all likeliness, saved my life. So I buried him. Or rather, I gave it my best, given the circumstances. Unable to make any headway with the shovel in the hard ground, I'd panicked that the assailant might think twice and return, and resorted to stuffing Roland's head into a cavity among the roots of the fallen eucalyptus – which was when I finally threw up. It was a ghoulish, far-from-fitting send off.

At least he was reunited with his brother.

Just then, two vehicles pulled up on the forecourt in quick succession, but they proved to be duds. The English couple en route to Naoussa weren't prepared to make the detour west, and the saloon car with a French family of four were headed in the right direction but were adamant they had no space, despite the empty boot.

However, no sooner had they sped off up the hill than a third car turned in: an open-top jeep with a cargo of tanned, twenty-something Americans. Two women, two men.

And space for a fifth.

I hopped up off the bench, took off my cap and shades and crossed to where the taller of the two guys, wearing a Dallas Cowboys tank top, tried to operate the pump. He was admonished with a whistle from the sweaty attendant in a sea captain's cap, who hurried over, snatched the nozzle off him and started the pump. As the American turned, I caught his eye and smiled. 'You guys go to Parikia?' I asked, German accent back in place.

He gave me a blank look and turned to the attendant. Before I could repeat the question, the ponytailed brunette in the passenger seat turned in her seat and flashed a set of flawless teeth. 'Dude, you wanna ride?' she asked, in a velvet, California drawl. 'Hey, Dan, we're going to Paros town, right?'

'Kinda. Wassup?'

Dan was enjoying the petrol fumes.

'Hop in man, no problem,' said the second man, in a high-pitched voice that didn't match his muscle-bound physique.

I gave my thanks and squeezed in the back between him and the woman I presumed was his girlfriend. 'I'm Alesha by the way,' she said, offering a heavily bangled wrist.

'Kurt,' I said, improvising.

'Hey, Kurt,' squeaked muscleman, offering his hand. 'Kelly. You from Germany?'

'*Ja*, absolutely.'

'Neat.'

'My room-mate's mother's German,' said the girl with the teeth. 'I was at the Munich beer festival last year. Totally

151

awesome. They have like a thousand different beers.' She tucked her chin into her chest and laughed. 'My name is Sally-Ann, but you can call me Sally, or Ann. Or both. You know – or whatever.'

I couldn't think of a response, so I reached forwards and shook her hand. 'Oh, and that's Dan,' she continued, 'but you knew that, right? Right.'

The entertainer of the group.

'We're good to go,' said Dan, returning from the office hut, jumping over the closed door in a *Dukes of Hazzard* fashion.

In a haze of gasoline fumes we pulled out of the siding, crunched our way over the fallen pine cones up the switch-back road to the Leftkes Monastery plateau, where the air cooled considerably, then wound our way back down into the valley to join the open coastal route to Drios. After more pleasantries, the wind soon swept away conversation and we occupied ourselves with the fly-by scenery and our private thoughts.

Fifteen minutes later, negotiating the road out of Drios, the traffic slowed down to a crawl until we were inching along through the village of Glyfa, on the southernmost point of the island. I'd never witnessed anything like a tailback on the roads before; I didn't think there'd be enough cars. But sure enough, we were part of a queue that stretched into the next village, Tripiti, a half-kilometre further along the road.

A festival, maybe?

'Looks like there's been an accident,' proffered Dan.

Water bottles were passed about – courtesy of self-appointed health and safety rep Alesha, who had a supply stashed under her seat – food supplies broken into, and conversation started up again. With nothing to contribute, I offered to pay towards the consumables, pretending to reach for my wallet, but luckily, they wouldn't hear of it. 'You can buy us all a drink some time,' said Sally-Ann with a smile.

'Dude, looks like you needed that,' said Kelly, watching me guzzle my water.

'Permanently dehydrated,' I replied, grateful for a chance to swill away the taste of vomit. 'Must be my kidneys. Too much booze.'

Alesha laughed, told me that I should take hydration seriously. She should know, she added – she was a physiotherapist back home.

'So, Kurt, where you from?' asked Kelly, passing me a packet of figs.

For some reason Cologne came into my head. Perhaps because my last assignment for the term was an essay on Cologne's famous philosopher, Albertus Magnus, the thirteenth-century logician and advocate of Aristotle – something I could digress on at least, if needed.

'There's a humongous cathedral there,' chipped in Sally-Ann, turning to face the rear and looking at me over the top of her aviators. 'The only building that didn't get bombed in the war, right?'

'*Jawohl*, a beautiful place,' I replied, wondering if I was about to be tested on German history. 'You must go there sometime.'

'Good beer, too,' added Dan from the front.

'You know it,' I said, grateful for the change of subject.

'You guys make the best fuckin' brew, dude,' said Kelly. 'The shit we have in the US . . .'

'Bud's good for me,' chirped Alesha.

'Budweiser is actually from Europe,' said Sally-Ann, flashing me another smile and tapping a finger on my knee. 'Budvar.'

153

'Half of America's from Europe,' retorted Dan.

'And we're all from Africa originally, so – Bud's African. Go figure.'

Before the discussion developed further, we rounded a corner and came face to face with the cause of the queue. 'Hey, it's the cops,' said Dan. 'Roadblock.'

Up ahead, two police cars were parked on either side of the road. The officers were letting the cars through from the oncoming traffic, but our lane was being stopped one by one. 'You think it's something to do with that murder?' said Alesha, craning her neck forward.

'I guess,' joined Kelly, before turning to me. 'Our hotel manager told us two tourists were found dead on a yacht. Like – a week ago. They don't know if it was murder or suicide.'

I pulled a face that suggested I hadn't.

'Looks like they know now,' said Dan, drumming his fingers on the wheel. 'Hey Kurt, you in the habit of chopping people up?'

As we all laughed along with Dan, the jeep rolled to a stop and an officer approached. Female. Had to be at least six feet tall.

'*Kalimera*,' she said, no trace of a smile. 'Identification?'

Despite her aviator shades, I recognised her instantly as the officer from the Parikia police station – Andreas's assistant. The one with the pale blue eyes who apparently spoke no English, who had lurked in the background as I was forced to watch Lucy's murder on the tape.

'*Kalimera*,' replied Dan. 'Driver's licence. That okay?'

Would she see through my disguise?

I pushed my sunglasses tighter to my face.

'Me too,' joined in Sally-Ann, 'My passport is at the hotel.'

The officer angled her head to one side and held out a hand, collecting three sets of licences. Kelly apologised that he had left his behind. She looked over at me and raised an eyebrow. I too told her that I'd also left mine behind.

For a moment she seemed puzzled by my accent, then she turned back to Dan. 'Where are you going today?' Her English was fluent. A trace of an accent, but it wasn't Greek.

'Parikia. Well, somewhere like that,' replied Dan. 'Just cruising, you know? Kurt, where was it you wanted to go?'

I watched another frown flit across the officer's face.

What if she asked me to remove my shades?

'*Ja*, going with the flow.' I said.

Thank fuck I didn't give them my real name.

'And you are staying where?' she asked, head turned towards me.

'Piso Livadi,' chimed in Kelly.

'The Aphrodite Hotel,' added Alesha.

'And you?'

'Camping at Naoussa,' I replied. 'They give me a lift.'

She asked me which campsite I was staying at.

I didn't know if there even was one in Naoussa.

'Camping Koula,' I said, finally.

'But this is in Parikia, not Naoussa,' she replied, checking over the driving licences. Her accent – it sounded more Dutch than Greek.

'That's what I meant, sorry.'

'Okay,' she said finally, handing back the IDs. 'Make sure you have identification with you at all times.' She gave me the faintest of smiles.

'*Viel Spass*,' she added, in German. Then she turned to the next car in line.

Have fun? What did she mean by that?

'She was totally checking you out,' said Kelly, as we pulled away and picked up speed.

'You think so?' I said, twisting around to look back.

But she'd moved on to the next car.

'What did she say to you?' piped up Dan.

'Ach, just − "good day",' I replied, realising in the same second that she must also have been the woman I'd seen at the hideout − the 'estate agent.' At a distance, as well as being out of uniform and wearing cap and sunglasses, I hadn't recognised her. But I was now in no doubt: the angular frame − her height . . .

'Way to go, Kurt,' cheered Sally-Ann from the front. 'Go local!'

'Local?' quizzed Kelly. 'She was like Scandinavian, or something. Right, Kurt?'

Possibly.

'Married to a Greek, though.' added Sally-Ann, not wishing to be outdone by Kelly.

'Most probably,' I agreed.

Reassuring, at least, that the officer had taken me for a German.

Dan eyed me up in the mirror and cracked a slow smile. 'You were so lying back there. You're the murderer, right?'

Everyone laughed. 'You should be a policeman,' I said, joining in, despite the sweat that had formed along the back of my neck.

'That is so funny,' said Sally-Ann, craning around.

Kelly and Alesha turned to me, smiling.

'Did I miss something?'

'I'm with the Drug Enforcement Administration − the DEA,' replied Dan, enjoying the attention. 'Don't worry, your secret is safe with me,' he added with a wink. 'Unless you're a drug dealer.' To which there was more laughter all round.

But my heart started its familiar arrhythmic beat. Not because of Dan, unnerving though it was to discover he was DEA, or a cop, or whatever he was: it was the officer – her smile. At first I'd taken it as a show of empathy – reaching out to a fellow northern European, far from his home turf. And yet the smile had seemed more loaded. Secret. As if she had recognised me.

Which made no sense, or she'd have stopped me.

We continued our way along the coast road and took turns having a guess at the nationality of the murderer – all of us apart from Dan, who kept quiet and from time to time threw me a glance in the mirror. I avoided staying centre of attention by asking Alesha about her work – a subject she was happy to expand upon. And as she gave me her beginner's guide to the ins and outs of physiotherapy, my thoughts drifted back to the policewoman . . .

Why the hell had she smiled at me?

Alesha dug me in the ribs. 'You okay, Kurt?'

I apologised for my distraction. 'Dehydration,' I told her. Upon which she produced another bottle of water from under her seat, insisted I take it, then reprised her speech on the importance of carrying a bottle of water at all times.

'Pounta!' cheered Dan, interrupting her flow.

At last.

We continued another fifty yards beyond the signpost and pulled in under a row of tamarisks. 'Guys, thank you. Really appreciate it.' I climbed over Kelly and slapped the side of the jeep, keen to get going immediately.

'No problem. Been fun sharing the ride,' said Dan, stepping out of the vehicle to stretch before shaking my hand.

'So, what goes on here, then?' asked Sally-Ann, peering through the trees to the water beyond.

Mind your own fucking business.

'Windsurfing,' I replied.

And the weather conditions were perfect.

'I don't feel much wind,' said Alesha.

'The onshores will kick in soon,' I fudged, hoping that would end the discussion.

'What do you ride, a sinker?'

Great, Kelly was an expert. 'Fun-board – well, I'm still a beginner, really.' My accent slipped again, but no one appeared to notice.

'I've never done it,' said Sally-Ann. 'Is it hard to pick up?'

'It's about balance. You'd find it easy,' encouraged Kelly, climbing up higher in his seat. 'You're a dancer, no sweat.'

'Let's go surfing!' cheered Sally-Ann, looking to Danny.

But Danny wasn't feeling it. 'Let's get to Parikia and have lunch. We can come back and hassle Kurt later on. You'll be here, right?'

'*Ja*, all day,' I said, shaking his hand. 'Thanks again for the ride.'

'No problem. See you later,' said Sally-Ann, waving goodbye, even though she was only two feet from my face.

'Cool.'

'Take it easy, man. Hope the wind gets up,' added Kelly checking the horizon. And with a honk of the horn, the jeep sped off, kicking a cloud of dust into the air.

Once they were out of sight, I cut through the trees down onto the shingle towards the rental shack, in the hope that Sadie, the Aussie windsurfing instructor, was still in charge.

She'd been happy to lend me the boards for free when Svenja and Jens had given me the lessons, and I was counting on a continuation of the favour.

Trudging through the shingle, I made my way round the beached boards and their flapping rigs to the makeshift office. To my left, across the channel, lay Antiparos island. Just over two kilometres away . . .

Should make it in less than half an hour.

There were only a handful of windsurfers out on the water – the wind wasn't strong enough yet for the hard core – but for the likes of me, who were still having to up-haul the sail rather than water-start, it was perfect. A steady, light breeze and plenty of boards to go around. I was in luck.

But where was Sadie?

I approached Sadie's assistant, Nikos, a young Greek god of a boy with a perfect Michelangelo physique, who was tinkering with the outboard engine of the rescue launch. When I asked of Sadie's whereabouts, he frowned and jabbed an oil-stained hand in the direction I'd just come.

'G'day, mate,' came Sadie's voice from over my shoulder. 'You wanna rent a board?' I turned and saw her pulling a hefty beginner's craft though the shallows to the shoreline. She hadn't recognised me. Neither had Nikos – the disguise was coming up trumps every time.

'Sadie. Long time no see.' I pulled off the cap and held out my arms for the hug.

'Haston?' She dropped the sail onto the shingle and stared.

'Busy times,' I said, hugging her. 'You know how it is.'

'What've you done to ya hair?' she said, returning the hug and kissing me on the cheek. 'That's a shocker. Ricky make you do that?'

'When you lose a bet,' I replied, 'gotta pay the forfeit.'

159

She laughed and ran a hand through my blue-black tufts. 'What's going on? How's Svenja – Jens?'

'Took some time off, been in Naoussa, chillin' out.'

'Yeah, I gather Ricky hasn't seen you in a while.'

My heart jumped. 'You've heard from him?'

'Yannis told me,' she replied.

I spun round and scanned the beach. 'When?'

'This was, what, three days ago? Said Ricky was caught up in crazy work shit. But he left you something – from Ricky. Asked me to pass it on when I saw you.'

'What did he say?'

Surely Sadie wasn't involved too?

'Just that it was something you might need.'

She smiled, loped through the shingle to the shack and returned with an envelope. 'I think it might be cash. Ricky's worried about you.'

I took the envelope and fingered the edges.

Cash?

'Any idea where he is now?'

'Ricky? Nah. Yannis said he was back and forth to Athens with work, and that he'd met a foxy chick he was all hung up on.'

'I thought he already had a girlfriend,' I replied.

'You kidding? Ricky's got a girl on every island in the Cyclades,' she said, dragging the beached board further up the shingle. 'Hey – if it's wonga, beers are on you.'

I took a deep breath and broke the seal.

No note, no caption. A photograph. Taken at some beach café: Ricky sitting with a beer, a girl on either side of him. From the lettering on a blue awning, it had to be Greece – couldn't tell if it was on the mainland or on one of the islands. The girl on the right was rotund with thick black hair and dark brown eyes, bedecked in gold jewellery. No idea who she was. But the other . . . she was also Greek. Well, of Greek extraction. Auburn hair and green eyes, olive skin, long slender limbs. Twenty-one years old. Capricorn. Studying anthropology at the University of St Andrews.

Ellie.

The world juddered to a halt.

Sadie edged over to me again. 'Everything all right?'

'Yeah,' I replied, managing a laugh. 'Just one of Ricky's jokes.'

Keep your head together, Haston.

'Look, I don't have any money on me right now, but d'ya reckon I could . . .' I broke off, gesturing to the windsurfers lying on the beach.

'Mate, take a board,' said Sadie, tying her hair up with a rubber band. 'Buy me a beer later. Or dinner. Looks like you could do with a meal, you've gone all skinny.' She smiled and held my gaze. 'Unless you got something better to do?'

Ricky had found Ellie.

How?

'You okay?'

'Sorry, yeah. Miles away. Beauty, you're on,' I said, scanning the horizon for the telltale white flecks of the onshores. 'I'll take the Bic, if that's okay. Looks like she's rigged to the right height.'

'Knock yourself out. But the wind's gonna pick up in no time,' replied Sadie. 'You don't want a smaller sail?' Then she disappeared into her hut to find the kit.

The day we'd recruited Charlene and her college friends, I'd told Ricky all about Ellie – how we'd planned to travel the islands together before we broke up. He'd offered to help

161

find her – to tap into his 'network of connections,' as he'd put it. But he needed a surname, so I gave it to him: Alexis. I hadn't taken him seriously. I'd assumed it was just another Ricky brag, and never gave it another thought.

He was planning it all along.

'No need, I can handle it,' I said, as Sadie returned with a smaller sail and dropped it in the sand at my feet. 'You haven't seen my gybes lately. I'm all over it.'

'She's all yours,' announced Sadie as she dragged the board to the shoreline. 'Just don't make me send a launch.' She flicked her hands dry and headed up the beach.

I turned to thank her, but she was already halfway up the slope to greet a gaggle of tourists making their way through the tamarisks. The Americans from the jeep.

Without hesitation, I rolled the tracksuit up to my knees, and without taking off my shirt or gym shoes, dragged the board into the water. Might've looked a little odd, but plenty of beachgoers used footwear while swimming on account of the sea urchins, and a T-shirt was obvious sunburn protection.

I ploughed on through the shallows and as soon as it was deep enough, jumped onto the windsurfer and bore away from the wind onto a broad reach.

The run didn't last long.

After thirty yards, the wind backed and pushed the rig into me, knocking me off the board into three feet of water. I scrambled back on, clothes clinging to me like cellophane, scooped up my cap – glasses had sunk – grabbed the in-haul rope, and pulled the sail out of the water.

Then there was a shout from the beach.

'Way to go, Kurt!'

Sally-Ann.

'Stylin'!'

162

Alesha.

Ignoring them, I kept my focus on pulling up the mast, hand over hand, and checked for the wind direction. It had reversed again and now favoured a direct tack out to sea. I wiggled the board round with my feet to face due west – towards Antiparos.

'Kurt, bro. I got some baggies if you need 'em.'

No mistaking Kelly's squeak.

Tilting the sail forward to catch the wind, I picked up momentum and travelled another fifty yards before turning back to look. Flexing my knees to ride out the gusts, I kept my head over my left shoulder and tried to pick out the conversation. But they were too far away. Had it been still, I'd have heard them, no problem – water magnified sound like a megaphone – but they were downwind, drowned out by the slapping of the board on the waves. All I could make out were gesticulations and head movements.

Then all at once they turned to look at me; Sadie and Dan standing side by side, a step forward of the others.

I took my downwind hand off the boom and waved.

It wasn't returned.

Sheeting in, I headed out to the open sea. I'd been busted.

No doubt the questions were flying thick and fast: Sadie wondering why I'd adopted a German accent and called myself 'Kurt' to a bunch of American tourists ... why I was windsurfing in a full set of clothes when I'd been doing it for weeks in only a pair of trunks ... DEA Dan and his twitching antennae filling Sadie in on the murder of two tourists on the yacht.

No matter. By the time Sadie realised I wasn't coming back, I'd be on Antiparos and out of reach.

Tightening my fingers around the boom, I lowered my

centre of gravity, locked my arms and set a course for the rocks on the opposing shoreline. And as the board picked up speed, heading out into open water, I could feel the edges of the photograph of Ellie scratching at my thigh through the sodden tracksuit . . . prodding me . . . cajoling me . . . daring me . . .

Fuck the British Embassy, fuck going home.

Ricky had laid his cards on the table.

My turn.

13

It took over an hour to make the crossing.

Eyes raw from the sea salt, I lowered my feet down among the sea urchins and took a moment to get my breath back, while out across the channel a splash of red cut furrows of white into the blue: the rescue boat, pulling expansive circles in the area downwind of where I had ditched my board.

Sadie was right; the wind had overpowered my sail. But I turned it to my advantage. When my arms gave out, I abandoned my board, kicked off my shoes and lost the cap, then swam the remaining kilometre to shore. As expected, she launched a rescue boat the minute I crossed the halfway point, but my abandoned craft quickly drifted downwind, proving a useful decoy while I struck out for Antiparos. It looked like they'd now found the windsurfer, and the circling of the rescue launch suggested they were searching for a man overboard, fearing that I too was drifting helplessly in a building sea. It was an dishonourable act, one that broke all rules of seamanship, but I didn't have a choice. If I'd stayed with the board, I'd be heading back to Paros and certain capture.

I slipped off the underwater protrusion, swam round the final twist of blackened rock that lay between me and the bay of Antiparos town, and crossed into the sheltered waters of the municipal beach. Passing through a line of naked tourists frolicking in the bath-warm shallows, I dragged myself out of the water, wrenched off my sodden shirt and tracksuit, and, staggering across the piping hot sand, collapsed onto a slab of rock.

Initially, my plan had been to hitch a ride on a private yacht north via the islands of Serifos or Sifnos, where the police wouldn't be on the lookout for me – or, at least, less so – and then beg or steal funds for a mainline ferry to Athens . . . Not any more. In light of the photograph, my destination was now to the east, in the opposite direction. It was part and parcel of an idea I'd first mooted at Roland's hideout – mulling over which of Ricky's entourage would have a vested interest in knowing of his whereabouts. And yet it was Sadie who had sealed it. Ricky may have had 'a girl on every island in the fuckin' Cyclades', as she put it – but I only knew of one: Amara, the daughter of a restaurateur . . .

On the island of Naxos.

A distant throbbing sound brought my attention back to the channel. Above the horizon, a helicopter was making a rapid low-level flight in the direction of the rescue boat now circling the water further and further south. The authorities had been alerted.

Up ahead I spotted a wooden railing running the length of the beach upon which, every few metres, a towel or shirt had been draped over, with the odd pair of accompanying sandals or flip-flops nearby. Stuffing my sodden tracksuit bottoms and T-shirt behind a boulder, I wandered in my underpants along the sandy track up to the railing, until I came across the first unattended towel, where, standing for a moment, hands on hips and staring out to sea, I checked no one was watching, then picked up the towel, wrapped it around my waist and continued along the path towards the town. Further along, I spied a pair of flip-flops that looked roughly my size, so once again I made a brief pretence of surveying the panorama, then surreptitiously slipped my feet in and walked away.

After a hundred yards, the dirt track eventually became a tarmac road and joined a tree-lined perimeter of cafés and bars where music was pumping and most of the holiday-makers were already half-cut. I skulked along a row of spindly cedars until I found an open-roofed beach bar draped with vine trellises that was particularly rammed, and soon iden-tified a gang of hammered football fans with Union Jacks painted on their faces. Their table was littered with ashtrays, cigarette butts and empty glasses, but also, close to the edge of the table, I spied a fat leather wallet, bulging with notes.

I tightened the towel around my waist, pushed through the crowd of revellers as they bobbed and swayed to Simple Minds' 'Don't You Forget About Me', and fought my way to the bar, where I was greeted by an Italian hipster covered in bangles and a shark's-tooth necklace.

I ordered six shots of tequila.

Once he'd poured them, I fumbled about my towel, cursed, and said I'd return with my wallet. He asked me where I was sitting, so I pointed to the group of drunken British lads, apologising in the process for having such boisterous mates. He laughed, told me to take the drinks and pay once I'd retrieved my money. I thanked him, and balancing the tray of drinks in one hand, approached the lads' table.

'Lads,' I yelled. 'Get involved!'

There was a moment's hesitation as the question filtered through their addled brains as to where they'd met me before, but I continued nonetheless, joined in with the anthemic Simple Minds chorus and edged round the table to where the wallet was perched. Stretching across the table, I landed the tray plumb centre. '*Yamas!*' I hollered, downing a tequila, and slamming down the glass. 'On the house.'

There followed a volley of joyful profanities – as well as the odd 'Cheers, mate' and 'Nice one' – and as they fumbled all at once for their shots, I pulled back from the table, slid my free hand over the wallet and tucked it away into my palm. I then weaved my way back through the crowd to the bar and returned to my Italian friend. Extracting a 2,000 drachma note from my newly acquired funds, I paid for the drinks, tipped him, and turned to salute the table of Brits. They'd already lost interest.

I thanked my unwitting accomplice and negotiated my way through the throng of bodies to the toilets, then slipped out of a side door into the open air. Flip-flopping my way through the dust, I searched the wallet and found a further 4,000 drachmas, along with a creditcard and driving licence:

Paul Gibb. From Maidstone, Kent.

I wasn't proud, but needs must.

Using Mister Gibb's funds, I stepped into a mini-market along the waterfront and procured pants, shorts, some cheap espadrilles and a plain T-shirt – all of which were on sale – along with a pair of imitation Ray-Bans, and a baseball cap. Ditching my redundant towel and flip-flops in a refuse bin, I picked up a chicken souvlaki and chips from a takeaway to replenish my depleted reserves, and, on the lookout for a chemist, chanced upon the telltale yellow sign 'OTE', which signified an international telephone service.

It was worth a try.

Within seconds of connecting, the operator gave me two listings for Alexis Shipping; one in Thessaloniki and one in Athens. I wrote down the number for the latter on the wall and dialled.

A woman answered in Greek.

'Hi, I replied, 'I'm trying to trace Ellie. She's the niece of your manager – sorry, owner. Mister Alexis?'

There was a flurry of Greek and then the line went dead.

I tried again.

Eventually a male voice answered. '*Kalimera*, can I help you?'

'This is Alexis Shipping, yes?

'*Nai*.'

'My name is Alistair Haston; I'm a friend of Ellie Alexis. I understand her uncle is the owner here. I need to speak with her.'

'But she is not here.'

'What about her cousin?'

'Anita?'

Thank you.

'Yes. Do you have a number for her? In Athens?'

'*Oxi* – I cannot give this.'

'It's urgent.'

'Who are you?'

'Alistair Haston, a friend of Ellie's – and Anita's – from university—'

But he cut me off: 'Call tomorrow. If Mister Alexis is here, he can talk with you.'

'Can you pass on a message?'

But he'd hung up.

I picked a piece of paper off the floor, and as I rewrote the number for Alexis Shipping down, it occurred to me I should put a call into the UK, but immediately thought better of it. What good could friends and family do at this point in time, and at such distance? Their advice would be to turn myself over to the authorities – which was a non-starter. A phone call would only worry them unduly, and would be of precious little help to me. As far as they were concerned, I was still on holiday, and no news was good news.

I paid the attendant then slipped back out onto the cobbled street and joined the tourists cruising the harbour front.

Pressing on through the busy port, I finally found a pharmacy, where I picked up a pack of disposable razors, a bar of soap and a pair of scissors. I paid for the razors – but not the latter items; the pockets of my shorts were ample enough to hide them – then, down to 500 drachmas, I headed for the marina where I found a café on the market square and locked myself in the unisex toilet.

Making use of its shiny steel plate in lieu of a mirror, I shaved my head, paving the way first with the scissors, and following up with the entire packet of razors. Having discouraged the approaches of two irate knockers on the door with strangled grunts and groans of dire stomach upset, I then emerged, cap and shades in place over my bald pate, set off to the other side of the square next to the marina, and took a seat at the Delos Hotel Café – one of the few places that had a Visa sign in the window. Ordering a bottle of water, I turned my attention to the harbour, and, confident in my newfound transformation, felt my shoulders drop.

Time to recce the boat traffic in the marina.

14

Three hours till nightfall.

Nearly all the yachts along the quay were occupied by couples or groups. Only two in the entire marina appeared to be singletons. It was possible I could hitch a ride with a couple, or indeed a group, but there'd be more opinions to consider. Also, I'd have little say in commanding my destination – which could result in a protracted journey, involving a second or even third change of vessel. The solo voyagers, on the other hand, were out for adventure: slower burning, answerable to themselves only and with fewer boxes to tick or timetables to fulfil.

If I could get in with one of them . . .

As the shadows lengthened, I got my hopes up for *Hasta La Vista,* a forty-foot boat with the British ensign on it, upon which a leathery man in his fifties was scrubbing away with a bucket and sponge. If he was heading home, I was scuppered, but if he was visiting anywhere else in the Cyclades, he'd pretty much have to pass by Naxos. The island lay only eight kilometres due east of Paros, and whether one's destination from Antiparos was north towards Mykonos or south for Santorini and Ios, you had to first circumnavigate the west coast of Paros; from there, the landmass of Naxos would be a slight detour, at worst. I wasn't expecting a lift to Naxos town itself, I'd be happy to be dropped anywhere on the island.

When he'd finished with his bucket, he went below and returned with a bottle of beer. I decided it was time to make a move, but as soon as I pushed back my chair, a silver-haired woman in a floaty dress emerged from below deck with a glass of wine and kissed him.

Clearly not going anywhere soon.

As I sat back down, a police car pulled into the square. Two officers emerged. One of them draped himself over the roof of the car and eyed the marina, the other set off for a café opposite, and returned with two ice creams.

I sipped at my water bottle and watched. Something about their laissez-faire attitude made me confident that word about my flight from Paros hadn't reached them yet. If, or rather, *when* they connected the missing windsurfer with the escaped murderer, there would be a frenzy of police activity. Perhaps the authorities were still under the impression I was drifting out in the channel somewhere . . . or, even better, had drowned.

In any case, in terms of scouts on the lookout, uniformed or otherwise, I had the upper hand. My appearance had undergone a double transformation; not even Sadie and DEA Dan could give an accurate description of me now the blue-black hair had gone. I was anonymous once again, provided no one asked me for my passport.

Eventually the officers returned to their ride and the car made a slow circuit of the harbour before disappearing into the side streets.

I returned my attention to the marina.

The other contender was moored at the furthest end of the jetty: a yacht sporting a German flag – twenty-odd feet. Less polished and glitzy than the former, with enough paraphernalia strewn about the deck to suggest there was no one else around to help out. The owner had made several sorties above and below deck, and at one point set foot on land and disappeared into the harbour master's hut, which stood halfway along the wooden quay, surrounded by sun-bleached crates of empty Coca-Cola bottles. He was a young man in his thirties, fit-looking, despite the cigarette hanging out of his mouth, wearing a pair of tight-fitting swimming trunks that didn't leave much to the imagination. A macho man, however, he wasn't. A lassitude in his limbs, along with a feminine gait, suggested any partner below deck was likely to be male.

When he returned to the yacht he took up position on the foredeck to sunbathe.

What would Ricky do?

Draining my water bottle, I left my table at the café and descended the steps to the quay. A quick scan of the area revealed no police presence, so I strolled along the decking and approached his vessel, *Etsi Ketsi*, from the stern. I knew the expression to be a Greek colloquialism, meaning 'so, so', and took his choice of a Hellenic name over a German one as an optimistic sign – that he was a fan of all things Greek and might jump at the chance of an impromptu detour.

Either way, it was a good opener.

I walked the length of the yacht, checking out the quick-release cleats and shackles on the halyards and forestays, the simplicity of the rolling genoa jib . . .

Eventually he noticed me and sat up. 'Pretty boat,' I said, Australian accent in place. 'Where's the name from?'

'It's Greek,' he replied.

I was right, he was German.

'It's er – how you say in English?' he continued, '"Okay" or, "whatever", "like this like that".' He scratched his ear and frowned.

'Gotcha, yeah.' I replied, moving closer to the paintwork, as if somehow that would clarify things. 'I thought it was maybe Italian, or something. You spend a lot of time in the islands?'

'*Oh, ja*. Every summer.' He smiled.

I wandered back to the stern and touched the hull. 'What is she, twenty-six feet?'

'Twenty-eight,' he replied, hanging over the railing.

I nodded and crouched down to check out the paintwork on the waterline as he followed me along the boat.

'You sail?' He sat down and stuck both legs over the side.

'Yeah. Not here, though. Back in Perth,' I said, standing up and strolling back to the prow. This time he didn't follow. He would have looked stupid if he had done so – but he knew I knew that.

'Perth?' He said, raising his voice over the cackling of a nearby pair of black-backed gulls.

'Australia.'

'I have never been.'

'So, where's next?' I asked, ambling back towards him, taking in the vista and breathing in the salt air. He didn't reply immediately, but emulated my actions in casting an eye about the harbour.

'Santorini,' he said finally.

'Tonight?'

'No. I will stay here two, three days. After that . . .'

I nodded and pressed both hands against the hull.

Two days wasn't an option, but I had to keep him in play. 'You reckon you could take me along with you? I'd pay you, but I'm strapped for cash. Happy to help out in other ways, though.' I held his gaze a fraction longer than necessary. Again, he didn't reply straight away, and I detected a flicker of suspicion in his eyes. Or was it excitement?

'You are working over here?' he said, standing up and moving to the stern.

I followed him down, affecting vague disinterest. 'Mate, you know how it is. No plans and shit. Bit of this, bit of that. *Etsi ketsi.*'

As he laughed, I removed my sunglasses. The cap, however stayed firmly attached; the cuts and scrapes on my sun-deprived scalp might attract unhelpful questions.

'Sure,' he concluded. 'I can use an extra pair of hands.'

I slapped the side of the hull. 'Awesome, let me buy you a beer.'

He bit his lip and scoured the messy deck.

'*Ja* – maybe later.'

'No such thing as "later" on the islands, mate,' I said with a wink.

It was half-five. Two and a half hours till sunset; at which point there'd be another hour and a half of twilight before night.

I had to work fast.

'Hey, why not?' he conceded, brushing his hands down his stomach. 'What's your name?'

'Paul,' I replied, kicking a stone into the water.

Thank you, Mister Gibb.

'Marcus.'

'Nice to meet ya, Marcus. Let's get a fuckin' beer, eh?'

There was no harm in emulating Ricky.

To catch a crook, you had to think like one.

*

Ouzo, at 80 per cent proof, was Greece's answer to tequila, but stronger. By seven o'clock, we were on to our eighth shot.

Well, Marcus was.

After an introductory Heineken, I'd suggested getting in the spirit of the islands with the local hooch. Marcus was all for it. But every time I went to the bar, I ordered an ouzo for him and filled my own glass with water. A wink to the Lisa, the Irish barmaid, ensured she was onside – 'Just a bit of fun with a mate' – and thanks to Paul Gibb's Visa card, I opened up a tab and didn't have to touch the remaining 400 drachmas. Marcus wasn't happy about me paying, but I had to be in control of the alcohol–water ratio, so I insisted I couldn't allow him to pay when he'd been kind enough to offer a ride to Santorini – *fair's fair.*

The problem was, he was still sober.

After we knocked back number eight, he slammed his glass on the table, let out a whoop, and suggested we move to his yacht. Understanding his intentions, I knew that timing was critical: get to the boat too early and I'd have to go through with it – or knock him out. Neither prospect was appealing. Ricky would probably have done both.

Either way, I needed him drunk.

I played on his pride, querying his willingness to be beaten by an Aussie in the drinking department. He called me a motherfuckin' pussy and insisted I order another round immediately. I complied. When I returned with the drinks, I suggested he sip his drink if he couldn't handle it – being a delicate German soul and all that. He swore again, tossed it back, and continued his tales of derring-do on the ocean wave.

I worked him well, fired all manner of questions about solo sailing in the Med. He couldn't get enough. During his

ramblings, I interrupted him from time to time to get clari-
fication on the mechanics and idiosyncrasies of the boat; how
his Duetta 86 shaped up against the Dufour 39 I'd come to
know under Ricky's tutelage.

He lapped it up. But he was still functioning on all
cylinders.

Having dispatched shot number ten, a groping hand
reached out under the table and landed on my knee. Resisting
the instinct to withdraw it, I listened attentively as he again
suggested we make a move for the yacht, stumbling on his
words in the process.

I returned the squeeze and agreed, on the condition that
we had one final drink.

Just to be sure.

'*Super, geil*,' he slurred, without hesitation. 'And I have *etwas
zu rauchen, selbstverständlich.*'

Great – he was now mixing his English with German.
Even better, he had something to smoke; if the drink didn't
finish him off, the dope would.

Flicking a cigarette butt from his fingers, he shouted the
drinks order at Lisa behind the bar, then stood and excused
himself – 'to urinate'. But before he left the table, he spun
around, a frown playing across his drunken brow, and
pointed a finger at me:

I waited for whatever he had to say, but nothing came.

He simply belched and staggered off.

Keep it coming.

When Lisa delivered the beers, I asked her for pen and
paper – 'for a game' – and once her back was turned, made
a few attempts on Gibb's signature. Moments later Marcus
returned, seemingly less drunk than when he'd left for his
piss, insisting we head straight for his boat.

I reminded him we had a drink to finish.

Reluctantly he agreed. And as I waited for him to finish his beer, I pumped him for further titbits; like how many nautical miles he could expect out of a full tank of diesel, and whether he had a depth finder. But he quickly became sullen and scratchy, bored by my questions, and then finally stood up and declared it was 'time'.

Worried he might cause a scene and draw unwanted attention, I told him to wait at the table while I paid – which calmed him down.

As extra insurance, I ordered a bottle of Metaxa, where-upon Lisa duly admonished me for getting my friend so drunk. I assured her he could handle it. Then I told her I'd put the whole lot on the credit card.

'You got ID?' she asked, handing me a pen.

'Shit, yeah,' I said, sliding across Paul Gibb's licence, grate-ful that I'd stolen from a Brit and not an American – at least I didn't have a photo to match up against.

But why was she frowning?

Aussie accent – English address. Was that it?

I signed the slip and waved to Marcus at the table.

Fuck.

When I turned back, she was still checking the signature. So I slapped my remaining 400 drachmas on the counter and told her to buy herself a drink.

She shrugged and thanked me.

But the smile had gone.

As I waited for her to return from the storeroom with the Metaxa I felt a flicker of guilt, but reminded myself I didn't have a choice. What ill was a missing wallet and a few lost pounds if someone's life lay in the balance? He'd have insur-ance. He'd get the money back. If it enabled me to find Ricky and save Ellie, it had to be a good thing. *Exitus acta probat*, as Ovid wrote.

The end justifies the means.

By the time I heaved Marcus into his boat, the sun had settled on a bank of cloud on the horizon and the wind was a mere whisper. Familiarising myself with the cockpit, I suggested he go below deck and roll a spliff. He acquiesced, on the condition I get down there pronto and join him. Then, as I fumbled about the control panel in an attempt to test the night-time navigation lights, he broke into song and started to remove his clothes.

When I returned to the cabin, he had smoked half the joint and was on his back, fully naked, one hand on his genitals, mumbling to himself. In an attempt to finish him off, I poured a large measure of Metaxa, propped him up and forced the glass to his lips, but he knocked it out of my hand, smashing it into the side cabinet, and insisted I get undressed.

I hesitated at first, but, faced with the alternative of physical combat, I risked the longer game. Stripping naked, I relit the joint and sidled up onto the berth next to him. Keeping his roaming hands at bay, I took a long drag – careful not to inhale any of it – then passed it over. I ran a hand through his hair as he took two long tokes, then poured us both a fresh Metaxa. I had to drink mine; there was no way round it. He followed suit. Then he rolled over onto his knees and tried to put his hands between my legs.

I removed them, reproaching him with mock outrage that we should surely finish the joint first. He agreed, but insisted he'd had enough – it was all mine. This time, unable to escape his scrutiny, I was forced to inhale more of the smoke than I intended, and quickly became stoned. As soon as I stubbed the thing out, he threw himself at me, clawing at my thighs with his fingers.

Out of options, head reeling from the weed, I improvised further, telling him that I needed to clean up and have a slash.

I locked myself in the toilet and sucked at the air through the tiny porthole in order to restabilise my brain. Each time he called out for me, I responded with assurances that I wouldn't be long – all the while accepting that I might have no choice but to satisfy him.

Eventually, however, he stopped calling and all seemed quiet. But when I crept back out into the galley, expecting to find him comatose, I was greeted instead with a rhythmic grunting. Turning to the reflection in the starboard window, I saw him crouched at the foot of the berth, tending furiously to his needs, a lopsided grin plastered across his face.

I withdrew into the shadows and waited until the noise stopped. And only when he began to snore did I finally enter the cabin, where I found him curled up in a foetal position, out cold at last. I slapped his face to check he was truly under, stuck my head under the kitchenette faucet in order to sober up, then pulled on my clothes, fetched the keys from his shorts and started up the engine.

Three quarters of a tank. More than enough.

I cast off from the mooring, still reeling from the marijuana, threw a wave to the harbour master's hut, and under a wheeling flock of swifts, guided *Etsi Ketsi* out of the marina.

We were soon clear of the harbour, heading north at a steady five knots towards the cliffs of Krios off the north-west coast of Paros. I tied off the tiller, retrieved the nautical map from below deck and attempted a few calculations – nothing fancy, I just needed to see how the drawings on the paper matched up with the lumps of rock in the sea and how to avoid running into them unintentionally.

I reckoned the port of Naxos town to be roughly forty kilometres away. At my current cruising speed, it would take me just over four hours – less if I burned more diesel – which meant I'd hit landfall on Naxos around midnight. Sunset was just after eight; twilight lasted another hour and a half. That meant I would round the northern tip of Paros off Naoussa as it turned dark, and would have only a further fifteen to twenty kilometres left to go. Provided there were no surprise storms in the offing, I'd be spared having to tackle complicated navigational equipment and would be able to steer my course by starlight.

Edging around the Krios peninsular, I motored steadily north, the sky weaving an ever-changing kaleidoscope of orange and purple. On reaching the mountainous headland of Monastiri to the west of Naoussa, I cut the engine, hoisted the mainsail to take advantage of the light offshore, and keeping the yacht on a gentle reach, continued eastwards, still lightly stoned, accompanied only by the lapping of water against the hull and the intermittent snoring from below deck.

Just before dark, a school of dolphins joined the boat, criss-crossing the bow in a game of tag, before dropping back to frolic in the ghostly wake. I watched them, mesmerised, until their shadowy forms were indistinguishable from the crumbling waves. Then, as night finally fell, they took their leave, at which point I reverted back to engine power, reefed the sail and turned south.

Alone in the dark, my thoughts returned to Ricky.

That photograph . . .

He was hardly going to go and hunt Ellie down just so he could pose for a snapshot and send it as a final 'fuck you';

he'd want more. He wouldn't be able to resist. Would Ellie have succumbed? Could she be tricked? She was on holiday, of course, out for fun – for adventure . . . But she was far less gullible than I. She would never compromise her integrity, or put herself in a vulnerable position – and she'd never ditch her cousin. In all probability, Ellie was safely out of harm's way, utterly oblivious.

But I couldn't take that risk.

Besides, I was now in full agreement with the unfortunate Roland.

One way or another, Ricky had to be caught.

The sea flattened, mirror calm, as the Milky Way blossomed in a great swathe across the firmament, adorning the canopy with a billion frozen lights. But there was no solace to be found. Emerging from the dark, a stark vision of Lucy loomed large before me, terror in her eyes as she desperately fought for breath, nails clawing in vain at her exposed neck . . .

The flash of steel as the blade sliced open her throat.

15

I drew level with Naxos lighthouse just after midnight.

Slipping through a line of sardine boats with their dazzling fishing lanterns, I stayed just shy of the harbour entrance, turned north, and motored at a snail's pace a couple of kilometres further along the coast until I found a suitable cove, where I hove-to and dropped anchor, barely fifty yards from land. The air was so still I could hear the thump of club music from the other side of the headland, while below deck the rhythmic snoring from the incapacitated German continued unabated.

I stripped off and wrapped my clothes, my espadrilles, a towel, and 3,000 drachmas from Marcus's pockets into several layers of plastic bags. Then, placing the stolen wallet in plain sight on the navigation table – the inference that I was a certain Paul Gibb would keep the police off my trail a while longer, buying me valuable time – I conducted a last-minute search of the cabin for any maps or literature on Naxos. But when Marcus rolled over and groaned, I aborted the plan and hurried back on deck.

Securing the bundle of plastic bags to my waist with a few yards of rope, I clambered down the ladder at the stern, lowered myself into the moonlit water and swam the short distance to shore.

Once on land, and reclothed, I scrambled over the thickets of thyme and myrtle to join a dirt road that wound its way south towards Naxos town, and after twenty sweaty minutes stumbling along the track, passed a straggle of partially constructed houses on a newly-planted olive grove, where I stopped to regroup.

At half one, the restaurants were beginning to empty out, the odds of finding Amara would be slim, and telephoning the shipping company in Athens would have to wait till after 8 a.m. at the earliest. More importantly, I needed rest. Twenty-four hours on no sleep was taking its toll, and a wheezing tightness in my lungs – exacerbated, no doubt, by the pot smoking – threatened the resurgence of the chest complaint that had dogged me since my days in the stinking Parikia cell. If I was to make any headway, I had to stay fit and keep my wits about me.

I turned into the olive grove and made my way to the middle of the building site. There was no point trying to find a hotel or camping ground at this time of night; they wouldn't accept me without ID, and anyway, I needed the cash for more pressing issues. A concrete floor was good enough as long as it was flat, above mosquito level, and open to the breeze.

Climbing an open staircase to the top floor of the innermost construction, well hidden from the road, I chose the least dusty spot available along one of the part-constructed walls, rolled out my towel, wedged the espadrilles under my head as a makeshift pillow and laid myself down. And as the aroma of wild rosemary and sage wafted over me, I shut out

184

the distant thud of techno music cutting through the crickets and tried to still my arrhythmic heart.

Tracking Ricky down was all well and good, but without an accomplice, how exactly would I 'catch' him?

I was kicked off my berth by an irate builder just after 8 a.m.

Apologising for my intrusion, I slunk down the steps past two other burly labourers ensconced in their breakfast of bread and cheese, and rejoined the dirt track to Naxos town. Half an hour later, the ground already throbbing in the heat, I reached the ferry dock at the north end of the harbour, where I stopped to wring out my sweat-drenched shirt and get my breath back. Sleep had restored my mind, but my body felt beaten up; my lower back and shoulders pinched, my legs were leaden and stiff. And in spite of the relatively short walk, I was already wheezing.

Sucking in the fishy air, I established my bearings.

The town was built mainly on a steep hill overlooking the harbour, but fell away in a sprawl of white and blue down to sea level, following a beach that curved around the headland and disappeared out of sight to the south. I assumed the layout would be roughly like any other tourist-orientated port: bars and restaurants to the fore, by the sea; museums, banks and residential areas to the rear. But from my angle on the docks I couldn't tell how far around the town stretched, and it was hard to see where the old quarter started. On Paros, some of the best restaurants had been further back, where the waterfront used to be before tourism extended the land with concrete and tarmac to allow for the ferries, yacht marinas and cheap waterside cafés.

I needed local intel.

With the onset of the first pangs of hunger, I followed

a signpost indicating the *paralia* – which I took to be the waterfront – and joined a paved walkway that weaved along the borders of the docks onto a promontory, at the far end of which was a string of bars. Passing Sanudos, perched closest to the seawall, I came across two competitors side by side: Joe's Pub and Mike's Pub.

Mike's Pub had a scattering of customers tucking into the 'Best Full English in Naxos' – as boasted on a plastic billboard along the café wall – and at only 350 drachmas, I decided it was worth the expense. In addition to having sleep deprivation, I hadn't eaten properly since my plate of stew with Roland two days earlier.

I ordered and took up my position at a table overlooking the marina. When a wiry, hungover Irishman returned with my sausage, egg and beans, I asked him where I'd find the best places to eat – excluding Mike's Pub, of course.

'Up by the castle,' he croaked. 'The *kastro*.'

I explained I didn't know my way around yet.

He beckoned me out from behind my table onto the paving, and brushing the tangled hair from his face, pointed a cigarette-stained finger towards the hill opposite. It took me a moment, but then I spotted it: just below the summit, standing out from the sea of blue and white constructs on all sides, a series of low-level, brownstone mansions, unmistakeably from another era. 'Not really a castle,' he declared, coughing up a chunk of phlegm and spitting it into the dust. 'But they're old, and fancy. Middle one's a museum. Load of restaurants near there. Pricey as fuck.'

I asked him for any recommendations, but the only name he could remember was Lucullus, supposedly the oldest on the island. He'd never been, but heard it was 'the dog's bollocks.'

I thanked him and sat back down.

'You want to know anythin' about Naxos, Alexandros is your man.'

I looked around for Alexandros, but the only other waiter was female.

'Owns the bike rentals by the docks,' he added, hoisting his jean shorts back onto his scrawny hips. 'Local legend. Knows everything and everyone.'

Alexandros Rentals was a block back from the sea, opposite a petrol station with a view over a building site. Whatever money had been made over the last ten years, it hadn't been invested in bricks and mortar; the joint was a corrugated-iron shack with a cracked forecourt, upon which half-a-dozen beaten-up mopeds awaited employment.

Alexandros sat drinking a Turkish coffee, reading the *New York Times*. He looked more western European to my mind: blond hair tied back in a ponytail, mahogany tan, hairless limbs and hooded blue eyes. A mainlander – from the north, perhaps. As I crossed the road, he dipped his paper and smiled. '*Kalimera,* my friend, *ti kaneis?*' he said, as if he'd known me all my life. 'Today is a good day for a bike.'

I laughed and shook his outstretched hand. 'It certainly is. Maybe later.'

'*Meta, meta,*' he said scornfully. 'I have good bikes. Great motorbikes. You will not find them any better. Or cheaper. Sit down. You wanna coffee? Beer?'

I thanked him, told him I'd just had breakfast and explained he'd been recommended as a good man to know.

'A woman told you?' he asked, his eyes lighting up.

'An Irish guy at Mike's pub.'

'Kenny?' He frowned and spat into his coffee glass.

187

'I dunno, but he was in pretty bad shape.'

'He has been fighting?'

'Hungover.'

'Ah, yes. Kenny.' He laughed, and tossed the newspaper to the ground. 'So, how can Alexandros help you, Mister ...'

'Gibb,' I replied. 'Paul Gibb.'

I should have kept the driving licence.

'English?'

I nodded and checked the vicinity for prying eyes.

'You have the most beautiful women,' he said, serious all of a sudden. 'This is the truth.'

I told him I agreed. 'Bar one,' I added. 'A local girl on this island. Amara.'

He looked at me blankly. 'This is a common name – I am not a magician.' Then burst into laughter.

'She works in a restaurant,' I said. 'Her father's. Studies English in Athens. Long dark hair, almond eyes. Eighteen, maybe nineteen years old.'

He held up a hand and turned his face away. 'Please, you are breaking my heart with this name,' he clamoured with melodramatic affectation – although I could have been mistaken. 'Amara Manolis?

I had no idea.

'Her father, Panos?' he continued, as if I had to know him. 'He owns Manolis Gardens restaurant. I have known her since she was a little girl. Now she is a beautiful woman. No man is worthy.'

I explained I'd met her briefly on Paros, at a party, that she'd suggested I look her up at her father's restaurant if I ever was in Naxos, but that I'd forgotten the name.

'You don't mess with her. Her father will cut your throat.'

188

Again, I couldn't tell if he was being serious. But it spurred the second question. 'You know a guy called Ricky?'

He held my gaze, fixed smile in place.

'Her boyfriend. Australian,' I added by way of a prompt. 'We spent some time together on Paros.'

'The lizard king of the islands,' he said finally, dropping his shoulders. 'He does not come here. Not to Naxos.' Sounded more like wishful thinking than fact. I was about to ask him why, but he stood up and lit another cigarette. 'You wanna bike, come back any time.' He walked into his office and slammed the door shut behind him.

I found Manolis Gardens tucked away in a small square at the foot of the hill, behind the *kastro*, opposite a more rustic restaurant, the Apollon. At first glance the place appeared deserted; tables on the shady forecourt covered with upside-down chairs and the gate shut. I was about to set up watch across the square by a children's playground, but a peal of laughter along with a waft of cigarette smoke from round the side of the building encouraged me to investigate.

Pushing the gate open, I walked through the myriad tables under the tangled vines, past the bar to a side door and called out a 'hello?'

At first, nothing.

The second time, I heard the scrape of a chair on concrete.

I hung back in front of the bar area, until a skinny Greek lad flip-flopped his way casually out from behind the door. When he caught sight of me he, took a drag of his cigarette and lifted his chin. 'We are closed before twelve.'

'I'm looking for Amara,' I said, taking off my cap.

'Who are you?'

'Haston. Alistair Haston.' I paused before adding the clincher: 'A friend of Ricky's.'

He took another drag, kicked at a one-eyed cat that had slunk in from the road, and beckoned me after him.

Weaving our way through empty crates and fruit boxes, I followed him along a narrow corridor to one side of the kitchen and out into a courtyard, at the centre of which was a long wooden table in the shade of an old eucalyptus. At one end sat a middle-aged man with a rotund, beaming face, wearing chef's trousers and an apron, one foot up on a stool. Next to him, in tight jeans shorts and a white T-shirt, her thick, chocolate-coloured hair tumbling to her hips, sat Amara. She was straddling her seat, smoking a cigarette.

When she saw me, she shot to her feet.

'Alistair?' she exclaimed, knocking over her chair.

'Long time no see,' I quipped, averting my eyes from her high-cut shorts as she rushed over, kissed me on both cheeks and threw her arms around my waist.

'*Panagia mou!* So skinny. What happened to your hair?'

After introductions, Dimitris – Amara's uncle and also the head chef – chased the young lad, Nikolas, her cousin, into the kitchen to peel potatoes, leaving Amara and I alone in the courtyard. 'I can't believe you are here,' she said, pushing me into a chair. 'I thought I never would see you again.'

I had no idea where to start.

'How did you find this place?' she continued, perching herself on my lap. 'Ricky told you, no?' She tapped a cigarette out of her pack and offered it to me. Despite the chest complaint and my vow to never touch the things again, I found myself automatically reaching out to take it.

'I haven't seen Ricky since the dinner party at the villa.'

I felt an overwhelming urge to pour everything out at once – instinct told me she was not of Ricky's kind – but I knew I had to tread carefully. Innocent bystander or no, she was Ricky's girlfriend nonetheless.

'He called me a few days afterwards,' she said, tossing back her mane of hair. 'Told me you had gone to England.'

'Yeah, I told him I was thinking about it,' I lied.

Apparently she was out of the loop.

Or was she dissembling too? She was a drama student, after all.

'I decided to stay a little longer,' I added. 'See more of the islands.'

'You must go to Santorini,' she said.

'Everyone says,' I replied.

'But here you are.' She beamed.

'I knew you worked in your father's restaurant. I asked around . . .'

'And it is a lovely surprise.'

'Is he here?' I continued, fudging.

'My father? No. He is in Athens. He comes down at least once a week. But my uncle – he runs everything.' Once more she gave me that electric smile. She was magnetic, irresistible, reeling me in as Ricky had done. Despite the questionable age gap, they were well matched.

'The dinner,' she continued, 'was it, you know – a success?' She sucked on her cigarette, a frown plastered across her brow. I had forgotten that she knew all about Operation Svenja. I remembered her telling me she wasn't going to stay around for that part of the evening because it made her uncomfortable.

I shrugged. '*Etsi ketsi.*'

'*Etsi ketsi*?' she coughed. 'You are now Greek!'

I laughed and changed tack. 'How did you and Ricky meet?'

I explained it was something I'd always meant to ask Ricky, but never got around to it.

Embarrassed at first, she eventually admitted he had tried to recruit her for Heinrich the year before on Naxos town beach. She'd resisted his advances but he wouldn't give up. It wasn't long before a family friend found out and told Ricky on no uncertain terms to leave her alone.

Perhaps because she was only seventeen?

'Alexandros, from the bike rentals?'

She laughed, inadvertently blowing smoke in my face.

'You know Alexandros?'

'It was he who told me where to find you.'

'You are like Ricky,' she said, running a finger up my chest. 'You come some place and "click", you know everybody. No, it wasn't Alexandros. But I have known him also a long time. It's a small town.'

'I don't think Ricky and I are so similar,' I said, looking around the courtyard and wondering if the Australian had once sat in the very same seat where I was – chatting idly, spinning his web of deceit.

'But Ricky didn't give up,' she continued. 'He's not scared of anyone or anything, you know? So I let him take me out on a date. He deserved it. My family wasn't going to tell me what to do.' She licked her lips and puffed her cheeks out. 'But no painting, I said. We became friends. Lovers. One night he told me how he and Heinrich were spending their time and money.' She paused and flicked her ash.

'It didn't bother you, what he was doing?'

She shrugged. 'Not my scene. But there is no harm in it.'

Present tense.

'Do you know where Ricky is now?'

'Ricky and I are relaxed,' she replied. Maybe I will see him before he leaves for the winter. Maybe I won't.'

'You haven't seen him recently?'

'Since the night at the villa he has been working. You know him. Always busy, busy.'

'But you speak on the phone?'

Odd that he wouldn't make a plan to meet her.

Unless he's with Ellie.

'He calls me sometimes, usually when he wants something,' she said, cocking her head on one side. 'I don't call him. He's always on the move. You have lots of questions.' She held my eyes and smiled. 'Ricky and I have no special commitment. We are friends. We are free.'

'Any plans to meet up?'

'He likes to surprise me. Comes for a night. Brings me presents.'

'Here?'

She shook her head and blew out a smoke ring. 'At my father's villa. On the other side of the *kastro*.'

'And you have no idea where he is?'

She shrugged and tapped her crimson fingernails on the ashtray.

'When did you last speak?' I added.

'Mister Haston the policeman,' she said, with a laugh. 'You are interrogating me. The day before yesterday we spoke.'

'What time was this?'

'After lunch. I don't know. Maybe two – three o'clock.'

I smiled. 'And he didn't tell you where he was?'

She pulled herself upright, and for a moment I thought she was going to tell me to piss off, but then she turned to me and tucked a lock of hair behind her ear. 'He said he had been in

Athens but was going to join Heinrich on the islands. And he would visit me soon.'

'Soon – when?'

A moment ago, she'd said he might leave for the winter without seeing her.

'I don't know. He said he would call again.'

'Which island?'

'You are the dog with the bone!' she replied, punching me on the arm. 'I have no idea. He has his own key. Sometimes he comes by when I am out, and is gone before I return. Depends on his work. But he said he wanted to see me, so ...' She tailed off and seemed suddenly far away.

'Always at night?'

'*Ti?*'

'Sounds dodgy, him sneaking about. Is that because he's not popular on Naxos?' I tried to keep the tone cheeky.

'What makes you say that?' She turned and studied me.

I laughed. 'He can be a little intense.'

'You mentioned Ricky to Alexandros?'

'To help find you. Six degrees of separation.'

The latter comment was lost on her. She shrugged and flicked her cigarette ash. 'He is jealous of Ricky. And he doesn't trust the quiet people.'

'I wouldn't have described Ricky as the quiet type.'

'You know Ricky, he likes to be secret. A man of mystery.'

Because he's a murderer.

'Right.'

'Is something wrong between the two of you?' she said, picking at a nail. 'Does he owe you money?'

'Absolutely not,' I protested. 'I wanted to surprise him, that's all,' I stubbed out my cigarette and reached for another. 'So, you have no idea where he might be?'

'You are smoking quickly,' she said, pursing her lips. 'Ricky told me when he first met you, you didn't smoke at all.'

'Yeah,' was all I could manage.

Always evading. Was she frightened of Ricky, or protecting him?

Once again, I felt the urge to tell her everything; there was no way she would side with Ricky once she knew about the snuff films – and at some point, I'd have to tell her, otherwise what was the point in seeking her out? But then she might want to confront him about it first – at which point it would be game over.

The time would come soon enough – I needed more intel first.

We sat in silence. As she flicked her cigarette lighter over and over on the table, I studied a pair of collared doves preening in the upper branches of the eucalyptus. Eventually she took my hand and squeezed it.

I returned the gesture. 'I know he and Heinrich were on Mykonos earlier this summer,' I continued. 'Then Santorini and Paros. Where else do they usually take a villa? Ios, surely – it's *the* party island.'

'I don't know anything about the other islands. Or the villas,' she exclaimed, her tone hardening. 'I only ever go to Paros. Because I have friends in Piso Livadi. I don't like to be around Ricky when he is working. I get bored of the bullshit.' With that she stood up, flicked a smudge of ash off her T-shirt and called out towards the kitchen.

'*Ti ora einai?*'

The switch was remarkable.

A shout came back that it was eleven thirty.

'I have to get to work,' she said. 'Come back at half past three and I will show you around.' Her manner suggested

195

it was the last thing she wanted to do. But then she turned and smiled. 'Haston, forget Ricky. He is not here. I am.' She dropped her hand and disappeared into the kitchen.

She reminded me of Ellie. Not physically: Ellie was all English rose – ethereal, feline, her smile more knowing. But they both possessed a volatility in temperament that was utterly compelling. One could never be sure what they were thinking. And with Ellie, that unpredictability became an opiate.

Time to try another phone call.

The OTE, where the payphones were, was further south along the *paralia* in the direction of the overpopulated town beach, Agios Georgios, by the art deco Hotel Hermes.

All booths were free. I borrowed pen and paper from the bearded attendant busy filling his pipe, chose the kiosk furthest away from the radio on the counter, and pulled out the scrap of paper with the digits for Alexis Shipping. It connected on the third ring.

Yes, they remembered me from yesterday. No, Mister Alexis was not in. But this time – my message must somehow have got through – the Alexis residential number was quickly forthcoming.

When I finally got through, I received a barrage of Greek.

'This is Alistair,' I replied. 'A friend of Ellie's. From university.'

There was a pause, followed by a hearty laugh from the other end. 'Alistair? I am Katerina, Ellie's aunt. *Ti kaneis? Kala?*'

'Very well, thank you,' I replied.

Why had she laughed so hard?

'I was hoping to speak to Ellie. She there?'

'She is on the islands with my daughter, Anita.'

'Which island?'

'I don't know. All of them. Party, party, party!' she replied, and guffawed with laughter.

'When are you expecting them home?'

'I have no idea. You are in Greece?'

'Naxos. Listen, if your daughter calls you, ask where they are. If they have met a man called Ricky – an Australian – they must be very careful. He is extremely dangerous. They must stay away from him.'

She laughed. 'This is Greece. All men are dangerous.'

I spent the next few hours at the southernmost end of Agios Georgios beach, away from the crowds, crouched under a lone tamarisk, keeping a watchful eye out for the authorities, as I revisited my conversation with Amara and tried to assimilate my concerns via a systematic dose of logic.

Amara was keeping something from me – of that, I was certain.

I'd sensed it most when questioning her about what contact, if any, she'd had with Ricky. She had been edgy and evasive in her replies, and the eventual revelation that Ricky had called 'the day before yesterday' to say he'd be 'visiting sometime soon' had set off alarm bells. First of all, it was all too vague. Secondly, there was the timing of Ricky's call: the day before yesterday was the day I'd left Paros. And Ricky had apparently called around lunchtime . . . After I had set off on the windsurfer . . . *After I had seen Sadie.*

Sadie tells Ricky . . . Ricky checks in with Amara . . .

But that was assuming Sadie knew where I was headed. And how could she possibly have known? I wasn't even sure myself at that point.

197

Maybe Ricky had no need of an informant . . .

The photograph.

It wasn't just a 'fuck you'. Ricky would have known all too well it would provoke me into coming after him. With Ellie's welfare at stake, it was a challenge I couldn't refuse. And having second-guessed I'd leave Paros via Sadie's windsurfing school, it wouldn't have taken much for him to deduce that I'd head for Naxos to track him down via the only lead I had – his sometime girlfriend, Amara.

Ergo had he phoned Amara because he was expecting my arrival?

And could that explain Amara's nervousness?

Possibly. It would depend on what had been said. Although her nervousness didn't necessarily mean ipso facto that she was complicit.

Complicit in what, exactly?

If Ricky was hoping to settle a score, why hadn't he done so when he'd had the perfect opportunity at Roland's hideout?

Unless it had something to do with Ellie.

Except Ricky's anticipated arrival on Naxos would suggest he wasn't with Ellie – whatever 'with' might entail. Ricky would hardly come to visit a girlfriend – ex or otherwise – with another woman in tow. There was every possibility that Ellie and her cousin were that very moment sunbathing, safe and sound, on a far-flung beach somewhere across the Aegean, oblivious.

But then there was the other, unthinkable possibility . . .

Enough.

I was floundering. Without a confrontation, there was no way of knowing Ricky's intentions, let alone Ellie's whereabouts. Neither could I be sure of whether or not Amara was complicit, or Sadie, for that matter, or even if the charismatic

Alexandros was somehow involved – despite his apparent dislike of Ricky. All I knew was that I'd escaped Paros, I'd found Amara, and that Amara and Ricky were in communication.

No – Amara claims they're in communication.

Fuck it.

Fuck logic.

I'd escaped Paros and I'd found Amara.

Everything else was conjecture.

Just before three thirty, I bought a loaf of bread and a slab of feta cheese from a convenience store on the *paralia*, donned my sunglasses and cap, and, pushing against the tide of beachgoers, wound my way through the network of cobbled alleyways back towards Manolis Gardens. As I hiked across the hill to the east, I joined a dusty footpath lined with poplars that led me downhill through a residential neighbourhood to the rear of a children's playground opposite the restaurant. Crossing the square, I spotted Amara at the front of the restaurant by the gate, talking to a man straddling a Harley-Davidson.

Alexandros. From the rentals.

When she saw me, she waved, kissed Alexandros on the cheek and took off her apron. Alexandros spun the bike around, looked me in the eye, then opened up the throttle and roared off down the hill.

'Friendly chap,' I said, climbing the steps.

Ignoring my comment, she tossed the apron at Nikolas, who was sitting sideways on a table, holding a broom in one hand and a cigarette in the other. 'I will take you to the *kastro*, to the museum,' she said, hitching up her shorts and taking me by the arm. 'If you have time.'

'Diary's empty,' I said, cracking a smile.

Nikolas slipped off the table, gave me a wink as he brushed past us, and trotted down the steps to a pristine moped parked up on the siding.

'Five minutes away,' she said, tugging me towards the gate.

'By bike?'

'Not everyone is lazy around here,' she shouted to Nikolas, as he revved the engine to full pitch, pulled a wheelie, and skidded off along the road.

'How old's your cousin?' I shouted above the din.

'Sixteen,' she replied, flipping Nikolas a 'V' sign as he gave a one-armed salute and disappeared around the corner in a cloud of dust.

'Nice bike,' I said. The restaurant was obviously doing well.

Amara turned to me as we set off in the opposite direction, towards the pine trees at the bend in the road:

'So, who is Paul Gibb?'

16

We never made it to the museum.

My association with Paul Gibb alone was enough to get me arrested, and if Alexandros was as connected as his reputation suggested, who knew where his snooping might lead? To enlist Amara's help, I'd have to come clean sooner or later. And even if she'd been compromised, or felt she owed allegiance to Ricky, I hoped that what I had to tell her would soon convince her to jump ship.

Besides, my gut told me she was to be trusted.

Sitting on a bench in a park behind the *kastro*, with a view across the windswept channel towards Paros, I told her everything: from the moment I met Ricky to stealing Paul Gibb's wallet and using his credit card to get Marcus drunk so I could commandeer his yacht.

To begin with, she spent most of the time looking out to sea, as if contemplating the view. A couple of times she asked me questions, to clarify a point – mostly to do with Ricky – otherwise she appeared quite still and relaxed, giving no indication as to what she thought. When I came onto the subject of murder, however – how Diane and Lucy's killings had been taped; how Svenja and Jens had been bludgeoned to death and hidden on board Heinrich's yacht; how I'd found Roland's severed head in the cool box at Yorgos's farm – her eyes grew wide, and her confident veneer disintegrated.

'You think Ricky does the killing?' she whispered, shifting in her seat and throwing a look down the street behind us, as if Ricky might suddenly materialise out of thin air.

I told her I didn't know. The point was that he'd orchestrated it: Diane, Svenja, Jens – Roland's missing brother, Michael, Lucy. They had all died because of him, if not directly by his hand.

'I've been framed, in the same way Roland's brother was,' I continued. 'And a handful of the police are involved, if not coordinating the entire operation.'

'Why?' she asked, her voice quavering.

I wasn't sure if she was referring to my being framed, or whether she was querying the complicity of the police force; still, I stuck to the point, explaining how the police were most likely getting protection money from Ricky and Heinrich.

'So they can paint portraits?' Again, she threw another glance behind her.

'The painting is a way for Heinrich to seduce the models,' I replied, reaching out and placing a reassuring hand on her arm. 'Prostitution – because he pays them for it. And he's paying the *police* to leave them alone.'

'But the films, the killing tapes,' she mumbled, clicking her fingers, trying to find the right word.

'Snuff films,' I said, studying her closely. 'The snuff films are the real reason behind all of this. They command vast sums of money from an underground market. That's how

Heinrich and Ricky earn their wealth. The painting and prostitution are part of the selection process for likely victims.'

'Ricky is organising this?' her face twisted in disbelief.

'They are in it together. But Ricky is at the centre of it. Without him there'd be no models for Heinrich to recruit, no tapes, and no need for police protection.'

'How many films?'

I told her I had no idea.

For a while we sat in silence, our thoughts lost over the horizon. Eventually, Amara leaned forwards, elbows on her knees, buried her head in her hands and let out a protracted sigh. I was about to wrap an arm about her in comfort, but she suddenly stood up, tied her hair back with an elastic band and lit a cigarette. 'I will tell my father,' she said, pocketing the packet without extending the offer. 'He will talk to the police.'

In an instant, the fear seemed to have left her, a cool steeliness in its place.

'No. You must say nothing to anyone about this,' I insisted. 'Not your father, and especially not the police.' I made a move to touch her arm but she flinched in anticipation.

I withdrew my hand. 'You said Ricky was coming to see you?'

'This is what he told me,' she murmured, staring up at a flock of swifts, wheeling in a wide arc above the *kastro*.

'You said he wants something?' I continued.

'I don't know. Clothes, sleep.'

Sleep?

'He has a key – what else does he keep there?'

She shrugged, took a pull on her cigarette, then turned away.

'Amara, we need to go to your father's house.'

*

The walk took fifteen minutes.

She didn't utter a word. Perhaps she was still digesting the horror of Ricky's actions, but I also felt she was keeping something back from me: the way she flicked the hair from her face when it wasn't actually in her eyes, sharp exhalations of breath, as if exhausted.

'My uncle Dimitri is having a siesta, so we have to be quiet,' she said finally, when we reached her father's house. Taking out her key, she opened the door and ushered me into the paved hallway.

And the cousin?

'Nikolas won't be here,' she continued, as if reading my mind. 'He is out, smoking marijuana.'

I followed her down a long hallway lined with photographs of Naxos from the sixties, then, passing an inner courtyard with an old fig tree set against a backdrop of tumbling hibiscus, she led me two floors up a stone staircase into an open-plan sitting-room-cum-bedroom with a large four-poster bed on a wooden plinth at the rear, beside a series of windows mounted with venetian blinds.

'Nice place,' I said, even though with all the shutters drawn it was hard to make much out. 'All to yourself?'

'Nikolas and Dimitri have the floor below,' she said, pushing the wooden slats open and flooding the room with light. 'My father sleeps downstairs in the guest room. When he is over.'

No mention of her mother.

I joined her at the window and stuck my head out. Just below the ledge was the concrete roof to the remainder of the house, with a square hole in the middle – a courtyard, presumably. A few feet from her window a set of chairs were placed either side of a small table underneath a row of potted cypress trees. The green-painted wood and chequered blue-and-white tablecloth, along with a trellis of honeysuckle along the entire outer wall was pure picture-postcard Greece.

'I like to hang out here when I need peace and quiet.' She turned to me and smiled. 'You want a beer?'

I nodded and breathed in the perfumed air: a combination of pine, vanilla and honey. 'Sure.'

'Go outside. We can talk more freely there,' she said, passing me the cigarettes and a lighter. 'I'll be back.'

But when she left the room I stayed put. Ignoring the plethora of cupboards and drawers, as well as a walk-in wardrobe at the side of the bed – I'd get around to those – I circled the room and cast an eye over the ceiling. It seemed solid enough. But in the corner above a dressing table the paint had worn away, and on closer inspection I found a series of panels. Pulling up the chair from the dressing table, I climbed up to see if the material would give at all, when Amara appeared in the doorway.

'So, you're a spy as well as a detective,' she said, deadpan.

Before I could explain myself, she put down the beers down and retrieved a suitcase from the wardrobe. 'This is what you are looking for?' she said, dragging it out and dumping it on the floor. 'It isn't locked.'

She took a sip from her bottle and eyed me steadily.

When I opened it, the first thing I saw was a pile of T-shirts and jeans, some underwear, and a pair of smart shoes – all neatly folded and squared away. But in the fold-down flap at the back was a packet of papers. And something else.

I reached in and took it out.

Ricky's passport.

It was definitely his photo – albeit from a long time ago, but the name James Richardson was obviously fake, as was, most likely, the Sydney address. Nonetheless it was the ID that must have allowed him into the country, and would be the one that got him out.

'So, he's leaving Greece,' I said, flipping through the pages. 'He's coming to say goodbye.' Why else announce his intention to visit? He had a key.

'Maybe,' she replied quietly.

Had I got this so wrong? Was Ricky simply shutting shop for the summer and doing a runner?

I looked over the room once more. It made sense that Amara should be the warden of his passport; Ricky was the definition of itinerant, his proclivities on and around the islands necessitated it — why risk carrying a valuable document around when he had the perfect safe place to stash it?

Although, I'd been hoping to find something else . . .

The tapes.

Without them, it was his word against mine.

Still, Ricky was heading to Naxos. He'd come within my grasp.

I turned to Amara, who was gazing out of the window. The fact she was harbouring his passport didn't mean she knew more than she was letting on; it didn't in any way implicate her in Ricky's crimes. She had been used, just as Ricky had used me.

And now he's planning his getaway.

She caught my eye and quickly turned away. 'Are you going to join me?' she asked, taking her beer to the window and climbing out onto the roof.

'You do believe me, don't you?' I replied.

To stop Ricky, I needed Amara one hundred per cent onside.

She nodded.

206

'You're aware of the danger – not just for me, but for you too?'

'I have to help you, yes?'

'You do.'

I climbed out of the window and took a seat, as she stared across the rooftops at the mirror-calm sea in the distance, twirling a lock of hair between her fingers. Perhaps the laissez-faire detachment was a defence mechanism.

'Now what?' She returned her attention to the table and handed me a cigarette.

I cupped my hand around hers as I lit up. 'We wait.'

There was nothing to do until Ricky arrived. I also had to figure out how I was going to physically restrain him.

And I need that evidence . . .

A gecko scuttled out from behind a shutter panel, down the wall and into a crack in the floor. 'Where are you staying?' she asked, letting go of my little finger and holding my gaze.

Her inscrutability was bewildering; I was quite sure she was withholding information that would be useful. But I knew I couldn't push it. Not yet.

I looked back through the window into her room. To duplicate video cassettes you needed a reliable master copy. Master copies were untouchable, irreplaceable. The golden goose. Where else to store such an illicit, lucrative legacy, except in a place no one would ever think to look?

I had to investigate further.

'I don't know,' I replied, with a smile.

Amara left for work along with her uncle and cousin at six o'clock.

She gave me a towel and a pair of her father's clean underpants and suggested I take a bath. I was to make myself at home, eat anything from the fridge, use any part of the house I fancied and to walk over to the restaurant after she finished work. 'But no spying, Mister Detective,' she laughed, as she hurried out to join her cousin on the back of his moped.

Nikolas gave me an upward nod of the head – a gesture that was lost on me, although it didn't seem unfriendly – then sped off up the hill.

I stood in the road, watching the dust settle. Amara was still impossible to read: she seemed to have overcome her shock at the discovery of her boyfriend's crimes all too easily. And yet, I had seen the look of terror in her eyes.

With such command of her emotions, she'd prove a consummate actress.

My thoughts returned to our earlier conversation: *Sometimes he brings me presents . . .*

What kind of presents? Cash?

I suffered a surge of paranoia: perhaps Ricky and Amara were using each other, their relationship a stunt – a mutually beneficial contract centred around money. It would explain the noncommittal air about her. Were the rest of the family party to his generosity? Had Ricky helped with the restaurant? Was that how he had won over her parents? No wonder Alexandros disliked him.

Stick with the facts.

After turning down the sinewy gardener's offer of eating a lemon fresh off the tree, I bathed, put on the loaned parental underwear and set about exploring the house. Every room was accessible apart from the guest bedroom, which was locked – her father's domain. But after an hour of checking every nook and cranny, every conceivable and inconceivable hiding place in the building, as well as outside in the gardens, I ended up back in Amara's room. It made sense that Ricky would hide anything of value where he'd have the right to come and go freely without questions being asked.

I checked every panel in her room; every inch of the floor, drawers, cupboards, mattress. I left nothing to chance. I pulled down the boxes and cases from above the walk-in wardrobe, inspected the lot. Finally, I ducked inside the wardrobe itself, checked all the shelves, kicked aside an open overnight bag with a couple of pairs of high-heeled shoes inside and foraged at the back, knocking against the wood for signs of false panels or hidden compartments.

Nothing.

Just before 1 a.m. I left the house and made my way up the hill towards the restaurant. Having eaten cold moussaka from the fridge, I'd attempted a nap on the sofa in the downstairs sitting room, but a fear of Ricky pitching up unannounced had kept me awake. I roamed the premises once again, this time paying particular attention to the grounds outside, and after further deliberation, came to the conclusion the tapes were most likely in Athens, where production and distribution would be more effectively achieved.

I needed a different approach.

I pressed on through the balmy air, saturated with the heavy scent of night-blossoming jasmine, as, around me, fireflies blinked in the shadows. Other than a lone tawny owl and a pair of roving stray dogs, I didn't meet another soul.

Passing behind the *kastro*, I approached the restaurant from the south and saw that there were still a few stragglers sipping their drinks. But the main lights were off, the kitchen closed up and in the dark; just the crackle of flies electrocuting themselves on the ultraviolet lamp hanging from the roof.

I climbed the steps and nodded to Nikolas, who was rolling a cigarette at a table to the rear of the restaurant, waiting

209

for the diners to leave. 'She's in the back,' he called across to me, as I approached the boarded-up bar. I thanked him and pushed open the side door as I'd done earlier in the day. A quick look behind proved my sixth sense was right; Nikolas was staring after me, a grimace slapped across his face. I gave a wave of thanks. No response.

He was sixteen. It was his prerogative to be a dick.

Making my way along the corridor, I entered the courtyard to find Amara at a table, feet drawn up to her knees on her chair, staring into the glow of a gas lamp on the table. I slid into a chair opposite to ask how the night had gone, but she got there first: 'I don't know,' she said without looking up. 'I'm worried.'

'About what?' I drew closer and tried to catch her eye.

'Ricky,' she replied, clicking her tongue. 'He called the restaurant . . . He will be in Naxos tomorrow afternoon.'

Back at the house, we sat on the stone floor of her room with the shutters thrown wide.

Amara's mood had plunged and the fear returned. She became ever more agitated, insisting we should call her father in Athens. I told her to forget about him and tell me exactly what had been said during the conversation.

She explained that Ricky had called around eleven and told her to meet him at the Ariadne café by the marina at five o'clock the next day. He didn't say how he was arriving on Naxos, or how he'd be leaving. All he said was that he would meet her for a drink, and that she should bring his suitcase with the passport and clothes. He had seemed upbeat and had asked after her family, hoping the restaurant was doing good business. That was it.

'You didn't ask him any questions?'

'He never talks about himself. Not on the phone.'

'Did you mention me?'

She shook her head, then reached for her cigarettes. 'My father. He will help.'

'Calling your father won't help, especially not at this time of night,' I stressed, as she picked herself off the floor and paced the room. 'If you tell him what I've told you, he'll call the police. If he does – it's over.'

She leaned back against one of the four-posters, lit by a shaft of moonlight across her face, and stared at me.

However . . .

'All you have to do is be there with the suitcase,' I said, half to myself.

'No – you think I should meet him?'

An idea had just taken seed.

'Absolutely. You go a little early, maybe five minutes, you order a drink and wait for him to arrive.'

Something I'd considered while still on Paros.

'And you?' she asked.

'I'll be close by. The minute he joins you, I'm there,' I said, walking over to the window to check the street.

'And then what?' she asked, unable to hide the doubt.

'Leave that to me.'

She kicked off her shoes, disappeared downstairs, and returned with a bottle of retsina, a plate of bread and some olives, which we took out onto the roof.

She didn't touch the food, but smoked several cigarettes while I helped myself. The first glass of wine she put down in a few hefty sips, and by the time she poured herself a third, her confidence had returned, and the sultry veneer began to reassemble itself.

211

'You have a girlfriend?' she asked, tapping her foot against mine.

To say 'yes' would be a lie, 'no' – a betrayal.

'I do.' I said, finally.

In my head, at least.

She said something under her breath, then leaned back in her chair and stretched. 'Café Ariadne is where I had my first drink with Ricky,' she began, turning to the crescent moon. 'It wasn't called that then, just the Harbour Café.'

'Right,' I said, averting my eyes from her tight T-shirt.

Stay on point, Haston . . .

My plan for catching Ricky was potentially catastrophically flawed. I still had a crucial decision to make.

She placed a foot in my lap. 'You know about Ariadne?'

Resisting the urge to hold her foot, I told her I didn't. My father had studied the classics. I'd taken the easier option – German.

'Goethe?' she asked, with a frown.

'That's right,' I replied, noticing that she'd painted her toenails different colours. 'Faust. He makes a pact with the devil so he can experience everything he wants in life.'

Then again, there was nothing wrong with a little conversation. Besides, it was important to stay relaxed.

She laughed and took another drink. 'The story goes that Ariadne, the daughter of the king of Crete, Minos, saved Theseus from her father's labyrinth. The boy promised to take Ariadne to Athens with him, but when they got to Naxos, he left her while she was sleeping and went to Athens alone. Dionysus found her and married her. When she died, he hung her bridal crown in the sky, and there it still shines. The Corona Borealis.' She turned to look up at the Milky Way. 'Somewhere up there.'

'Juliet says that of Romeo, doesn't she?' I said. 'If he should die, she'd cut him up into little stars and hang them in the heavens to watch over her.'

'That play has nothing to do with love,' she said, leaning forward and rubbing her thumb across my lips as if to dislodge a speck of food.

'Right.'

Was she deliberately fucking with my head?

'It's all about identity,' she continued, twirling her glass. 'The danger of defining yourself through someone else.'

Been there, done that. 'Someone once said there are only seven original stories in the universe,' I offered, squeezing my thighs to stop the rush of blood. 'Everything else is a variant.'

She hesitated, then blew a column of smoke and shuddered, as if cold. 'So, I told Ricky the story of Ariadne and Dionysus the day I met him. He liked it so much, he persuaded the owner of the Harbour Café to change the name. Café Ariadne.'

By paying him, or holding a knife to his throat?

She refilled my drink and moved closer, so that her hair brushed against my neck. 'But Shakespeare is the best, no? When I am an actress I will play only Shakespeare.'

I raised my glass. 'Here's to that.'

'What happens to Faust?' she asked.

Her foot returned to my lap; her painted toenails gently flexing against my inner thigh. 'I only read the first book,' I said, taking a drink. 'Part two is incomprehensible.' I checked my watch. 'It's nearly three, we should get some sleep.'

'Your girlfriend, she has a name?'

'She does.'

She ran a finger down her neck. 'You know *Zorba the Greek*?'

213

'Seen the film,' I replied, thinking of Ellie. We'd watched it together at a classic film night at the New Picture House at the end of my first term.

'It is written by Nikos Kazantzakis,' she continued. 'When he died, he had put on his gravestone: "I hope for nothing. I fear nothing. I am free."'

'I must read the book.'

'He had a theory about numbers. He didn't like even numbers. Too safe, too predictable. Like standing on the ground with both feet. It roots you to the spot and you are stuck. He preferred odd numbers. Standing on one foot, the other raised in the air, not knowing where you will put it down ...'

With that she pushed back her chair and stood up.

'My bed is big enough for both of us.'

Not quite, as it turned out.

Once sated, the cotton sheets embalmed with our mingled sweat, I spent the remaining hours of the night stretched out under a thin blanket on the roof terrace. Our mutual needs had been met, appetites slaked. Sex had been unavoidable, medicinal almost; without the soporific effects of orgasm, sleep would have eluded us. Having achieved it, however, I had to remove myself from her physical presence – to remain within six feet of her would have foiled any attempt at rest.

At least, that's what I told her.

The truth was otherwise. Halfway through the act, the moonlight caught her face as she writhed above me, and in that instant, she transformed. Everything: her face, her eyes – the grunts and moans, her touch, the smell of her skin ... those lips.

I was making love to Ellie.

The hallucination eventually released me, but I couldn't shake the ache in my chest, so, once replete, I smoked a cigarette then dismissed myself, kissed Amara goodnight, and climbed out of the window to find a new berth.

In the end, I didn't sleep a wink.

At daybreak, the effects of the episode thawing with the growing light, I stumbled to the edge of the roof and sat with my legs hanging over the edge to watch the sunrise. My fear of heights would ordinarily have stopped me, but on that morning it had no effect.

A pair of bright blue birds, almost aquamarine, alighted on the telegraph wires opposite. Rollers, I believed they were. Svenja had mentioned them to me once, but I'd never had the privilege to see them. They sat with me for half an hour, with only the odd flick of the head, waiting for the insects to rise with the impending heat. When they left, I stood up and faced out to sea.

It was time.

Crossing the roof, I stuck my head through the bedroom window.

Amara lay wrapped in the sheet, her shoulder and a bare breast visible beneath her locks. I stared at her as you would a painting, wondering where the artist might have begun. Then she opened her eyes and lifted her head.

'You're awake,' she murmured.

'I am.'

Amara was the last to leave the house.

I waited ten minutes, then picked up the phone on the hallway table. I didn't need the operator; the number was listed at the front of a well-thumbed directory in the drawer.

As the call connected, I studied my face in the hall mirror. It was an impossible decision. Ultimately a coin-toss . . .

'*Chairete. Astynomia tis Paroikias?*'

'Hello,' I replied.

Mihalis had been the more pleasant of the two; Andreas was mean, shifty and brittle.

'Yes? This is Paros police station.'

Andreas had taken pleasure in my discomfort . . .

'Can I help you?'

Mihalis had offered to help.

'Who is this?'

Mihalis was the boss.

'*Nai, ti theleis?*' The man yelled.

'I need to speak to Andreas,' I said, finally.

Mihalis had reneged on his promise.

'Your name?'

'Is he there?'

'Who is this?'

'A friend from England.'

'Who is speaking?'

I hung up. Waited a few minutes . . .

Then dialled again.

It connected on the third ring:

'*Nai. Astynomia tis Paroikias.* Andreas speaking.'

'Andreas. This is Alistair Haston.'

III

17

According to the English family under the neighbouring olive tree, the temperature was going to reach 40°C – the hottest day of the year so far. The boy was ecstatic – it meant more ice cream; the father used it as fodder to berate his wife for having chosen a hotel room without air con. The mother was happily indifferent, her attention taken by a pair of Greek gods playing frisbee by the water's edge.

I checked my watch: four forty. Time to move into position.

Keeping an eye out for the police, I left the town beach and approached the southern end of the harbour, crossing the street with a group of middle-aged Germans before disappearing into the myriad network of pontoons. Through the forest of yacht rigging, I located Café Ariadne on the south-facing promenade between O'Tsimis and Platanos. There was no shortage of tables; other than the hardcore drinkers and late lunchers, everyone was down at the beach.

No sign of Ricky.

And still no police.

I retraced my steps along the wooden walkway back to the line of cafés, took a seat under a slow-rotating fan at the Agora Taverna, two along from Ariadne, ordered a large ouzo and settled in for the wait.

The sea breeze died, the temperature soared, and a stillness settled in on the island, while on the western horizon, beyond the backlit silhouette of Paros, a bank of cloud climbed into the stratosphere.

I'd laid the foundations and set the ball in motion. For the plan to come to fruition, I was counting on a whole host of different elements to pull together – all of which were now out of my control.

I could only wait.

At five o'clock, my nerves got the better of me.

Amara was late. The 'Greek way' or not, I'd hammered home how critical it was that she be on time – early, even . . .

Traffic?

There wasn't any.

Where the fuck was she?

Unable to sit still, the sweat pouring from my forehead, I began to panic. She must have changed her mind. More than that – she had contacted Ricky, and he'd aborted, otherwise he'd be at a table, waiting for her.

The paranoia grew. Scratching furiously at the back of my neck, I watched the minute hand steal across my watch face a further agonising four minutes.

Without Amara, without Ricky – no Ellie.

Two more minutes . . .

To have come so far . . .

Run.

Another minute . . .
Get out of here, Haston.

Heart racing, I pushed my chair back and rose to my feet.

The plan wasn't just tenuous, it was insane.

But before I could take a step across the café floor I saw her, riding across the square on a moped, the orange suitcase upended and strapped onto the rear pannier.

Amara . . .

My clothes sodden from perspiration, I clutched the table-top and watched as she parked by an ice-cream stall under an ancient eucalyptus at the top end of the pedestrian zone, un-tied the suitcase and dragged it behind her along the cobbles towards the row of cafés. In her simple white dress, heels and blood-red lipstick, she sashayed down the path, turning the heads of everyone she passed, until she reached the vine-trellised terraces of Café Ariadne, where, dismissing three salivating waiters vying to carry her luggage, she took a table near the front of the courtyard, kicked off her shoes and lit a cigarette.

I gripped the chair tighter.

Still time to make your escape . . .

But then, as if on cue, a lone figure appeared on the far side of the quay, strolling along the boardwalk between two rows of yachts, sporting jeans, a white T-shirt and a wide-brimmed suede hat.

I rose from the table, my spine stiffening.

No mistaking that swagger. Strolling along the walkway, pinging the halyards of the boats as he passed through the maze of hulls and masts, Ricky descended the steps onto the promenade, slipped his hands into his pockets and sauntered towards Café Ariadne, kicking away the loose stones with idle stabs of his cowboy boots.

When he reached the restaurant, Amara stood up, smoothed down her dress and folded her arms. Without quickening his pace, Ricky pushed through a clutch of prospective diners studying the menu, and with the Hollywood grin spreading across his tanned face, wrapped her tight in his arms.

Then came the kiss . . . Unabashed. Endless.

Once the show was over, they sat down and held hands across the table as their admiring neighbours got back to their own business.

Fuck it.

I left my table at the Agora and walked over.

'Snapper's off,' I said, removing my cap and shades. 'Stick with the lamb.'

Ricky looked up, and for a millisecond his face froze, then he let go of Amara's hands and sprung to his feet. 'Haston, ya Pommie bastard! How the fuck are ya?'

Ignoring him, I flopped into the chair and banged the tabletop with both hands, matching his gusto. 'Fifteen bloody islands to choose from . . .'

'Alistair? Oh my God!' exclaimed Amara, open-mouthed.

'Mate, don't leave me hanging,' said Ricky, arms stretched wide.

As actors, they were evenly matched.

'You don't deserve it,' I replied. 'You, on the other hand,' I added, leaning over to Amara and kissing her on the cheek, 'you're all right.'

Amara summoned a bashful laugh, then sat back in her chair. 'But you are so thin,' she said, reverting to a script she'd used before. 'And your hair – what happened?'

I turned to Ricky. 'You gonna tell her?'

He rescued himself by grabbing the arm of the waiter and ordering two beers, for himself and the 'whingeing Pom'.

'He shaved it off,' I continued. 'At my leaving dinner.'

Ricky jumped in: 'If you're gonna get shit-faced and hit the sack before the party has really started, whaddya expect?' he laughed, sticking his feet up on an empty chair.

Cool as fuck.

But he must be wondering.

'At your leaving dinner?' chimed Amara.

'You'd already gone,' I replied.

'Punishment,' Ricky said. 'For being a pussy.'

'Does that sound brotherly to you?' I pulled out a cigarette and tossed the pack to Ricky.

'But you're okay?' asked Amara, touching my arm.

'Just need to quit these,' I replied, exhaling a lungful of smoke in Ricky's direction. 'But we're not done yet. He owes me.'

Ricky slung his free arm over the side of his chair and helped himself to the packet. 'He's a plucky fucker,' he said, lighting up without taking his eyes off me. 'I taught him well.'

I picked up a knife off the table and pointed it at him. 'You didn't teach me anything I didn't already know. Except how to lie.'

He laughed, but the eyes were dead. I'd forgotten how translucent they were.

'Boys will be boys,' Amara chided, lighting first Ricky's cigarette then mine. 'So, what are you doing here?'

'Took the words out of my mouth,' said Ricky, scratching at his tattoo while scanning the marina.

Planning your escape route?

Not on my watch.

'Haston?'

'Sorry. It's my last night on the island before I leave for

223

Santorini. I hear your father cooks the best fish on the island. Thought I'd check it out.'

Ricky grunted and kept his eyes on the yachts opposite.

'Oh, but you must,' said Amara, clapping her hands together. 'We can have a reunion dinner.'

'A return match,' I said, turning to Ricky.

'Where are you staying?' he replied.

'Behind the *kastro*.'

Amara brushed a finger over her ear. 'That's near the restaurant.'

'And your house,' Ricky added, with a smile.

'Yes,' she continued. 'If I had known . . .'

'Three's a crowd,' I replied, cutting her off.

Ricky pulled his chair closer. 'I'm not staying. Got work to do.'

'Great,' I replied.

'You know me. Always on the move,' he continued, acknowledging the suitcase with a casual tap on the handle. 'Renting a new property out to a couple of chicks from the mainland.'

'Uh-huh.'

Ellie and her cousin.

'Yeah. Big old house. Miles from anywhere. Gets lonely up there. I'm heading along to help out. In any way I can.' He knocked back his beer, sucking the froth through his teeth.

'Well, guys,' I said, standing up. 'I won't keep you.'

Are you watching, Andreas?

It was time.

Ricky lurched to his feet, cigarette hanging from his jaw.

'It's good to see you,' I added, opening my arms.

Stand by . . .

'You too, mate,' he replied, with his trademark wink.

With that, we finally hugged.

It was as if someone had thrown a switch.

Two officers jumped out from behind a moored fishing ketch, guns raised, screaming at us to get our hands up. Then a police car howled up the promenade, slamming sideways to a halt opposite the entrance.

Panic exploded across the terrace.

Wailing sirens, flashing blue and red lights.

I seized Amara by the arm and dragged her to the ground, as terror-stricken customers dived for cover. Ricky leaped up from behind a fallen chair, grabbed the suitcase and made a break for the toilets.

No fucking way.

I threw myself at his heels and brought him crashing down on the concrete. He spun over onto his back, tearing with his free hand at my throat, as his boot connected with my groin. Fighting the stabbing pain, I ripped the suitcase from his grip, rolled away from his thrashing limbs, and struggled to my feet, but before I could travel a yard, I was knocked to the ground as police stormed the café.

I twisted back towards the hysterical Amara, yelling at her to stay down. Then a second policeman barrelled up the steps, gun levelled, hurling obscenities.

I ducked and dropped the case, hands in the air. But he planted a kick to my chest and knocked me to the concrete, punched me twice in the ribs and rammed the barrel of his pistol into my jaw.

Andreas.

I hauled myself to my feet but he shoved me backwards. I called his name, tried to connect. Nothing. His mouth

225

moved, but the words never reached me. Another set of hands grabbed me from behind and slammed my face into the ground. Then came the cold steel of handcuffs crushing into my wrists. Gasping for breath, I lifted my head off the concrete.

To my right, two officers beat Ricky, kicking him in the stomach as he writhed on the ground. Then a blur of white from my left, as Amara leaped out from under the table, hurled herself across the terrace and grabbed at one of the men. She didn't stand a chance. Swatting her away with the back of his hand, he knocked her to the floor like a moth. Then a female officer scooped her off the floor by her hair and hauled her down the steps onto the promenade.

Lying with my face pressed into the ground, strength fading, I watched Ricky succumb to the handcuffs. Finally, he stopped struggling and looked over at me, unblinking, blood spilling down his face from a cut above his eye.

Not a trace of emotion.

We were driven in two separate police cars along the water-front, through the new town and on to the docks where a police tugboat was waiting. On arrival, Andreas stepped out of the passenger seat, and with the aid of his chubby junior colleague — one of the two officers who had led the charge from behind the yacht — hauled me from the back of the car and pushed me through a crowd of gawping tourists to the boat.

Dragging me on board, they manhandled me into a stifling, low-ceilinged cabin and shackled me to a steel girder before returning to the jetty to meet a second unit pulling up on the harbour concourse. Through the cabin windows I watched them drag Ricky out of the vehicle and jostle him along the quay towards the tug. Moments later, the three of them appeared in the doorway, accompanied by yet another officer, hanging back at the stern. Andreas's sidekick shoved Ricky forwards and secured him to a handrail opposite me, where, once restrained, he sat perfectly still. Then, as the two officers filed through the cabin out onto the stern deck, the third stepped forward from the railing and fixed me with a steely glare.

In the confusion earlier, I hadn't clocked it, but in close quarters there was no mistaking that angular face: she was the blonde from Paros police station – Andreas's assistant. The officer who'd stopped us at the roadblock . . . the 'estate agent'.

As a smirk stole across her leathery features, she turned, ducking to avoid hitting her head on a crossbeam, and joined the others on deck, where, after a team briefing, Andreas disappeared around the side of the tug towards the bridge.

Then the engines fired up and diesel fouled the air. Reappearing through the rear doors into the cabin, Andreas took a seat a couple of yards further along from me on the wooden bench, followed by his chubby junior, who sat down close to Ricky on the opposite side. The blonde maintained her position at the stern.

Where was Amara?

On land, a motley gathering of locals and port-authority officials had grouped in front of a convoy of police units, lights pulsing all at once, while behind them the pack of tourists grew, pushing and shoving each other along the concourse to get an angle on the action.

I tried to meet Andreas's eye. His aggression towards me at the café had been overt and unrestrained. I knew he had to keep up appearances and play his part, but the violence was all too convincing, and I was beginning to wonder if, in fact, he had believed none of the phone call. As far as the authorities were concerned, I'd committed murder, assaulted an officer, broken out of a police cell, resorted to theft and kidnapping to flee Antiparos on Marcus's yacht, and I was undoubtedly the prime suspect for Roland's beheading. I needed a sign that Andreas had believed my version of the events – that I hadn't walked into a trap of my own making.

I edged forwards, kicking out a leg in the hope of catching his attention, but a rattle of Greek from the stern pulled his focus outdoors. He grunted and passed a hand lightly over his ever-pristine parting, then hauled himself to his feet and pushed through the doors to investigate. Moments later he returned with the orange suitcase.

But no Amara.

What had they done with her?

As Andreas shuffled back to his seat, the blonde relieved him of the case, pinned the rear doors open and took up position in the corner of the rear gunwale, shouting further instructions to the bridge.

Amara was part of the deal.

My key witness.

The engines roared and the boat shuddered to life, churning the water on all sides of the vessel as we inched away from the harbour wall. Mooring ropes were untied, coiled and tossed on board, fore and aft. As the crowd surged forwards hoping for a glimpse of the criminals below deck, a flock of scavenging seagulls homed in over the oily water, diving and screeching in their quest for anything edible.

Then I saw her, emerging from the throng, a policeman on each arm. No cuffs. No restraint. Chaperoned only.

Shading her eyes with a hand, she peered through the windows before one of the cops pulled her back. Not that she would have seen anything. No matter how close she came to the tug, the glare of the sun would have rendered the inside of the cabin pitch black.

But I could see her.

Was that a smile?

The sun was in her eyes; she might have been squinting.

As the boat pulled away from the dock, she shrugged off the officer's arm, lit a cigarette, and, running a hand through her hair, gazed at the seagulls jostling for position above the stern. If there was any regret or trepidation for what she had done, it wasn't apparent. Far from it: in her brilliant white dress, standing one arm folded under the other, cigarette pointing to the sky, she had all the composure of a film star. Triumphant. Basking in the knowledge that she was not only free from her murderous boyfriend, she'd also been instrumental in bringing him in.

This was her show.

Clearing the harbour entrance, we ploughed into the channel and I lost sight of her. From my shackled position, I had restricted views to the sides and rear of the boat only, but I could tell from the way the horizon swung that we were turning south.

Odd. The quickest route to the Paros capital, Parikia, was to the north, via Naoussa. Our current heading meant we would travel the length of Paros to the southernmost tip, and then backtrack the same distance all the way up the western side of the island.

To avoid the shipping lanes?

After a few hundred yards, we turned parallel to the Naxos shore and the boat picked up speed. The blonde moved along the gunwale to the starboard rail and cast her gaze to the distant shores of eastern Paros, her hair working its way loose under her cap as the headwind strengthened. Andreas had dropped his customary military poise and was now hunched forwards, head bowed, still refusing to make eye contact. To his left, across the cabin, his fat colleague dabbed at his brow with his sleeve.

As for Ricky . . .

Curled up against the handrail he appeared a ghost of his former-self. Shrunken. Bereft. A beaten, abandoned cur.

Drawing level with the southern tip of Paros, we left the Naxos coast and turned into deeper water to begin the crossing that would take us past the windswept headland of Drios and on towards the entrance of the choppy channel between Antiparos and Paros.

As the boat began to pitch and roll, the junior officer looked like he might be sick any minute. But he pulled himself together when the blonde stuck her head through the rear doors and called for Andreas. After a brief exchange, the latter reluctantly dragged himself from his seat, muttered a few words to his junior and staggered across the heaving floor to join his colleague outside, where they continued their conversation out of earshot.

Andreas seemed preoccupied. Morose, even.

Was it surprising? Earlier that morning he'd learned from me that one of his men, most likely his boss, Mihalis, was the ringleader of a prolific criminal organisation across the Cyclades. Bringing in Ricky was one thing, but it opened a Pandora's box that would spell an untold amount of shit for the man. He'd be lucky to come through it in one piece.

Then a voice called out from across the cabin: 'Bet you're chuffed to fuck.'

Junior told him to shut up.

Ricky ignored him.

'Didn't think you had it in you.'

I knew I shouldn't engage, but I couldn't resist.

'What can I say? You taught me well.'

His face pressed to his handcuffs, Ricky picked at the cut on his forehead and swivelled round to face me. 'That's what I love about you, Haston. Not a bad bone in your body. Always ready to give the benefit of the doubt.'

'*Skase, malakas,*' said the officer. 'No speak.'

He pulled his weapon into view to show he meant it.

'*Mihn anisycheis,*' said Ricky, straining against his chains with an upheld, bloodied hand. 'We're just chewing the fat.'

'*Ti?*'

'Catchin' up,' replied Ricky, smiling. 'Been a while.'

The officer threw a nervous look towards his colleagues smoking at the starboard rail. With the drumming of the engines, there was no way we'd be heard on deck, even with the doors open. He'd have to handle it alone, or embarrass himself calling for backup.

Ricky tapped his fingers on the steel girder. 'Andreas, eh?' he slurred. 'Lucky shot. Could have gone tits up.'

I kept my eyes on the seagulls, tried to shut him out.

But I couldn't. 'Where's Mihalis?'

'Who?' grinned Ricky.

'Easing your passage out of the country?' I continued. 'How much do you give him for that?'

Ricky sighed and slid back down to the bench. 'Mister Haston-like-the-car-but-without-the-H, you're quite the detective.' Then he turned to the chubby officer. 'This guy should be in your shoes. He's a fuckin' genius.'

'Where were you heading?' I asked. 'Where does a

sociopath overwinter nowadays? Back to Thailand, the old hunting grounds?'

'See?' he said to the officer. 'Got it all figured out.'

'Heinrich, too?'

Ricky nodded. 'When he's finished babysitting.'

Ellie.

'And where is Heinrich?' I asked.

He winked, then turned to the policeman.

'What's yer name, fella?'

'*Ti?*'

'*Pos se lene?*' he asked again.

'Stelios,' he replied, caught out by Ricky's Greek.

Ricky smiled.

'Nice to meet you, Stelios. This ismy friend Haston.'

Stelios pulled himself to his feet and peered through the porthole above Ricky's head, then crossed over to the starboard side, where, after a moment muttering to himself, he hoisted up his sagging trousers and pressed his nose against the glass.

Ricky never took his eyes off him.

'Ellie – where is she?' I demanded.

Ricky lifted his handcuffs and scratched at his tattoo.

'I'll find out soon enough,' I added.

Pursing his lips, he checked his watch, then splayed his legs wide, turning his body towards me as much as his shackles would allow.

'What did you say to Andreas?'

I shook my head. 'Tell me where she is.'

'You trust him?' he continued, leaning forward to wipe his hand on the back of his mouth. 'I mean, we're both wearing cuffs.'

'Tell me,' I insisted.

'Hey, Stelios,' he grunted. 'Any idea where the Pom's bird is?'

The officer spat on the floor and continued to stare at the backs of his comrades at the stern, willing them to return. 'Stelios doesn't want to play,' said Ricky, twisting his neck to look out of the porthole. Then he checked his watch once more and slid off the bench onto his feet.

Why the obsession with the time?

'Come on, Haston, I say we get off this fuckin' thing.'

'*Katse kato!*' barked the officer from across the cabin.

Ricky ignored the instruction and lifted a leg onto the bench.

'Tell me about Amara,' he said, bending his head towards his knee in an attempt to stretch his hamstring. 'Man to man. Did you fuck her?'

Stelios kicked Ricky's leg off the seat and drew his pistol.

Undeterred, Ricky lifted it straight back up. 'You must have screwed her,' he continued, resuming his stretch. 'You expect me to believe that bullshit about you turning up out of the blue? To eat fish at her old man's restaurant?'

Stelios stepped in towards him, gun at the ready.

He was starting to panic.

'Hey, fat guy,' said Ricky gesturing to his foot. 'Grab hold of this bro, I'm all tensed-up here.'

Stelios stared at him, baffled.

'Come on, man, I got the cramps,' Ricky persisted.

'Get back!' I snapped.

But Stelios had frozen. I looked for his colleagues – no sign. They must have moved up to the bridge.

Fuck.

If Ricky was shot, we'd never find Ellie.

'Andreas!' I yelled.

Distracted, Stelios turned to me, and in doing so came within reach of Ricky, who thrust his feet forwards and clamped them around the officer's leg, pulling him off balance and towards him.

'Mate,' pleaded the Australian, straining against his cuffs, inches from his face. 'I'm gagging for a fag. Got a light?'

What the hell was he doing?

'*Gamisou!*' bawled Stelios, holding his gun above his head while trying to wriggle himself free.

Again, I called for Andreas.

'*Echeis anaptira?*' spat Ricky.

Where the fuck were they?

'*Oxi,*' replied Stelios, panicking. '*Den boreite na kapnisete etho.*'

'Amara's a pretty girl – he should've nailed her!' ranted Ricky, 'She gives great head. Fuck, man, she can't get enough.'

Stelios finally freed himself and turned, looking for back-up, but Ricky hounded him further. 'It's her speciality. Her party piece,' he panted. 'And she's got these great fuckin' tits—'

Without warning, Stelios smashed his elbow into Ricky's face.

'Bravo,' roared Ricky, as blood spurted from his lip. 'About fuckin' time.' Then he lunged out again with his boot and caught the officer on the shin. 'Thanks for nothing, ya fuckin' prick.'

Stelios cocked his pistol.

'No!' I screamed.

'Do it!' jeered Ricky, ecstatic.

But as Stelios levelled his weapon at Ricky's head, Andreas barrelled in, followed by the blonde.

'Come on, motherfucker!' bellowed Ricky.

'*Malakas!*' screamed Stelios.

In a lightning move, Andreas kicked his colleague to one side, drew his pistol and clubbed Ricky across the face.

Ricky buckled and collapsed on the seat.

'Bunch of fuckin' amateurs,' he screamed, levering himself back to his feet as blood poured from his nose. 'Finish the job!'

Andreas took another swing, but Ricky was too quick. As he ducked out of the way, Andreas's hand smashed into the wooden panelling. 'Come on, you pussy,' taunted Ricky, howling with laughter, offering up his chin. 'I'll make it easy for you.'

Andreas spread his legs and lined up for another strike.

But the blow never came. Drawing her weapon, the blonde took two paces forward, and from point-blank range shot Andreas in the head.

The air in the cabin exploded.

Clawing at my skull, I flung myself backwards as Stelios ran for the doorway. The blonde turned and followed him with the muzzle of her gun, squeezing off two more rounds: one into his back, knocking him sprawling to the floor; the second, a coup de grâce to his left temple. Then she bent down to Andreas's decapitated body, took the keys from his belt and unlocked Ricky's cuffs.

The bloodied Australian rose to his feet and stretched.

'Don't think you've been officially introduced,' he said, wiping bits of Andreas's brain from the corner of his mouth.

'This is Heinrich's sister. Annika.'

18

Ears ringing from the percussion, I tore my eyes from the dead officers on the floor and stared transfixed as the blonde approached me through the pall of gunsmoke, dropped the pistol by her side, and took my chin in her bony fingers.

Heinrich's sister?

I recoiled, pushing back against the hull, but she tutted and knelt down beside me, her face centimetres away from mine. Then she ran a finger under my jaw and inserted it into my mouth, thrusting it back and forth over my tongue.

I stared into her ice-blue eyes, fighting a gag reflex.

'Finally,' she murmured. 'You have come home.'

Holstering her weapon, she withdrew her finger, and stepping over her dead colleagues, slipped out through the doorway and disappeared on deck. 'Not as chatty as her brother,' drawled Ricky, hooking his arm through a crossbeam to steady himself against the pitching deck. 'But she's all heart.'

I slid down the steel girder to the floor as my legs gave out underneath me.

It was all over. I was as good as dead.

*

Unhooking himself from the beam, Ricky dropped to the deck and flipped over Stelios's head. 'Looks like the bullet went straight through the floor,' he said, lifting the officer's torso. 'This one, on the other hand,' he continued, feeling under his stomach, 'must be out there somewhere.' He turned and gestured through the doorway to the stern. 'Along with his spleen.'

He jumped up, made his way over Andreas's headless body and pulled a lighter out of one of the pockets. 'You can never have too many of these,' he said, lighting up.

As the engines shifted up a gear he took a seat on the bench opposite, stuck his feet on top of Andreas's back and studied me while he smoked. I turned away and stared out of the starboard porthole, as it dawned on me that despite the shots, the tug hadn't slowed or altered its course.

The captain must be compromised.

Then Annika reappeared in the doorway.

'Christos up to speed?' asked Ricky, dragging himself to his feet.

'He's nervous,' she said, brushing her hair from her eyes.

Christos must be the captain.

'I'll deal with him,' snorted Ricky, collecting Stelios's weapon from the floor and handing it to Annika.

Then he turned to me and winked. 'Leave you guys to it.'

Stepping over the bodies, he disappeared out on deck as Annika brought Stelios's gun over to the bench.

'*Heinrich hat gesagt du kannst Deutsch?*' she murmured.

I nodded, sliding to my left to keep the girder between us.

'An ugly language, no?' she continued, holding her ground. 'But it can come in useful.'

Her brother had said the same thing.

The family resemblance, along with her German accent,

238

was now all too clear: the Amazonian features, jutting jaw and her high forehead. Unlike her brother, however, she was all sinew. '*Mach dir keine Sorgen*,' she smiled. 'I am not going to shoot you. You are – *wie soll ich sagen?* – family.' She unclipped the magazine, emptied the bullet from the firing chamber, then sidestepped the girder and seized my T-shirt.

I jumped backwards, slipping in a slick of Andreas's blood as my wrists yanked against the cuffs.

Family?

'Be still,' she snapped.

Using the shirt, she wiped the gun and thrust it at me.

'You're trying to frame me for this?' I said, taking the pistol by the butt. 'No one will buy it.'

She took hold of my shirt again, ripped off a piece from my midriff, then wiped and re-slotted the magazine clip, followed by the bullet. Wrapping the gun in the fabric, she placed it on a shelf, picked up Andreas's pistol from under his arm and withdrew to the stern. 'Perhaps you are right,' she said, tossing the weapon overboard and assuming a position in the doorway. 'But it will give forensics something to think about.'

The tug ploughed on through the windblown channel, but instead of bearing north towards Paros's capital, we maintained a westerly course. All the while, Annika remained silent, watching the spindrift as we drew ever closer to Antiparos.

This was no ad hoc detour. There was a cold inevitability about the proceedings that suggested prior planning.

Thanks to Amara.

At what point she had betrayed me, I couldn't be sure.

But I was now in no doubt that she'd tipped Ricky off, and he, in turn, had given the heads-up to Annika on Paros. Which meant that by the time I called Andreas, Ricky and his accomplices were already ahead of the game, their own preparations in place, ready to strike.

Although Amara wasn't entirely to blame. In my telephone call, I'd instructed Andreas not to tell Mihalis about the sting, on the grounds that I believed him to be the ringleader. Andreas had no reason to take orders from a suspected criminal, but he'd trusted me and kept true to his word. Who else could he turn to but Annika? She was the obvious alternative to Mihalis; apart from being Andreas's number two, she'd been involved in the case from the outset. Under the guise of sharing his burden, she'd have easily engineered a hit squad to suit her own needs.

The dead men's blood was on my hands.

By the time we rounded the church on the cliffs off Antiparos's southeast peninsular, the sun had dipped behind an ominous band of cloud in the west, and the wind had backed. Heavy weather was on its way.

Hugging the barren coast, the rhythmic chant of cicadas drifting across the water from the sprawling olive groves, we glided through calmer seas towards the narrow strip of water between Antiparos and her sister island, Despotiko, a deserted islet that lay a kilometre offshore. And as we passed the scrubby landmass to starboard, the tug swung left and entered a sandy cove, which narrowed until it became a gorge just wide enough for the boat to squeeze through.

Edging through the turquoise water, we travelled a hundred yards up the ravine and emerged into a crystal-clear lagoon framed by a wall of crumbling ochre rocks that fell away into the water and tapered out onto a carpet of sea urchins nestled between banks of spindled seaweed.

'You have been to the stalactite caves on Antiparos?' Annika asked. 'The ones at the top of the mountain, they are acceptable. But here on Despotiko island, they are *spektakular*.'

I'd stopped listening. We were slowing down.

The boat reversed its engines and we ground to a halt. There was a bump, followed by a muffled exchange of voices from above as Annika threw a rope to shore. Then Ricky bounded into the cabin, followed by a new addition to the party: not the captain of the vessel – I could still hear the footfall above as he shuffled about the bridge – but another face that was all too familiar . . . Yannis, the sous-chef from the Dubliner.

The man who'd cooked my departure dinner at the villa.

'*Kali spera, malakas, ti kaneis?*' he roared, slapping me on the shoulder, before peering round the cabin. Then his eyes narrowed on Andreas's mangled body. '*Panagia mou*,' he declared, scratching his stubbled chin. 'But he has no head.'

'Hour and a half till dark,' chimed Ricky. 'Let's do it.'

He pulled out a set of keys and unlocked my cuffs.

'Behave.'

This time there was no wink.

I slumped back onto the bench and, feigning cramp in my legs, weighed the odds: I was out of the handcuffs, the gun on the shelf was less than five feet away. Then again, even if I beat Ricky to it, I'd have no time to pull the trigger, let alone take aim. Annika was around the corner, and there was Yannis to contend with. Besides, the last time I'd fired a gun was on an army-cadet field trip while still at school – a bolt-action Browning 303, the kind used in World War I. I'd never fired a pistol . . . Was there a safety catch?

Before I could look up, Ricky grabbed me by my neck and hoisted me off the bench, drawing a hunting knife from a strap above his boots. 'Don't make me use this, bro,' he snarled, slamming me up against the porthole.

At which point Annika reappeared with the orange suitcase.

'*Alles klar.* We go?'

'*Endaxi*, boss,' growled Yannis, holding up a brown package.

Ricky turned to Annika. 'Perfect. Meet you there.'

Where?

As Annika disembarked off the stern, Ricky scooped up the gun from the shelf and marched me round the side of the boat up to the bridge, followed by Yannis.

'Ready?' barked Ricky, from behind.

I froze, expecting a bullet.

But he shoved me into the wheelhouse.

'Hey, Christos,' he yelled. '*Eisai etoimos?*'

When the officer twisted around, one hand gripping the steering wheel, I recognised him instantly as the thug who'd attacked me in the prison cell. 'You might get some pleasure out of this,' said Ricky, handing me the pistol as Yannis slid in from behind and squeezed into a corner.

'*Ella*, new boy, you are one of us now, *nai*?' Yannis chuckled, patting me on the head. Then he tossed the package at Christos's feet. Christos snatched it up and stashed it behind the wheel.

'Take the gun!' snapped Ricky, raising the knife to my throat.

'*Tora!*' yelled Christos, bracing himself.

What the fuck?

'*Malakas!*' cheered Yannis.

242

'Steady now,' Ricky said, as I pulled the weapon from the scrap of T-shirt. 'Point it at his kneecap.'

Hand shaking, I lowered my arm.

Christos threw up his hands, hollering expletives.

'He thinks you will miss,' jeered Yannis, sticking a wad of gum in his mouth. 'Come on, motherfucker!'

'Shoot him, Haston,' murmured Ricky into my ear as he pressed the blade into my neck. 'In the kneecap. Now.'

Fuck.

I raised the gun and squeezed the trigger.

The explosion sucked the air out of the wheelhouse and I fell backwards into Ricky as the officer crumpled to the floor. 'Spot on,' cheered Ricky, edging me backwards to the door while Yannis thumped his appreciation on the window. 'Now drop the gun, kick it into the corner and cuff him.'

Head spinning from the blast, I rid myself of the weapon, then, as Ricky released the knife from my neck, I staggered forwards, scanning the floor for a set of handcuffs.

'On his belt, dickhead,' laughed Ricky, kicking me from behind.

I hauled the groaning officer onto his working leg, and, propping him up against the control panel, threaded the shackles through the wheel and cuffed both his wrists. Or so I thought. As the second handcuff popped open, he wrenched his arm away and slammed a fist into my groin. '*To mounai tis manas sou, poustis!*' he cried, tumbling to the floor, as I doubled up, clutching my stomach.

Yannis pushed away from the window, howling with laughter as I crawled across the floorboards towards the threshold and retched. 'Hit the fucker,' snorted Ricky, pulling me to my feet as the puke dribbled down my ripped shirt. 'He told you to suck your mother's cunt.'

Then he turned to Christos.

'*Sto kalo*,' Ricky said, slipping a chair under the stricken officer and nudging him closer to the wheel. 'Yannis will help you guide the boat in. When they find you, you know what to say, yes?'

'No problem,' replied Christos, wincing through the pain.

'Right, let's get out of here,' snapped Ricky.

He dragged me around the side of the tug onto dry land.

Which was when I saw the yacht ... It was moored to a tree stump protruding from a thick belt of thyme a few yards further along the bank; a sleek ocean-going vessel, some fifty feet long. Yannis must have delivered it.

Ricky turned back to the tugboat. 'Take her in as far as she'll go. Get back ASAP,' he yelled, returning his knife to its holster above his boots. 'Storm's on its way.'

I scanned the vicinity for Annika and saw she was already on board the yacht.

'*Endaxi!*' shouted Yannis through the window.

As Christos fired up the engines, I peered through the twilight to the far end of the lagoon and saw a sliver of black in the towering crags that I presumed was the entrance to the cave. Or was it a shadow? In the half-light, it was impossible to tell.

Ricky tossed a stone into the water. 'Nice work, back there,' he said, his eyes following the tug as it pushed away from the bank. 'But I'd have put the gun closer to his leg. You could have hit an artery.'

The pain in my stomach subsiding, I pulled myself upright. 'So, how much does Christos get for a shattered kneecap?' I asked, searching the ground for a sizeable rock. Ricky's knife was safely sheathed; Yannis and Annika were otherwise occupied. 'Isn't that the story?' I continued. 'I disarm an officer,

244

shoot my way out of the boat, incapacitate the captain, cuff him, and what – kidnap the rest of you?'

There, five feet away, towards the water . . .

An egg-shaped stone. A perfect palm fit.

'Something like that,' chuckled Ricky. 'The kneecapping was Christos's own idea. Team player.'

'They'll never believe it,' I said, drifting to my right, taking in the brooding cliffs of Antiparos.

Almost there.

'They'll never hear it,' he grinned. 'But if they ever find the boat, your prints are on the gun.'

If they ever find it?

I kicked at the stone, lining it up. But before I could reach it, Ricky lurched forwards and grabbed my arm.

'Check this out.'

Pulling me back towards him, I turned to see the tug headed for an overhang on the far bank, to the right of a twisted solitary cedar. But at the moment of impact, instead of breaking up, the boat simply melted into the rocks. There was a flash of red and yellow, as a pair of bee-eaters shot from their sandy burrows in the cliffs and dived into the myrtle, then the moonscape terrain was still once again.

'A thing of beauty, those caves,' chirped Ricky, dusting down his hands and lighting a cigarette. 'Won't stay secret for long. They'll sink the boat and turn it into a fuckin' tourist attraction.' He picked up my stone and tossed it in his palm. 'Smugglers' Cove. Or some such shit.'

Then he hurled the rock into the water.

'Try that again,' he growled, squaring up to me, 'and I'll gut you like pig.' He turned away and we stood in silence, waiting for Yannis to return as lightning flickered through the thunderheads on the horizon.

Eventually there was a shout from the far bank; seconds later, the Greek's rangy figure emerged through the gloom, loping steadily closer, cigarette hanging from his jaw, the brown package still tucked under his arm.

And something else.

'All taken care of?' asked Ricky, scratching at his tattoo.

'Of course, boss,' grinned Yannis, striding past without stopping. 'But this is mine, *nai*?' he added, waving the package above his head.

Then I saw the bloodied knife in his other hand.

'Cheeky bastard,' said Ricky, exhaling a smoke ring. 'Let's roll.'

Fighting the urge to run, I dug my heels into the ground. 'What happens now?' I asked, wondering how long the police would wait before they mobilised a search party.

'Now?' he replied, swatting away a fly.

Breathe, Haston.

He smiled and put a hand on my shoulder.

'D'you seriously think I'd leave without saying goodbye?' he asked, flicking his cigarette into the water.

'It's party time.'

I was escorted at knifepoint to the yacht and dragged through the interior to a cramped twin-berth cabin at the bow. Hands and feet summarily bound together with nylon cord, they then dumped me on the floor between the two bunks. 'Get some beauty sleep,' said Ricky, pushing Yannis through the door into the main cabin. 'Big day ahead.'

But there was no sleep to be had.

Nor was there time to regroup; once the yacht left the sheltered waters of Despotiko, we sailed straight into the teeth of the storm. For three gut-wrenching hours, I was hurled across the deck from the foot of one bunk to the other as the boat slammed head-on into wave after furious wave. Powerless in the pitch black, I fumbled for hand-holds, trying to second-guess which way the heaving boat would plummet, then discovered I could jam myself sideways between the two beds and attain brief respite until the next rogue wave tossed me loose and the battering resumed.

By the time the storm blew itself out, it was almost dawn.

Overcome with exhaustion, I nodded off, but was roused from slumber when the door creaked open, flooding the cabin with light. Shuffling onto my side, I craned my neck off the floor and saw Ricky in the doorway, and in his hand, the video camera.

'Rough night, eh?' he mumbled.

I shunted backwards into a lopsided sitting position in the 'V' of the bow and squinted into the light.

'I'd have come down earlier,' he continued, pushing the cabin door to until only a chink of light shone through. 'But I had my hands full.' Then he slid across the floor and stepped up onto the starboard bunk. 'Yannis has been chucking up his ugly guts for most of the night. Now the lazy fucker's back on the job I thought I'd check in on you.'

With the video camera?

'Don't worry,' he said, lifting the machine and pointing it at me as the red light illuminated. 'I'm not recording sound. You can think of something witty to say later.'

He filmed for thirty seconds then killed the tape.

'So, how long were you working together?' he asked.

I stared at him, uncomprehending.

'The Scottish guy.'

'You mean the guy whose head you ripped off and stuck

247

in a cool box?' I grunted. 'He had a name. Roland. And no, we weren't working together. You cut that short.'

Ricky laughed and stretched out on the bunk. 'The day after I bring you to the villa, the guy shows up in the area like a fuckin' rash. Popping up everywhere we look. Along with the fat Greek bloke.'

'Leo.'

'Whatever.'

He turned on his side and propped himself up on an elbow.

'I had no idea,' I said. 'I was oblivious.'

'Save it,' he coughed. 'So, Annika checks him out. Turns out he's the brother of the guy we worked with two years ago—'

'Worked with?' I snorted. 'You killed him.'

'And that he hired a PI and had been snooping around the islands for the last two summers.'

I pushed away from the hull and edged into the light. 'I had no idea about Roland, or what he was up to,' I protested. 'Not until he took me into his hut on the night I was ambushed at the villa. You were the one who picked me out as fair game on the ferry. You followed me. You tricked me, lured me into your bullshit entourage. Stole my passport. You brought me into the villa so you could use me, stitch me up, as you did Roland's brother. You played me. But what you didn't know – nor did I – was that Roland was playing you too. He was one step ahead of us both.'

'I could have cut your fuckin' throat, right there and then—'

'But you didn't,' I said, interrupting him again. 'Because *you* didn't cut Roland's throat, did you? One of your monkeys did.' I wasn't just trying to provoke him; I'd been harbouring the suspicion for some time now. I'd seen the German woman kill. Yannis had surely murdered the captain of the tugboat in the caves. But Ricky? He was always in too many places at once.

'You don't get your hands dirty, do you?' I persisted. 'Question is – is it an issue of delegation, or are you just chickenshit?'

He slammed his fist into the ceiling. 'I trusted you,' he cried. 'I looked after you. Treated you like my own brother. I set you up with a fuckin' bonzer job and all the time you're waiting to stab me in the back. You and your Scottish sleuth.'

'No,' I said. 'You betrayed me.'

'You left me no choice,' he bellowed. 'You were my protégé. I turned you from a green, snivelling little fuck into the man you are now. And you fucked me over. Your own flesh and blood!'

He lunged forwards and grabbed my jaw. 'I saw the power in you,' he hissed. 'Fuck it, I saw me in you, Haston. Not like that Scottish guy's brother. He was nothing, a nobody. But you ... I had faith in you. Trusted you. And then the day word comes through that the Kiwi chick's body is found on Santorini, you tell us you're leaving the fuckin' islands!'

'Coincidence,' I gasped, as his fingers clawed into my mouth.

'You were with that geek from the start,' he screamed, grabbing me by the throat and lifting me to my feet. 'You shared his tent. He groomed you. Trained you.'

Then he dropped me and kicked the bunk inches from my face. 'You think I'm stupid?' he bawled, slapping my face with the back of his hand. 'Yannis tailed you the minute you stepped off the ferry. You and Roland set me up – the pair of you. The moment you set foot in Greece.'

'Ridiculous,' I blurted, shielding my face from his blows.

'You shacked up with him in his fuckin' swamp hut,' he continued, punching the hatch. 'Don't fuck with me Haston. I was there.'

'For one night,' I protested. 'He came and picked me up after I was ambushed at the villa. When you tried to have me killed.'

'Because you're a traitor!' he howled.

I shuffled deeper into the shadows, pressing my back to the steel.

'I took you in,' he drawled. 'And you spat me out.' He hung there, panting, sides heaving like an enraged bull, as the moon slid into view through the hatch, bathing the cabin in a silver glow. Then the door swung open.

'*Alles in Ordnung*?' purred Annika, waving a cigarette.

She'd changed out of her uniform into a full-length dress.

'Everything's fine,' muttered Ricky, straightening up.

'I heard a disturbance,' she added, stepping in and perching on the end of the bunk. 'I was worried.' Then she rolled across the bed and sat with her legs folded up beside my head. 'Please, don't let me interrupt.'

I recoiled and shunted backwards into the hull.

'So, here's the thing,' said Ricky, staring up at the moon. 'Thanks to your handiwork, we've come up short this year. Down on last year's production. I'm not gonna disappoint my clients, so we're gonna squeeze in one last film. A signature dish.'

'A snuff film,' I retorted.

'I don't like that expression, it's undignified. But yes – if you like, a "snuff film".' He picked up the camera and switched it on. 'Come forwards, mate, it looks great when the moonlight catches your face.'

I stayed put, until he walked over and swung a foot at my

head. 'You wanna test me?' he growled, as I ducked out of the way. 'Go ahead.' Annika shifted her feet to one side to allow Ricky through as he knelt beside me on the floor and brought the camera closer to my face.

'I have this one client,' he continued. 'A Yank. Lives in LA. Into all kinds of weird shit. He came over last year to watch us making one of the films. Wanted to understand more about the process. Reckoned too many films were cheats – you know, where the victim doesn't actually die. So, he insists their throats are cut, on top of whatever else we do to them. Just to be sure.'

He turned the camera off and stood up. 'We never got the chance to do a decent job of Svenja and Jens,' he said, taking a cigarette from Annika and lighting up. 'Thanks to your fat Greek friend getting in the way of the dinner. Once he left, we knew he'd raise the alarm, so we did a rush job. Fucked it right up. Strangled Svenja and had to beat her boyfriend's head in with an oar from the boat. The Yank didn't buy it. Reckoned we'd rigged it. He wanted to see the knife go in.'

He held out an arm and lifted Annika off the bunk.

'So, I figured I'd make amends,' he continued, tapping the camera against his thigh as a ray of moonlight fell across his drawn face. 'Serve up something special.'

He walked Annika to the door before turning back to me.

'After all, I got the ideal leading man,' he said, exhaling a column of smoke up towards the open hatch while wrapping his arm around Annika's waist. 'And the perfect co-star.'

19

Moonlight gave way to a magenta dawn.

Having tried yet again to loosen the knots around my wrists and ankles, I shuffled about on my elbows and knees, quartering every square inch of the cabin for an object or surface that might serve to cut my bonds. But it was a fruitless exercise. Aside from a solitary chair, an empty cupboard and a plastic light fitting in the ceiling, the berth was empty.

One more film . . .

I understood now why I hadn't been killed along with Roland; why I had been engineered safely off Paros and allowed to escape unharmed. Ricky had been biding his time, concocting his revenge. His malevolence towards me wasn't rooted in my attempt to bring him to justice, to overthrow his operation and bring his sick proceedings to a close – although that was all part of it – but rather because he had failed. He had failed to corrupt me, to turn me into him. I'd eluded him. I'd been a devoted dog to his addiction, food for his compulsion to control and dominate everyone around him. But that dog had broken away, turned around and bitten him. A simple execution wasn't enough for Ricky. This was personal.

Around 10 a.m. we picked up a breeze and, reverting to sail power, wound our way in a northwesterly direction through a string of deserted islets.

The sun climbed higher, the temperature soared, and the cabin began to cook. Unable to force the hatch open any wider, the combination of dehydration and exhaustion got the better of me: I abandoned my post at the skylight and crashed out on the starboard bunk, where I drifted in and out of sleep until, at midday, a mechanical grinding inches from my head wrenched me from my slumber.

We were dropping anchor.

Hauling myself off the sweat-soaked bunk, I lowered my tethered feet to the deck, hopped back to the hatch and peered out.

To port, there was nothing to be seen but an expanse of aquamarine stretching to the horizon beneath a blazing noonday sun, but when I shuffled around to my right, I discovered we had hoved to off a horseshoe-shaped cove. It was perhaps a kilometre in width, with a crescent-shaped stretch of golden sand in the centre and reddish cliffs on its western promontory, the tops of which were covered with myrtle, thyme and a scattering of stubby olive trees. Further inland a flock of swifts wheeled above a verdant plateau that fell away to sea level on the eastern shore along an incline populated with lemon and peach trees. At the foot of the slopes, tucked in behind a row of poplars and cypresses, I could make out the cuboid whitewash of a sizeable villa nestled amid a swathe of bougainvillea.

Why had we stopped?

254

Other than the lone building, the cove appeared devoid of human existence. Not a soul on the beach, no huts along the shoreline, not a single fishing boat, nor any kind of leisure craft. From my restricted view, I was unable to tell the size of the landmass, although I felt sure we couldn't have reached the Greek mainland in the six or so hours we had been sailing. It had to be an island. How big was impossible to tell.

I lurched over to the cabin door and pressed an ear to the wooden panel, straining for clues, and just as I realised they must be all on deck, I heard the distant whine of an approaching speedboat.

After an animated exchange of shouts from the stern, there followed a bump, whereupon the speedboat's engine cut out. The yacht rocked and juddered along with a resurgence of activity on deck, until, eventually, the engine sputtered to life once again and resumed its waspish drone as it throttled away across the water. I hopped back to the hatch in the hope of establishing a visual, but the launch had retreated in line with the stern, remaining hidden; I then understood the boat must have travelled beyond the cove – otherwise the journey would have been significantly shorter.

I stayed motionless, wondering which one of them would have stayed to keep watch over me; but after several minutes' stillness, realised I was quite alone.

Where the hell had they gone?

Confined to my claustrophobic berth, I felt the silence thicken and the heat become unbearable. It started to dawn on me that I'd come to the end of the line – that I wouldn't be going home. When would anyone hear of my death? How long would it take for the police to find me? Would they ever find me? Chances were, like Diane – and, most probably,

Lucy the New Yorker – I'd end up as food for the fish. Except this time, they'd be sure to dump me further out to sea; no danger of my body being washed up on the shore.

But as I blinked through the sweat towards my cabin door, wondering what sort of funeral my family would give me – how long they'd wait before they gave up, and whether they would eventually bury me, or cremate me – I realised, to my disbelief, that there didn't appear to be a locking device. Just a handle and a catch, hanging free.

I rolled over to the door, and once upright, gave the handle a twist, which resulted in the panel opening a few milli-metres before being stopped by, presumably, another catch on the other side. But certainly there appeared to be no lock. Which made sense: fastening doors on yachts was more about stopping them swinging wildly in rough weather than being anything to do with security. A catch on either side would suffice.

Hoping against hope, I dropped to the floor, raised my tethered feet up to my chest, and in one swift donkey kick, slammed my feet into the door.

It flew open without resistance.

I lay there stupefied, wondering if it was a trap, but a quick scan of the main cabin confirmed I was alone. I lurched to my feet, bounced into the main cabin and stumbled upon the detritus of what looked like dinner: scattered sheets of greasepaper littered the central table and seats, along with the remains of salad leaves, half-eaten strips of fried chicken, a crusty bread roll, some cheese and tomatoes. In addition to the food, stacked on the kitchenette counter was an array of empty beer bottles and cigarette packs, as well as a quarter-full bottle of Metaxa brandy.

A quick glance towards the companionway established they

had secured a hatch-board in place, a two-panelled wooden affair with a central lock – and, presumably, a set of bolts on the opposite side. It would be harder to break than my cabin door, certainly, but the hatch-boards weren't heavy-duty – it was doable.

I made short shrift of the scraps on the table, slaked my thirst with fresh water from the tap at the sink, then, after several failed attempts to sever my bonds on the blunt knives in the kitchen drawer, returned to the companionway, where, edging up the steps to the hatch, I wedged my elbows into the narrow passageway to stop myself from sliding back down, and repeated my tactic on the inner-cabin door – attacking the wood with a series of donkey kicks. After only a few minutes, a crack spidered across the wood. Moments later, the hatch-board split with a resounding crack and light poured in. Three further jabs of my feet and there was hole large enough for me to crawl through.

Shit, yes!

I scrabbled up through the hatchway onto the open deck of the cockpit, but my burst of optimism was short-lived: there was still nothing with which I could cut my shackles; the cockpit was all hard plastic. The only metal objects were the smooth fittings for the shrouds, winches and halyards. Nor was there any sign of a compartment that might conceal the hoped-for toolkit.

I clawed myself to my feet and, shading my eyes with my bound hands against the dazzling light, discovered we were moored in maybe thirty feet of crystal-clear water, which shelved gradually towards the shoreline some 150 yards away.

Still no sign of the others.

Had they gone for good? Or were they already making their way back?

Clambering on my hands and knees over the tiller to the transom, I lowered myself down the rear stepladder until I felt the limpid water cover my feet, then stopped to calm the palpitations in my chest. Once I stepped off, I knew there'd be no getting back on. If I couldn't keep myself afloat then I would drown.

But there was nothing else for it.

I filled my lungs with air and launched myself backwards into the water.

Twisting over onto my front as I sank, I managed a series of porpoise-like undulations, gaining ground towards the shore, until I ran out of breath, whereupon I rapidly pumped my tethered legs in short, sharp jerks to bring my head above the surface long enough to snatch a couple of mouthfuls of air . . . and then gravity beat me and I slipped back under.

Again, I undulated my body through the brine, and again gained ground. After some twenty yards, to relieve the pain in my lower spine engendered by the door-kicking, I spun over onto my back and attempted the same move, inverted; except it only exacerbated the pain even further, making me involuntarily gasp for air, upon which I took in a lungful of water. Coughing and spluttering, I fought a rush of panic and inadvertently discovered I could bob backwards through the water, inch by inch, using a minimal flapping of my tethered arms along with vigorous thrusts of my knees, while holding my breath to aid buoyancy. Not so effective in gaining distance, but it took less energy.

I proceeded with a combination of the two techniques until I was in around ten feet of water, and then turned to face shore, using the sea floor as a springboard to pogo my way to standing depth. Finally, balanced with outstretched, tethered arms, I shuffled, zombie-like, up the shallows and hit dry ground,

258

where, pausing momentarily to overcome a sudden dizziness, I hopped, lurched and rolled my way across the sand and pebbles to the bottom of the cliffs, dispatched my shackles with a jagged lump of flint, and disappeared into the wall of bamboo that lined the upper beach until I hit the trees. Once safely in the shadows, I collapsed, wheezing, to the dusty ground.

Fuck you, Ricky.

For once, he'd underestimated me.

Keeping the villa several hundred yards to my right, I pushed on through the rambling undergrowth accompanied by the chant of cicadas overhead and the rustle of lizards underfoot. When the poplars gave way to a trail of olive trees, I found myself heading once more uphill, until I eventually broke through the parched grove at the side of the plateau and stopped to recover my breath.

Turning back to face southeast, I picked out the villa in all its rambling glory, although at such distance it was hard to make out any detail. Shading my eyes against the glare, I thought for a moment that I'd caught a movement on the patio, but nothing materialised – it was most likely a swift, chasing flies over the pool. Although there was nothing to say Ricky and his crew weren't already inside. Either that, or they were back at, or en route to, the yacht. There was nowhere else for them to be – except hiding in the trees, and I wasn't about to believe they'd stopped off for a picnic.

Pushing on around the edges of the plateau, wheezing on a heady cocktail of thyme and wild sage, I eventually came to the cliff edge, which fell away in a sheer drop of a hundred feet or more to the water below.

Besides the fruit plantations I had spotted from the yacht – which from my position on the side of the plateau were no longer visible, being now above me – I could now see the island in its entirety. It was perhaps some eight to ten square kilometres in area, and around seven or eight kilometres distant from a larger, equally verdant landmass that lay across the water, directly to the north. My knowledge of the Cyclades was limited, but I was confident that I was looking across at one of the larger islands. It couldn't be Mykonos; we had travelled west into the storm and had continued northwest once morning had broken. I knew that Mykonos lay due north of Paros – too far to the east. Ios was way down to the south, along with Santorini; again, not possible. Serifos, perhaps. Or Sifnos?

One thing was for sure: whatever the landmass, I wasn't about to try swimming across. A couple of kilometres was doable, but eight, or maybe more, was too much – leaving aside my weakened physical state and the glaring heat from the sun.

Could I wait until night? And risk being run down by a ferry, getting caught in a storm, drifting off in the wrong direction?

Only as a last resort.

And how long before Ricky found me?

Returning my gaze to my immediate environs, I scoured the plain below, and through the wheeling swifts I eventually detected the roof of another villa nestling in the middle of a vineyard, alongside which a tiny stream meandered. The building appeared Venetian in style, with a terracotta sloping roof, not the typical cuboid Greek design. It was too far in the distance to tell if it was occupied, but it was my only hope. Yes, I'd have to retrace my steps and pass by the first villa at the cove – the cliffs prohibited any further forward travel in any direction – but it was a necessary risk. I'd reached a dead end. To gain access to the remainder of the island I had no choice but to follow the eastern perimeter.

I skidded back down the parched earth of the plateau, sending a pair of hoopoes flapping for cover, and soon re-entered the plantation of poplars and olives on the flats, where I checked my progress to reassess: unless I wanted to risk breaking cover along the beach, I'd have to pass close by the villa to the inland, northern side.

It was the lesser of two evils; no way could I risk being out in the open.

Keeping within the shadows of the trees, I stole my way through the brush and, spotting the walls of the villa looming ahead through the cypresses, stopped once more to listen.

Apart from cicadas and swifts, there was no sign of life.

I continued on through the grove until I came to a sharp incline, which compelled me to come within a hundred feet of the premises. Creeping across the tinder-dry terrain, pungent with the scent of dried pine needles, I passed along the northern edge of the property and emerged on the far side, with a direct view over a tangle of honeysuckle cascading from the perimeter wall across the patio to the pool.

What I saw took my breath away.

She was sitting on a sunlounger, towelling herself down after having taken a swim, her auburn locks falling down to her waist. Long, slender limbs oozing from a snug-fitting bikini. When she sat back in the lounger and removed the sunglasses from the top of her head, the sun caught her hair, radiating red and gold. In the same moment, I saw her eyes. A flash of emerald in the slanting light. Only for a fleeting second, but it was long enough.

I stood rigid in disbelief.

Ellie.

20

As a pair of swifts chased each other through the shimmering air above the pool, I momentarily forgot myself. Everything faded into static as Ellie's feline form crystallised in front of me. My heart swelled in my chest, my throat tightened . . . How could I ever have moved on? How could I have forgotten her, or believed the world would continue to turn without her?

I unrooted my legs from the cracked earth and slid through the hibiscus into a thicker hedgerow of oleander to give me more cover, as well as a better angle.

She had lost weight. But her body had sharpened and tautened, and had been ripened by the kiss of the sun. Was she the same woman? Despite the tan, she remained the elegant English rose . . . cool as ever, all-knowing, oblivious to how her form charged the air around her, yet comfortable in the knowledge she could conduct anything or anyone with the flutter of an eyelid.

Then came a crack behind me.

I spun around, heart thumping, expecting to find Ricky,

but the noise proved to be the ramblings of an untimely hedgehog marking his territorial boundaries in preparation for the night's hunt.

It was enough of a jolt, however, to snap me out of my stupor.

One more film.

Whatever Ricky had in mind, it was to involve Ellie.

I shrank back into the hedge as she peeled herself off the sunlounger and stretched, then wandered over to the pool, studying the refracted light in the water.

Ellie . . .

How Ricky had achieved it, I couldn't fathom. Up until now a small part of me had clung on to the belief Ricky had been bluffing. Yes, he'd had a photo taken with her – and her cousin – but I'd been convincing myself that it had merely been a ruse to make me go after him, to ensnare me for his revenge. I never believed Ellie would fall for it – for him.

I threw another look around the grounds. Other than the ripples dying on the surface of the pool there was no other movement from the villa. She appeared to be alone. Where was Ricky now? From the direction of the disappearing engine noise, I had reckoned the speedboat to have landed at a mooring around the headland. But it couldn't have been that far away; at least an hour had passed since they'd left the yacht.

But as I waited in the undergrowth, legs cramping from the prolonged squatting, the truth suddenly dawned on me . . . My escape from the yacht had been stage-managed, just as my breakout from the police cell on Paros had been. They could have held me in lockdown on the boat had they wanted to, but instead they'd allowed me to slip away with relative ease, providing a token set of hurdles for me to negotiate to keep up the pretence, going so far as to leave me food and water to encourage me on my way and engender the belief that I'd outfoxed them, knowing full well I would only walk from the frying pan into the fire.

Why?

Because it was all part of the game. Ricky never did anything straightforward; he prided himself in the practice of enigma and theatrics. He saw himself as an artist, a modern-day Mephistopheles. The great manipulator.

And he was close by: hiding, watching. Awaiting my arrival.

I ducked back into the bushes and considered my options.

Attending to an itch on her right shoulder blade, Ellie tore her gaze from the reflections, tugged her bikini bottoms back into place and ambled along the side of the pool. Stepping up onto the diving board, she tiptoed to the end, cast a quick look about her, then turned a somersault into a flawless dive, popping up seconds later in the shallow end, lips parted, smoothing her hair back from her face.

I never knew she could do that.

She swam a length of breaststroke and then for no apparent reason froze, looking directly at me.

I stayed stock-still.

But it wasn't me. She had spotted a lizard asleep in the sun on the flagstones. Easing herself half out of the water, she folded her arms under her chin, and with her head tilted to one side, studied the somnolent creature, a smile playing on her wet lips.

A sudden squawk from above sent me cowering to the ground. But it was only a magpie, calling me off his turf. As it flapped higher into the foliage to preen itself, I cast my eye

265

back to Ellie in time to see her pull herself out of the pool, drip her way across to her towel and begin to dry off.

Whatever means Ricky had used to entice her to an effectively deserted island, I could only infer from her relaxed body language – by the way she massaged the sun cream into her thighs – that she was blissfully ignorant of his machinations.

Again I checked my surroundings.

No sign. But they were out there somewhere.

I couldn't simply grab her and run. Even if we escaped the wrath of Annika's pistol, there was nowhere to go; the yacht was as good as useless without any wind, and I had no way of starting the engine without a key. Equally, I couldn't remain in hiding. Ricky was forcing my hand, waiting for me to make the first move. And he could wait all day; the cards were stacked in his favour. We were hapless inmates of his open-air prison, outnumbered by his armed entourage with nowhere to run; he was at liberty to indulge in voyeuristic pleasure and watch the drama unfold – to sit back, play God, and admire the fruits of his labour. Eventually I had to break cover.

But what was I supposed to do? Without a weapon I was impotent. Annika had a gun, and both Ricky and Yannis had knives.

I turned back to Ellie. She finished applying the sun cream and adjusted the towel on the sunlounger in preparation for her next tanning session. Picking up her paperback, she straddled the lounger, one hand pulling at the strands of her wet hair as she leafed through the pages to find her place.

How would she react to my out-of-the-blue appearance?

There was only one way to find out.

I pushed aside the oleander branches and stepped into the sunlight, making a split-second decision not to tell her why we'd been brought together. To instigate panic would only accelerate our fate and shut down options. Ignorance had its advantages; it would give me room to manoeuvre.

Ricky wanted a show?

I'd give him one.

Striding out across the flagstones, half-expecting a bullet at any moment, I came to within fifteen feet of Ellie before she raised her head from the novel. Stopping in my tracks, I thrust my hands in my pockets and, affecting a carefree non-chalance, kicked away a stone.

'Ellie Alexis, I presume.'

She shot bolt upright and tossed her book to the ground.

'Alistair bloody Haston,' she replied, a Cheshire-cat grin spreading across her freckled face. 'Took your time. How's the head?' With a shake of her hair, she stepped off the lounger, and balling her fists, stood defiantly in front of me, hands on hips.

Not the response I was expecting.

I stalled, surveying the terrace as the cicadas in the nearby cypresses fell silent, disturbed by my arrival. 'You know how it is,' I replied, scrambling to think what story Ricky might have spun her. 'Boys will be boys.'

Let her take the lead.

'What have you done to your hair?' she exclaimed, putting a hand to her mouth as she eyed my sunburned, stubbled scalp. 'And you're soaking wet.'

'Yeah.'

I'd forgotten how her sheer presence could destabilise me, an irresistible magnetism sucking me in.

Eye on the ball, Haston. Ricky is watching.

'Actually, the bald look suits you,' she murmured as I

267

stopped in front of her, hands still in my pockets. 'Makes you more distinguished.'

'Thought it was time for a new image,' I replied, searching the cypresses. 'Nice place you got here,' I added, keeping my back turned as a flotilla of swifts shot over the villa roof and disappeared over the poplars to the east.

No 'How've you been?', or 'Fancy meeting you here' . . .

What had Ricky said to her?

'It's good to see you, Alistair.'

It sounded more like a question than a statement.

But as I turned around, she held out her hands and smiled.

Fuck.

Her dimples brought the world to a halt, and all sense of danger dissolved as I was overcome by vertiginous longing. Dizzy. Desperate. As smitten as I'd felt the very first day I set eyes on her. 'Hug me, for Christ's sake!' she chided, misconstruing my silence as reticence. 'You can manage that, can't you?' But before I could take an in-breath, she threw herself at me and wrapped me tight in her arms, pressing her hips into me. 'My God, you're skeletal,' she muttered. 'When did you last eat?'

I closed my eyes and breathed in her scent, unable to prevent a rush of blood to my groin. I felt suddenly powerless. It wasn't love; it was a drug, an addiction.

'Is this sweat?' she asked, tugging at my T-shirt. 'Or did you swim across?'

The spell broke. She knew about the yacht.

What else?

'Ricky bet you'd swim,' she continued, pulling herself away from me an inch and taking my chin in her hand. 'Said you wouldn't know how to work the tender boat.'

'Figured the water would clear my head,' I quipped. 'And my clothes needed a wash anyway, so . . .'

268

I broke away, turned to the villa. How could she act so cool? Four months ago, she had broken off our relationship out of the blue and refused me audience. My pretence was born of a need to survive the next few hours. What was her excuse?

Focus, Haston.

A quick scan of the vicinity for possible weaponry revealed nothing of use; the only objects on the terrace were the sun-loungers, a dining table and half a dozen chairs. I'd have to find something in the villa – a knife from the kitchen.

Or was Ricky already inside, waiting for me?

'Stunning place,' I mused, walking over to the pool. 'How long you been here?' Agonising though it was, I had to keep my feelings for Ellie in check. I needed facts. Fast.

'Five days. I think. Maybe six,' she replied, turning away and reaching for her bottled-water. 'It's hard to keep track of time.'

I dipped a hand into the pool. 'On your own?'

Six days . . . I'd have still been in the cell on Paros.

'God, no!' She spat out a mouthful of water. 'With Anita. I'd go crazy here all by myself. There's nothing to do. It was Anita's idea to come here, not mine – because of Yannis.'

'Right.'

Yannis?

'No one else?' I asked.

But I was thinking back to the night of the ambush at the villa. The final piece of the puzzle had fallen into place: Ricky's men had been lying in wait for me, yes – but not to kill me. Having broken me out of prison, they were to ensure my escape, to eliminate Leo and Roland – and possibly any legit police who might have been in pursuit. To make sure I got off the island safely in order to be lured to Amara, then Ricky and, ultimately, Ellie.

269

She blew a strand of hair from her eyes. 'Well, there's the artist. You know, the German guy. Heinrich.'

'Uh, huh.'

A falcon swooped in low from the southern garden wall, chasing the swifts from the terrace.

Babysitting, Ricky had said.

'Extremely talented,' added Ellie. 'And he only has one eye.'

'Clever man.'

A full house.

I hauled myself to my feet, brain racing. 'So, where the hell is everyone?' I retorted. 'I could use a drink.'

I had to get into the kitchen . . .

'I'm not sure,' she replied. 'Heinrich's asleep downstairs in his studio. Anita's gone off with Yannis to pick up the lamb for tonight. Heinrich's sister and Ricky went for a walk – I think.'

A walk?

Right. Annika's pistol was surely trained on me that very second. 'Pick up the lamb from where?' I asked. 'There's a village nearby?' I stood up and walked round to the deep end of the pool, catching a glimpse of movement out of the corner of my eye from the villa. Someone was at the window.

I didn't turn, kept my eyes on Ellie.

'No village,' she replied, joining me by the diving board and wiping the grit from the soles of her feet. 'The island's private. Yannis took Anita in the speedboat over to Serifos.'

'Okay,' I replied.

Serifos. Halfway between Paros and Athens, roughly a day's sail in good weather. 'Takes about half an hour to get there,' she added, stepping up onto the board. She walked to the tip and began to bounce.

'Is this Anita's place?' I asked, tearing my eyes away. I knew the answer, but I had to keep up the pretence. And it was a fair supposition; Anita was the daughter of a wealthy shipping magnate.

'She wishes,' laughed Ellie, bouncing higher.

'How did you find it?'

It was extraordinary that she wasn't in the slightest bit curious as to the coincidence – as to how we had ended up on the same tiny island.

She gave up and sat down on the board. Lowering her legs into the water, she told me how Anita had met Yannis in a bar on Ios when they'd been island-hopping, and that the two of them had hit it off. Yannis bought her drinks all night and told her about a private villa he knew of that she could stay in for free. The next night Anita introduced Yannis to Ellie, then, a couple of days later, Yannis introduced them both to Ricky.

'Ios? And this was – when?' I asked, trying to do the maths.

'I dunno. Ten days ago,' she replied, staring over to the cypresses.

Before my arrest . . .

I was right, Ricky had been planning this since way back. He must have assigned Yannis the task of tracking them down in Athens and tailing them; then later – not long before the housewarming – joined them on Ios to set up the next phase.

'Ricky told us he had a friend who was an artist,' continued Ellie, kicking the water with her tanned feet, her ankle bracelet catching the sunlight. 'Said he owned an island. Private. Totally remote. And that we could have the place to ourselves. Well, share it with him. Wouldn't have to pay. All we had to do was let the artist paint our portraits – if we were comfortable with it.'

271

'And were you?' I retorted, scanning the row of cypresses to the west of the gardens.

'What?'

'Comfortable with it?'

'I haven't let him paint me, yet,' she sniffed, tightening the cord on her bikini bra. 'Anita has.' With that she slipped off the board into the water. 'It's a great likeness.'

I felt a surge of relief; the thought of her sleeping with Heinrich . . .

But she was hiding something.

'When we got here,' she continued, swimming side stroke to the shallow end, 'Heinrich gave us a tour of the place. Showed us his studio. That's where I saw your portrait.'

Mine?

He'd never done one, to my knowledge.

'I mean, what are the chances?' she mumbled, reaching the far end and standing up to wring out her hair.

Zero.

'Ricky came over with you, then?' I asked, casually as possible, although I could feel my gut tightening.

'Yeah,' she replied, without looking at me. 'The day after we met on Ios, he left and said he'd come back in a few days to collect us. Offered to bring us over in Heinrich's yacht – wanted to help us settle in.'

And what else did he offer?

More to the point, what had Ellie offered to bring to the table, if not her portrait? She would have known nothing was for free.

'Anyway,' she continued, 'when I told him I recognised you from Heinrich's painting, he said you guys had hung out together – that he'd met you on the ferry from Athens, and that you'd worked together. Then later, over dinner, he told me how you'd confided in him about me.'

'It's true,' I replied.

No lying necessary. I had the urge to tell her everything there and then, to expose the man who had deceived her and won her confidence. But it was too great a risk. I couldn't count on her ability to dissemble. She wore her heart on her sleeve; and, unlike myself, she hadn't had ten years of boarding school to teach her the ways of duplicity and self-preservation.

'He got all excited,' Ellie continued, levering herself out of the pool, her wet body glistening in the sunlight. 'Kept boasting he could fix anything, find anyone. He said he would prove it and bring you to me. He'd taken a photo of the three of us – him, me and Anita – said he'd give to you, in case you didn't believe him either.'

'I saw it,' I said, forcing a smile. 'Ios looks fun.'

'Paros,' countered Ellie, raking her hair with her fingers. 'It was a last-minute idea. Anita's dad owns a restaurant in Naoussa – remember? The Tamarisk? I told Ricky about it and he reckoned we could drop in for lunch on the way up from Ios.'

'Must have been a short lunch.'

I was locked up at the police station by then. Ricky would have known the police would be after him too . . .

Ellie wrinkled her nose. 'Why d'you say that?'

'Long trip from Ios to Serifos,' I said, backtracking.

'True. Ricky was keen to get to the island in daylight. We pretty much ate on our own, in fact. He went off to catch up with some business stuff.'

Yeah, to get Yannis to develop the photo and deliver it to Sadie.

'You never went to the Tamarisk in all your time on

Paros?' she added. 'I'm surprised.' She sounded disappointed almost.

'Never got around to it,' I lied.

She didn't need to know that not only had I been there, I had also made a fool of myself falling helplessly for a Dutch woman who was already attached, but being on the rebound from Ellie, I was too blind to see it.

'You were saying,' I continued, 'about Ricky asking if you wanted him to find me.'

She picked up her towel and dried herself off. 'He was pretty insistent. Kept asking me, over and over, if it was something I wanted,' she said, avoiding eye contact.

'And you told him "no"?'

She wouldn't have wanted to put me through the heart-break of seeing her. Whatever her reasons for dumping me, she wasn't cruel.

She nodded. 'We had a moment together,' she murmured, eyes fixed on her painted toenails. 'A kiss in the bar the first night we met. On Ios. We were all drunk on tequila. You know . . . just been offered a private island to stay on for free, and stuff. It was one of those things. Meant nothing.'

Then she looked up and bit her lip.

Jesus fucking Christ.

I held up a hand. 'I don't need to know.'

'We slept together.'

I couldn't breathe.

'I was drunk,' she mumbled dropping her shoulders, as if having shifted a terrible burden. 'I don't really remember it.'

Speechless, I felt the ground tilt; the thought of Ricky's slippery tongue kissing her, licking her, exploring her curves . . .

She took a step back and wrapped the towel around her. 'I thought it was the right thing to do,' she stammered.

274

'Of course – a "thank you fuck".'

'That's unfair,' she replied, jutting her jaw. 'I don't owe you anything.'

'I didn't say you did.'

'I'm being honest with you.'

'I don't want your honesty,' I exclaimed bitterly. 'I want you!'

There it was. I said it. Done.

She made to speak but, again, I cut her off: 'I just – forget it.'

Embarrassed at my outburst, I strode to the edge of the pool and scanned the trees again as Ellie crept over to the sunlounger and sat, knees drawn up to her chest.

What the fuck was Ricky waiting for?

'I'm sorry, Haston,' she murmured.

'For what? Fucking him or for telling me?' It was childish, but I didn't care.

She looked up at me with bloodshot eyes and shook her head.

The swifts returned to the garden, tumbling and whistling as they fought over an errant butterfly above the swimming pool. 'It's all good,' I lied, dismissing an eternity of heartache with the wave of a hand. 'Shit happens.' Excruciating though it was, to hear of her and Ricky, Ellie wasn't the enemy. At some point very soon, the Australian would step in and talk would turn to action. There'd be blood. I just had to make sure it wasn't Ellie's. Or mine.

Without a weapon, however . . .

I resisted asking if she had considered why Ricky had disobeyed her wish not to bring me to her; it would only escalate into me revealing Ricky's true intentions. Instead I focused on our options for escape.

275

'You're sure this island's private?' I asked, staring at the reflections of the hibiscus in the pool. She must have known something about the other villa: did they have a boat? A telephone?

But she had her head on her knees.

Was she crying?

I asked her a second time. This time she looked up, but before she could answer, a voice boomed out across the patio from the direction of the villa:

'I share the island with a film star.'

It was Heinrich. Panama hat in place, cigar in hand. Navy blue eyepatch.

'An Italian,' he beamed, his one eye twinkling. 'He's hardly ever there. Too ill to fly most of the time. I've offered to buy the place, but he won't hear of it.'

Bumbling over the flagstones, walrus-like, he lifted his hat and ran a hand through his silver hair as he turned to face me.

'Mister Alistair Haston. What a wonderful surprise.'

21

It was no time to be backward. I had to take a leaf out of Ricky's book.

'Heinrich, my good man,' I drawled, striding towards him along the edge of the swimming pool. '*Wie geht's? Gar nicht schlecht, dieses Villa.*'

'*Vielen Dank,*' he replied, all charm, as he returned the hat to his head. 'It is not a bad spot, if I say so myself. But it is just a house. Bricks and mortar. These ... *possessions* are not so important. People. That is what counts, yes?'

'Couldn't agree more,' I replied, turning to Ellie.

'*Seit langem, nicht gesehen,*' continued Heinrich. '*Ich hab' mich gefragt – na also, was macht denn der Jungs Haston in dieser zeit?*'

We shook hands, his left arm straying onto my shoulder.

How was I doing?

'Pretty good,' I replied, turning back to the pool. '*Eine Freude, deine Schwester zu treffen.*' And yet, as pleasurable it had been to meet his sister – or so I'd made out – she couldn't have been further from my mind ... I was thinking about the pool.

How far was it from the table – twenty feet?

'*Bin froh darauf*,' he replied, releasing my shoulder. 'She and I are very close.'

'Hey, guys,' said Ellie, grabbing the end of the towel and dabbing at her face as if drying herself off. 'I don't speak German.'

All trace of her upset had vanished in an instant. Had she sensed something, or was she saving face?

'Quite right,' apologised Heinrich, adjusting his eyepatch. 'How rude of me—'

'I was just complementing him on his sister,' I interrupted. 'Say, anyone else thirsty?' Heinrich was the perfect host; he wouldn't refuse.

'A drink, of course,' replied Heinrich. 'You are reunited at long last – a truly splendid occasion. We must have champagne!'

Reunited . . .

I turned to Ellie, but she gave nothing away. Perhaps she hadn't heard it.

'Champagne, or whatever you would like,' continued Heinrich. '*Mi casa, su casa.*' He turned and doffed his hat to Ellie. 'This is Spanish, of course.'

'I'll do it,' laughed Ellie. 'It's my *casa* too. For now.'

'Excellent. Haston?'

'I'll have an ouzo. With water,' I said. 'Thanks.'

Usually served in a tall glass to release the aroma. But would Ellie know that?

'*Annika schiesst gut*,' I added, turning to Heinrich. *She's a good shot.*

'You must pay her that compliment yourself,' he replied, glancing towards Ellie with his one eye. 'For me, a Metaxa would be fine.'

Ellie smiled and with a quick look over her shoulder disappeared into the villa.

What's she thinking?

'I look forward to the opportunity,' I said, through gritted teeth.

'Well,' he countered, hauling his shorts up on his hips and adjusting his eyepatch. 'You can tell her now.'

I turned to see Annika and Ricky approaching the border of the gardens from the direction of the cypresses. Ricky held the video camera in his left hand – and what was that in his right? As they passed through the gate, he handed it to Annika . . .

The pistol.

Annika dropped back, and turning to the trees, lifted the hem of her dress and slid the gun into a thigh-strap.

'The man of the moment,' exclaimed Ricky, placing the camera on a sunlounger and pulling out a packet of cigarettes. 'You guys work well together. Great chemistry.'

Work well together?

'Wanna check it out?' he asked, lighting up. 'Got the whole thing on tape. You swimming across from the yacht. Scrambling through the undergrowth. But the stuff with Ellie makes for the perfect trailer—'

'We were about to have a drink,' I said, cutting him off.

'Sweet,' said Ricky, with a wink. 'Where's ya gal?'

'Inside,' I replied, my eyes flicking back to the pool.

If I could engineer a toast around the table . . .

'Told her yet?' he added, walking forward to offer me his packet of Karelia Lights. 'Course you haven't. Didn't want to spook her. Needed to time to figure your game plan – await an opening.'

'Something like that,' I replied, raising my voice as I took a cigarette and lit it. Now wasn't the time to reveal what I knew about him and Ellie, although he may well

279

have attributed our argument to the issue. 'So, Yannis and Anita,' I continued, 'I take it we won't be seeing them again.'

'Not what you think, mate,' Ricky slurred, checking to make sure Ellie was out of earshot. 'They're all loved–up. He wouldn't do that. But you're right. Yannis has taken the tapes to Serifos. Someone's gotta keep the business running while we're away.'

'In the suitcase, right?'

Amara must have packed them at the last minute.

'Right again, detective,' jeered Ricky.

'I must make sure our guest is okay,' interrupted Heinrich. 'Perhaps we might refresh the topic of conversation?'

'Ouzo,' I repeated, as he wandered to the patio doors. 'With water.'

'Yes, you have already told Ellie,' he chirped.

'She's a tourist, she'll only fuck it up.' Heinrich was a stickler for form; he'd never serve it in a tumbler.

I was counting on it.

'I'll have beer,' added Ricky with a nod of approval.

'*Nichts für mich, danke,*' replied his sister.

Being the marksman, she had to stay sober.

'But I'll let you into a secret,' Ricky added, pulling up a chair as Heinrich went inside. 'It wasn't Amara. It was her cousin, Nikolas.' He kicked off his shoes and stuck his feet on the table. 'Who d'ya think bought him the new bike?'

I blew out a stream of smoke and eyeballed him.

'Looks like you made an impression on her after all, eh?' he said with a wink.

Right now, the tapes were moot – so too, was Amara's innocence . . .

Annika had a gun, Ricky, a knife . . . *Heinrich?*

'I say we get down to business,' I declared, positioning myself closer to the table. 'Losing the mood.'

'That's my man,' laughed Ricky.

It wasn't enough to think like him. I had to join him.

He turned to Annika: 'Hey Anni, bring over the camcorder, will ya?'

She slid over to the sunlounger, collected the camera and, placing it on the table, took up position behind Ricky as Ellie and Heinrich arrived with the drinks. We were now all present: Heinrich to my immediate left, Annika beside him and Ricky at the head of the table, closest to the pool – Ellie was hovering on the other side of the table opposite me.

'Say hi to your friends back home,' cheered Ricky, switching on the recorder and pointing the lens at Ellie. 'Looking hot in that bikini.'

'Since when did you smoke?' retorted Ellie, catching my eye, unable to conceal a blush as she placed the drinks on the table.

My glass was a highball, about five inches in height.

Thank you, Heinrich.

'Ever since I taught him,' said Ricky, standing up and backing around to his left with the camera. 'Minimal movement please, sweetheart. You're in close-up.'

Annika took a step backwards, as the rest of us, bar Ricky, picked up our drinks.

'Reckon now's the time to tell her, mate,' he purred, his face pressed to the viewfinder.

'Tell me what?' said Ellie, sipping her wine.

'Haston has a surprise for you,' he continued, turning the camera on me.

'I love surprises,' said Ellie stepping up to the table.

I slid Ricky's beer across. 'Don't spoil the party.'

281

'Thanks,' he said, catching it but leaving it untouched. He threw a look to Heinrich, who in turn nodded to Annika. She took a step closer to the table and placed a hand on her dress, above the pistol.

'You're recording this, right?' I asked, giving Ricky a wink.

Fine, leave the beer.

As long as his hands were occupied.

'Wouldn't miss it for the world,' he grinned.

But I could see him wondering.

'It's pretty simple really,' I began, turning to Ellie as Ricky pointed the lens back at her. 'Ricky and I have spent the summer working for Heinrich, recruiting models for him to sleep with.'

'You mean, paint, milord,' interrupted Heinrich.

His breeziness was a lie; I could tell he was nervous.

'Sorry, my mistake,' I replied. 'Paint.'

Dismissing it as a joke, Ellie laughed and took another sip of her drink, then flicked me a look.

What did that mean?

'Indeed. Heinrich paints them,' I continued, studying her, 'then *afterwards* he sleeps with them.'

I turned to Heinrich. 'Better?'

Heinrich looked over to Ricky . . . Ricky looked up from the camera and gave him a nod – *let him finish.*

Ellie still appeared to be under the impression we were joshing. 'But that's by the by,' I continued, feeling Annika's stare boring into me. 'Some of them end up in the gallery that you've seen. Although how my portrait ended up there I have no idea. I can honestly say I've never sat for Heinrich, nor have I slept with him.'

Ricky laughed, along with Ellie. The siblings, however,

282

remained silent. 'Others, the more fortunate ones,' I continued, taking a sip of my ouzo, 'end up in his films.'

The swifts left the pool and flew out to sea.

'Films?' asked Ellie, wrinkling her nose.

'Porn films,' I replied. 'Right, Ricky?'

'Spot on, mate,' he replied.

Chipper enough, but I could see the cogs turning.

'Shut up!' said Ellie, bursting into laughter. 'Seriously.'

But I could see it in her eyes – the doubt.

'The less fortunate ones, however,' I said, moving closer to Heinrich, 'end up in another kind of film altogether. And, I have to say Ellie, you're not going to like this.'

Ellie's smile finally dropped. She turned to the others for support, but found none. Still Ricky kept his eye to the viewfinder, swinging the camera alternately between me and Ellie.

'That's right,' I continued, knowing that Ricky was trying to second-guess me, but failing. 'The victim is forced to have sex and is then killed. On camera.' I turned to the Australian: 'Whaddya call 'em?'

'Snuff films,' he replied, edging closer to Ellie.

Annika glanced over to Heinrich and gave him a nod. He shook his head and took a sip of his Metaxa. She then moved to her right to give her a clear line of sight to Ellie ... but Ricky was still hovering in the foreground.

Any time now.

'And that is why we are here on this beautiful island,' I continued. 'So you can star in his latest film. Sorry – snuff film.'

'You can stop now,' snapped Ellie, tightening the towel about her waist. 'Not funny any more.'

'I agree,' I said. 'No one is laughing.'

Still Ricky kept the camera rolling.

Heinrich shifted uneasily on his feet, looking like he was

about to call a halt to my speech. 'And I hate to break it to you,' I continued, 'but it was all my idea.'

It was a gamble, but I knew Heinrich and Annika were waiting on Ricky's word, and that the Australian was too fascinated by the impending car crash to stop the proceedings. This was gold for him; as far as he was concerned, it would only end one way. All he had to do was catch it on camera.

'What the fuck is going on?' stuttered Ellie, her eyes flicking about the gathering. 'Ricky?'

Losing patience, Annika took another step around the table, fingering her dress, desperately awaiting a sign from Ricky, but he'd returned his attention to the viewfinder. Sensing her approach, however, he raised his beer bottle as a sign for her to stay put.

Another metre . . .

'I'm sorry, baby,' I said, as Ellie retreated backwards along the patio. 'And now I find you fucked Ricky.'

'I don't understand,' stammered Ellie.

In my peripheral vision, I saw Annika shift again to her right.

It was enough.

'Then, understand this, you fuckin' whore,' I said, tightening my grip on the tumbler. 'Strip.'

Ellie froze.

'Strip. Now!'

She hesitated a fraction of a second, then dropped her glass and ran for the trees.

As Annika reached for her gun, I spat out my cigarette, smashed my glass against the table and slammed the jagged edge into Heinrich's good eye.

He howled, threw his hands up to his head and staggered forwards into Annika as blood spurted across the table.

284

Distracted, Annika hesitated. And in that moment, I threw myself at her, rugby-tackling her around the waist and pinning her right arm against her thigh to stop her withdrawing the gun as I swept her across the patio. With her feet off the ground, she was unable to check our momentum ... seconds later, we barrelled over the edge of the pool and into the water.

She wasn't prepared for the submersion.

Locked in an embrace, we quickly sank to the bottom. As we rolled over the mosaic tiling, I squeezed her rib cage tighter, forcing the remaining oxygen from her lungs. Unable to move either arm, she resorted to trying to headbutt me, and managed to sink her teeth into my cheek. But her struggles grew weaker until I heard the telltale clang of the gun hitting the pool floor. Still I hung on. Only when I was on the verge of blacking out did I let her go. Clawing the pistol from the pool floor, I tore for the surface and exploded into the sunlight.

I heard the howling first, then caught sight of him out of the corner of my eye: Heinrich – clasping his mangled eye as he slithered through a puddle of blood away from the table. In the foreground stood Ricky, video camera in hand, at the water's edge ... filming me.

Chest heaving, I twisted around to find Annika floating face down, her dress fanning out like a giant waterlily in the crimson water.

Of Ellie, there was no sign.

'Awesome,' cheered Ricky. 'You're a natural.'

'She's dead,' I panted, hauling myself out of the pool and pointing the pistol at his head. 'Drop the camera.'

I could barely breathe. My heart was on the verge of collapse.

You've committed murder ... killed a woman ... killed ...

A bellow of anguish erupted from the German and he crawled blindly in the direction of the water, calling for his sister.

'Mate, you should see your face,' drawled Ricky, stepping out of Heinrich's way. 'That's gotta hurt.'

'Hands up. Now!' I screamed, wiping the blood from my jaw.

'Or what – you gonna shoot me?'

'Fuck, yes,' I replied, shaking with adrenaline.

'Good luck with that.'

'Water won't affect it,' I snapped, tightening my grip on the gun.

Firing mechanisms for rifles and handguns were the same, surely?

'Put the fucking thing down, ya dickhead,' barked Ricky. 'Have some respect – you just killed his sister. Let's at least get the guy comfortable.' I stared dumbfounded, the gun quivering in my hand, as Ricky set the camera on the table then dragged the jabbering, bloodied German to his feet, slipping him into a chair at the table.

'Easy, mate,' Ricky purred. 'Just a scratch.'

'I can't see,' hollered Heinrich. 'Annika! *Liebchen*!'

Was I wrong about the gun? It wasn't just wet – it had sunk to the bottom of the pool.

'Enough,' I yelled. 'Get your hands on your head.'

'Sit down before you hurt yourself,' Ricky jeered.

I felt another rush of blood to the head. 'I'm going to count to three,' I cried, shaking with rage.

'Go ahead.'

'One . . .'

He walked over to Heinrich and leaned on the back of his chair. 'You're right about the gun,' he said, spinning the knife in his hand. 'They'll even fire under water. A few feet, until they spin off track . . .'

Stay on it, Haston.

'Two . . .'

'But if there's already a bullet in the chamber, you gotta clear it.'

'Three.'

'Otherwise it could jam.'

I pulled the trigger.

Click.

Nothing happened.

And again.

'But that's assuming it's even loaded.'

I froze.

Ricky had emptied it.

In the trees, when he was watching with Annika.

'You think I'd let a crazy Sheila loose with a loaded gun?' he continued, flicking his cigarette across the table. 'She might have shot you before I got the footage. And to be honest, I never trusted her anyway. No offence, Heinrich.'

I turned to the bleeding German. But Heinrich hadn't heard him. Rocking back and forth on the chair, he clawed at his eye, groaning and chanting his sister's name as the tears mixed with his blood.

'But you never got your footage, did you?' I said, finally.

I wasn't only stalling for time; it didn't make sense. All that effort to bring Ellie and me together – to film us – had gone to waste. Ellie had escaped; I was still alive.

'Ya kidding?' he grinned. 'I got you killing Annika on tape – that's a snuff film in my book.' He slid an arm around Heinrich's shoulder and stepped towards me. 'But the question remains – what are you gonna do now? Empty gun versus a hunting knife? I don't fancy your chances.'

'I'll take them,' I said, casting an eye to the eastern border of the terrace where Ellie had disappeared. 'You're going to pay for this.'

'Yeah, right,' he said. 'But if you lose, Ellie will be alone with me on the island.'

Shutting out the bellowing Heinrich, I weighed the odds. The thought of walking away, of letting him go and conceding, was unthinkable. But if I took him on and lost, there was no telling what he would do. Ellie had no way off the island except by yacht; he'd find her eventually.

Ricky drew his arm tighter around Heinrich, pulling him closer. 'Want a hand with that decision?'

Then he spun around and plunged the knife into Heinrich's heart.

The German jerked bolt upright, then collapsed.

No scream this time.

Twisting the blade, Ricky tugged the knife out of Heinrich's chest and let his body slide to the ground. 'Time's up, detective,' he said, as Heinrich's blood crept across the flagstones. 'What's it gonna be?'

I was prepared to gamble my life. But not Ellie's.

Dropping the gun, I backed away across the patio.

'That's right, ya fucker. Run.'

22

Breaking through the trees, I ran across the shingle down to the water, and scanning the length of the shoreline, called out once again for Ellie . . .

But there was no answer.

Unless she had witnessed the proceedings by the poolside, she'd still believe I was out to cause her harm. She'd never give away her position – rather, she would aim to put as much distance as possible between her and the villa.

I called out a final time – for Ricky's benefit – then back-tracked through the trees until I could make out Heinrich's villa.

I now understood Ricky's motive for killing Heinrich and why he'd let me take out Annika: it was every man for himself. Whatever bond of trust had existed between Ricky and the Germans, it had been severed by the need for self-preservation – in Ricky's head, at least. And as for letting me go – he wasn't afraid of taking me on, nor was it an issue of mercy; he'd left me alive as the fall guy. And he had good reason to be confident: he possessed filmed evidence of me killing Annika; an anonymously delivered copy of the tape to the police would ensure I'd spend the rest of my life in prison.

I wasn't about to let that happen.

Earlier, he'd had the upper hand, so taking him on would have been suicide. But the balance had since been redressed. He believed I'd backed down in order to protect Ellie, which meant I now had a crucial advantage – the element of surprise.

For now, Ellie was safe.

I had to go after Ricky.

I edged closer to the villa and peered through the oleander shrubbery.

Ricky's departure from the island had to be imminent – it made no sense for him to burn time at the crime scene. Yannis had taken the speedboat, which meant Ricky would have to commandeer the yacht . . . But how would he reach it? Swim? What about the cassette, the snuff film? He'd be unlikely to risk sabotaging such a lucrative commodity by getting it wet. Then there was the camera, and what about provisions? The cupboards in the yacht were bare – he wouldn't pass up an opportunity to pilfer supplies from the villa. Water, food, clothes – he'd never be able to swim those across.

There had to be another boat.

Keeping low, I set off through the trees in search of the mooring for the motor launch, which I knew lay somewhere on the east side of the island. It was the perfect opportunity for an ambush: while Ricky was tending to manning the craft and embarking, he would be distracted, his hands occupied . . .

Twisting through the plantation, scratched and torn by the low-lying branches and thistles, I continued downhill towards the eastern shore. But just before I reached the treeline, I drew up short and, wiping the blood from my cheek, turned back towards the villa.

It was something Ellie had said . . .

That Ricky had bet I'd swim across, because I 'wouldn't be able to work the tender boat'.

The yacht didn't have a tender. At least, I hadn't seen one.

It made sense for there to be such a vessel: most leisure yachts had them – either inflatable dinghies or a small skiff-type affair. Moored offshore, it was the only way to get to dry land.

Unless . . .

I doubled back and fought through the undergrowth towards the cove, stopping momentarily to pick up a fist-sized rock along the way, before breaking back through the treeline and traversing the boulder section of the headland. When I reached the point at which shingle gave way to sand, I took up position behind a thicket of bamboo and scanned the beach.

The yacht was at its mooring, no sign of Ricky on deck.

Yes! There it was – a hundred yards up the beach, lying on its side under a lone carob tree, half obscured by sea grass: a sun-bleached rowing boat with a tiny outboard engine mounted on the stern.

I hadn't seen it earlier, because it was already on shore. I'd assumed all three of them had disembarked the yacht onto the speedboat with Heinrich, but Ricky must have taken the tender. On my swim across I had been too consumed with fighting just to stay afloat to notice it, and once on land, I was too focused on trying to cut free my shackles.

But where was he?

Keeping as low as possible to the ground, I made my way

along the scrub to within fifty yards of the boat and dug in behind a pair of stunted palm trees.

Any second now.

As the first puffs of air rattled the fronds above my head, I remained immobile, barely breathing, listening out for Ricky's approach – the snap of twig, a disturbed bird or lizard . . .

But with each passing minute, the doubt grew. A rock was better than nothing, but Ricky had a knife – he could even have reloaded Annika's gun. Then what?

Don't think. React.

Nothing. Just cicadas. And the rustle of rising wind.

Had I been right the first time – had he gone to the mooring?

Too late now. I'd committed.

But what was that?

Ricky suddenly broke through the vegetation less than thirty yards away, cigarette hanging out of his mouth, a hold-all slung over his shoulder and sporting a clean T-shirt along with his trademark suede hat.

Turning away from me along the fringes of the seagrass, he sauntered up to the tender, lowered the holdall into the bottom and, taking hold of the painter rope at the bow, raised the outboard motor up on its mount, then dragged the skiff to the water's edge. Twice he looked up to check his direction – there was a line of semi-submerged boulders towards the centre of the beach – otherwise he appeared relaxed and unhurried. No sign of the gun. Nor his knife. The latter was probably back in his bootstrap.

From my position behind the palms I calculated it would take me six or seven seconds to reach him . . .

Too long. He'll see me coming.

Removing his boots, he rolled up his jeans and waded out through the shallows until he was in deep enough to lower the propeller, then hopped onboard.

I'd frozen – my mind a blank.

But as he turned his back and pulled the starter cord, my lizard brain kicked in. Jumping to my feet, I clawed a handful of pebbles from the ground and hurled them as high as I could muster over the top of the boat, then set off towards him.

Before he could put the motor in gear, the pebbles struck the water on the far side of the tender, and he turned briefly away from the outboard, distracted by the splash, buying me a further vital second.

I lunged through the shallows, and wielding my rock, launched myself at Ricky's head. Wrenching himself around to the outboard, Ricky finally saw me, but by the time he had released the throttle arm and bent down to withdraw his knife, I was upon him.

Except I had misjudged the distance.

I fell short, landing in the sea with my arms over the side of the tender, the rock smashing harmlessly into the gunwale as the boat tipped underneath me. There was a flash of silver in the sunlight as Ricky flew over my head into the water. Kicking off the seabed, I used the momentum of the vessel as it rolled back upright and slid over the rail into the bottom of the boat. But as I scrambled frantically about the hull for my rock, I discovered to my dismay that it had fallen overboard. I was now unarmed and helpless.

Elbowing my way across the transom to the outboard engine, my feet sticking out over the side, I grabbed the throttle arm and tried to engage the clutch, but Ricky was too quick. I felt his blade puncture my right calf and rake down through the muscle towards my Achilles. I froze momentarily, then a reflex jerk of my other foot connected with his arm, dislodging the knife. Screaming to overcome the searing pain, I drew my legs into the boat and, scrambling to the stern, rolled the throttle into gear and revved the engine.

The tender shot forwards into deeper water.

Too late.

'Checkmate, ya fuckin' Pom,' came a voice by my ear, as a fist slammed into my left kidney.

I collapsed into the hull, along with several gallons of blood-infused seawater slop. 'Snake in the grass,' spat Ricky, as the boat, unhelmed, began to circle wildly. 'Is this what I get in return?'

'Return for what?' I yelled, pulling myself up on my knees as a fresh surge of blood gushed from my calf. 'For killing Heinrich? Roland? Svenja . . .?'

Before I could finish, he leaned back and thrust his foot at my face, his boot connecting with my jaw. I felt a tooth snap, followed by the tang of iron as blood spurted forth from the open gum. 'I let you go,' he stormed, slithering through the boat towards me. 'I show you fuckin' mercy, and this is how you repay me?'

Reaching again for the outboard in an attempt to steer the boat onto the beach, my fingers slipped across the plastic engine housing and caught the starter cord. Ricky dived onto me, and yanking the cord out, wrapped it around my neck. Twisting me onto my back, he tightened his grip on the cord, then headbutted me. My skull ricocheted off the transom as a flash of white momentarily blinded me.

I couldn't breathe . . .

I was going to die.

Sucking on a vacuum, my tongue glued itself tight to the

roof of my mouth. Ricky pressed his mouth against mine. 'Don't fight it, mate,' he whispered, his tongue flicking over my teeth. 'You're gone.'

And as the boat continued to corkscrew, my vision grew dark. There was no fear, just disbelief. I was twenty-two years old; I had to finish my degree . . . I had to say goodbye. Goodbye to my family . . . to Ellie.

In a final bid for freedom, I jerked my body sharply to my right. The throttle slipped and the boat suddenly slowed, the nose digging into the water as forward momentum was lost. In that split second Ricky's body lifted infinitesimally from mine, briefly releasing my feet. My left leg was in shreds, but the other still worked.

Drawing on the last atom of air in my collapsing lungs, I thrust my right knee into Ricky's groin. He howled, and for a millisecond relaxed his grip on my neck.

It was enough.

Jamming my fingers between the cord and my throat, I sucked in a lungful of air, and as his hand shot to his crotch, I kicked again and rolled out from under him in the direction of the motor.

Last chance.

I grabbed the handle and twisted the accelerator. The boat jumped to life, unbalancing Ricky, who teetered for a moment, a frown stitched across his face as he flailed his arms to stop himself falling overboard.

I threw my weight to my left.

In he went.

Gunning the engine, I powered the boat hard into a 180° turn. Ricky swam towards me, eyes wide with adrenaline, but when I aimed the bow at his head, he stopped, trod water, then duck-dived.

He was too slow. As I ran over him, the propeller struck his upper back before he could complete the dive. The engine screamed and cut out as the boat juddered to a wavering halt, nearly throwing me over the side. Thrashing at the cord, I tried to restart the outboard, but the choke had flooded. I scrambled to the rail, preparing myself for Ricky's return, but when I saw the blood spreading through the water, I crossed to the opposite rail and found him floating face down, his shredded shirt revealing his lacerated back, open across his shoulders like a gaping, purple mouth.

No movement from the man.

Just the wind in my ears and the lap of water on the hull.

I slumped onto the rear seat and watched the waves roll Ricky inexorably over onto his back. In only four feet of water, his legs were nudging the bottom, buoying him up, and it didn't take long for the wind to push him into the shore, where, with a final sigh of sea foam on sand, he became beached, half in, half out of the water.

Was he dead?

His eyes were closed, his body inert . . .

Holding my left leg out of the bilge water, I shuffled to the seat at the bow and opened the holdall. I tore out a shirt from the top of the pile of clothes and fashioned an impromptu tourniquet to stem further bleeding from my calf. Incredibly, the knife had missed the main artery and vein, and most of the blood was already in the slop at my feet, but the wound was deep enough. I had to protect it against infection, or risk losing a leg.

Rifling further through the bag, I found the camera, various items of clothing and a set of keys that I presumed were for the yacht, but no sign of the tape. No food, no

296

water. He must have been planning a short trip – to Serifos, perhaps . . .

Was Yannis waiting for him?

As for the tape, it must have been on his person.

A gust of wind rocked the boat, and I looked up to find I was drifting closer to shore. Ricky's body had encroached higher above the waterline, the growing onshore breeze pushing the flotsam further up the beach. I was about to make another attempt on the outboard, but then I spotted a silhouette on the rocks at the eastern headland of the bay: tall, still, immovable as a cypress.

Ellie.

I raised my arm in salute, but she didn't return the gesture. Instead, she picked her way across the point, through the bamboo and onto the beach; head down, hair blowing in the wind, her arms hanging freely at her sides. She had changed out of her bikini into a pair of cut-off jeans and a tank top – which meant she'd been back to the villa. She must have seen Ricky leave. Had she also witnessed the events at the pool? Her body language gave nothing away; her gait was relaxed – purposeful, even.

Ellie . . .

A few months back, her very name had been a passport for my identity. But as I watched her kick through the sand, blood dripping off my chin into the shapeshifting sea, I had the epiphany that she was, for all intents and purposes, a stranger. My mistake had been to believe I knew her, understood her, and that the knowledge spelt ownership. It had nothing to do with love, just obsession. Ellie. Only a word, composed of everything and nothing. Like the wind.

My throat tightened and I felt the sting of tears prick in

the corners of my eyes. Was it guilt? Relief? Or something more visceral?

As the tender swung round in the wind-chop, Heinrich's yacht slid into view.

It wouldn't be such a challenge, despite my leg; two hands would make light work of the sails. Even if I couldn't helm the boat – the cockpit was small enough to allow me to control everything from a sitting position if called for – Ellie would be able to take the reins. She was an experienced sailor, as she'd boasted back in April. Now she'd get the chance to prove it.

The boat ground to a sudden halt, beaching on the sand. I heaved myself around towards the bow, turned and came face to face with Ellie . . .

And a gun pointed at my chest.

Uncomprehending, I froze, as her eyes bore into mine.

'Let me explain,' I lisped, my tongue fat from Ricky's kick.

Annika's pistol. Ricky must have left it behind as evidence; my fingerprints were on it.

'Why?' she whispered, her jaw clenched tight.

I could see the artery pulsing in her neck.

Other than that, no outward signs of panic.

'Why what?' I replied, wincing as I lifted myself higher on the wooden seat. 'Could you point that thing the other way?' She wouldn't know the gun was empty. I had to play along.

'Why did you bring me here?'

'I didn't,' I slurred, keeping my eyes on the weapon. 'Ricky set you up. Just like he did me.'

'I don't believe you.' She raised the pistol and levelled it at my head.

Or had she found the missing bullets?

'They were going to kill us both,' I stammered. 'I had to get you to run. Please, drop the gun.'

'Snuff films?'

'Nothing to do with me. I swear.'

'How can I trust you?' she said, throwing a look towards the yacht.

Her voice was strong and steady. No trace of fear.

'Take the yacht,' I implored, reaching out a bloodied hand towards her. 'You can handle your uncle's catamaran – this one's a walk in the park. Tie me up and hand me over to the police on Serifos. I'll tell them everything. But I'm innocent. I did this for you.' I nodded to where Ricky lay on the beach, legs rolling in the surf.

'Bullshit.'

A seagull's cry cut through the wind.

'It's not loaded,' I said, changing tack. 'Gun's empty.'

She brushed away a strand of hair from her eyes. 'It was,' she replied, taking a step backwards. 'I found the bullets in the kitchen.' Then came the 'click' as she pulled back the hammer.

Fuck.

'Don't do it, Ellie,' I urged, preparing to throw myself to the bottom of the boat. 'I'm innocent.'

'Liar.'

Her composure was cracking.

'You have to believe me!'

The gun was now trembling in her hand.

'Ricky's dead,' I urged. 'It's over.'

Again the screech of a seagull, high overhead.

'Turn me over to the police,' I cried. 'I'll go. Willingly.'

'Enough!'

She was about to pull the trigger . . .

'Take the fucking yacht!'
'Shut up, Haston.'
'Save yourself!'
'Haston, for Christ's sake ...'
She dropped the gun in the sand.
'I can't sail.'

Epilogue

It took two days to sail to the island of Aegina, some twenty kilometres from Athens, where we were intercepted by an industrious coastguard outfit carrying out routine checks of the Piraeus harbour vicinity. Not ready to trust the police, we decided it was best I should remain mute – *in shock, owing to a nasty boating accident* – until I was standing before a British Embassy official. Ellie handled the Greek authorities with aplomb – my fears that she'd be incapable of duplicity had been unfounded; itturned out she was a born actress – and by the time the police discovered that the yacht had been rented out in the name of a certain Roland Jenner, and that I was *the* Alistair Haston, wanted for six counts of murder on the islands of Paros and Santorini, as well as the murder at sea of two officers on a police launch, I was drinking tea in the reception room of the British Embassy, having recounted the entire sequence of events to an able and willing deputy ambassador prepared to give 'one of our own' the ear and counsel of Her Majesty's representatives.

Not that they could do much.

I spent four weeks under police watch at an infirmary on the outskirts of Athens undergoing reconstructive surgery to my leg, as well as treatment for severe delirium and insomnia, and the next seven months in a high-security prison, awaiting first bail – which was denied, on account of my admitting to killing both Annika and Ricky in self-defence – and then my impending trial.

Ellie was sent straight home on the instruction that her presence would be required once my trial date had been set. Meanwhile, I counted off the interminable days and nights in a single cell and spent every waking moment trying to survive to the next mealtime – which I did, thanks to a massive Albanian who had sworn to protect me after I'd prevented him from hanging himself in the showers. It was no great feat; all I had done was talk him down. At any rate, the speed at which I achieved his change of heart suggested he'd been bluffing. What he really wanted was a friend.

Eventually I was appointed a lawyer who had relations in the police force and who, in the end, might as well have been working for the prosecution. But salvation finally came in the form of Mihalis, the chief of police from Paros, who had interviewed me all those months previously. He had found the evidence on the walls of Roland's hideout, as well as the latter's decomposing head under the eucalyptus in the grounds of the farm. Piece by piece, he started to collect evidence that he believed would prove I had been framed.

After six months of graft, however, we hit a brick wall. There was no substantial evidence of a criminal organisation like the one I'd been decrying; furthermore, the prosecution threatened that, should proof of the organisation in fact come to light, it would only contribute to my downfall, as it

302

appeared that I had been working alongside them – if Ricky was to blame, then so was I. Damned either way.

It was further complicated by the fact that Heinrich's and Annika's bodies were recovered at the villa off Serifos, but not Ricky's. Official word had it that a storm had most likely swept his cadaver to the depths, to be eaten by the fish. Nor was there any evidence of the snuff films that I'd been insisting were being sold on the black market. The camera itself was no proof, and the final tape that Ricky had made seemed to have perished along with his body.

There was simply no evidence and no one willing to come forward and testify. I kept insisting that Amara would talk, and gave them her address on Naxos, but somehow the police were unable to track the family down. According to Mihalis, who had had dealings with him over two decades, it appeared that the head of the Cyclades police force was under pressure from someone higher up the chain of command in the government to preserve the reputation of the nation's chief source of income at all costs.

Just as it seemed I was looking at life behind bars, fate intervened.

Yannis was caught crossing the border into Albania in a stolen car. When they searched the vehicle, the customs officials found the orange suitcase containing the snuff tapes hidden in a false compartment under the back seat, along with over $10,000 in cash. Cross-checking him with Interpol, officials found he looked sufficiently similar enough to the Yannis I had mentioned in my many interrogations, of whom an artist's impression had also been filed, so he was summarily extradited back to Greece. At the recommendation of his defence lawyer, he offered to name and shame all the members of the police force who had been involved – including those on Santorini and Mykonos, as well as Annika and Christos in the Paros department – in exchange for a reduced sentence for his participation in the crimes, which included the murders of Michael Jenner, Roland Jenner, Diane the Kiwi, Svenja and Jens, Lucy and finally, Christos, the driver of the police tugboat. The murder charges were dropped and he ended up facing a sole charge of manslaughter for the 'accidental' death of Christos, for which he received eight years.

The Greek authorities duly released me, issued a new passport and put me on the first available Olympic Airways flight to Heathrow.

Over a final glass of Mythos beer in the airport departures lounge with Mihalis and his teenage son, I learned that Leo had recovered from his shooting at the villa on Paros – he'd come forward and offered his services to the police when he saw a news item about the impending murder trial on national television – and that Amara had been tracked down at a distant relative's house in Sparta, on the mainland. Turned out she'd been forced to delay her studies when she confessed her association with Ricky and me to her father, who had immediately put her under house arrest with her cousin, once removed, until the trial was over and any danger to the family name had passed.

Arriving back in the UK on 23 May 1989, I spent the summer at my parents' house in Rye, attending therapy while accruing funds for my last year at uni. Then in October, having been given the green light for extenuating circumstances, I returned to St Andrews to recommence my final year of studies.

Throughout my time in jail, Ellie wrote to me almost every week. It wasn't in any way a romantic affair; our communication was a mutually cathartic need to exorcise the horror of the

304

summer. Something, it turned out, that was more keenly felt by me, for in early February she abruptly ceased correspondence. I could only assume she had met someone.

When I returned to the campus, Ellie, along with all my other contemporaries, had graduated. There were still enough students from the year below with whom I had friendships and some rapport – chiefly on the squash court, although that was a thing of the past; according to the doctors, my limp would remain with me for a further six months – but I had so much work to catch up on that I became a recluse.

I continued to suffer nightmares and would wake up yelling on most nights, the bed drenched in sweat. Eventually, I found that if I slept on the floor I could get through the night without interruption from my mind.

In early 1990, I received a letter from Ellie saying that she was planning on visiting the university to see a friend who had stayed on to do her Ph.D., and would I be interested in meeting up? I wrote back to her address in London and told her I would of course love to see her.

She arrived on a blustery February afternoon as the sleet drove in off the North Sea, sending the students deep into their lairs. I met her at the desolate Leuchars station on the moors, and we took a taxi directly to Ma Bells pub opposite the Old Course Golf Club for a beer, before a mutually agreed on walk by the sea.

After two warming pints for me – she was back on her favourite Malibu and Coke – we walked arm in arm up to the black-stoned castle on the cliffs and threw stones into the crashing waves below. I put forward the proposition that one day we would get a group of friends together and revisit the Greek islands. Perhaps not Paros.

305

She agreed. And promised to take sailing lessons in the interim. She also agreed to dinner that night: Jack's diner on South Street.

We set a time to meet, then I returned to St Salvator's Hall.

When I entered the lobby, I found I had post. Scraping it out of the wooden cubbyhole, I bounded up the stone steps to my room on the top floor and, excited by the prospect of spending an evening with Ellie, let myself in and tossed the mail across the room onto the bed.

I sparked up the kettle and threw a look outside: the wind had picked up, the sleet now fully turned to snow, hissing against the rattling, ancient window frames.

Darkness was only an hour away.

Turning back to the mail on the bed, I found a letter from my parents, an invitation to the German department's annual ball and, at the bottom of the pile, a postcard from Paros.

A sunset photo of the famous windmill in Parikia.

I turned it over and read the message:

Missing you.
Rx

There was a gust of wind as the window shook and the room grew darker.

Impossible.

Then I noticed there was no stamp.

It had been delivered by hand.

Acknowledgements

I'm eternally grateful to Sarah and Kate Beal at Muswell Press for their unstoppable belief in *The Lizard*, and also for their endless enthusiasm, encouragement and support. I'd also like to thank Kate Quarry for her ruthlessly forensic editorial eye; Fiona Brownlee, of Brownlee Donald Associates, for her fathomless skill and drive in marketing the novel; and also, Tine Nielsen – Muswell Press's foreign rights agent, based in Denmark – for working her magic across several continents. An enormous thank you, also, to William Boyd and Charles Cumming for their support and kind words of praise for *The Lizard*. Their writing has been an endless source of inspiration for me, and I remain in awe of their phenomenal abilities as storytellers. I'd also like to thank the inimitable Simon Williams, who pointed me in the right direction at the very start. I owe an untold amount of thanks to my wife Penny for her never-ending support; for agreeing to read every micro-permutation of the novel along the way; and also for introducing me (via Sara Alexander) to The Write Workshop, where I met Jeff Ourvan, of The Jennifer Lyons Literary

Agency NY. To Jeff – my agent, mentor and friend – I am hugely indebted. Without Jeff's skill, tenacity and commitment, this story would never have been written.

A Note on the Author

Dugald Bruce-Lockhart was born in Fiji in 1968. The son of a diplomat, he attended boarding school from the age of nine; spending his holidays in Cyprus, Vienna, Lagos (Nigeria), and Bonn. He graduated with a degree in German from St. Andrews University in 1990, then trained for a career in acting at The Royal Academy of Dramatic Art in London. A professional actor since 1994, Dugald lives in Kent with his wife Penny and their two children, Mackenzie and Cassidy. This is his first novel.